PRAISE FOR *KILLER MARKET,*
THE LATEST MYSTERY FROM
MARGARET MARON,
WINNER OF THE
EDGAR, AGATHA, ANTHONY,
AND MACAVITY AWARDS

"I recommend Margaret Maron's well-mannered Southern mysteries. . . . The real attraction is her polished style, a high-gloss combination of original observations and clever turns of phrase."

—**Marilyn Stasio,** *New York Times Book Review*

"Maron continues her usual warmhearted approach, tempered with observant detail, infectious enthusiasm, and light humor. Highly recommended."

—*Library Journal*

"The author is known for making North Carolina the 'co-star' of her novels. Her books are filled with details about the state's geography and culture, from the Atlantic coast to the Smoky Mountains."

—*Baton Rouge Magazine*

more . . .

"A classic whodunit."

—*Dispatch* (Lexington, NC)

"Ms. Maron's intelligent and personable detective is making her fifth appearance in a series noted for its Southern charm. She has created an atmosphere loaded with Southern traditions and a character who uses them to suit her own needs and inclinations."

—*Dallas Morning News*

"Deborah Knott [is] as winsome and admirable a character as the genre has to offer."

—*Raleigh News & Observer*

"One of the best writers of what are sometimes called regional mysteries is Margaret Maron. . . . Maron is an excellent writer, who gives readers an insight into the way furniture is marketed while bringing her story to a satisfying conclusion."

—*St. Louis Post-Dispatch*

"Margaret Maron's the queen of the mystery genre. . . . Like her other Deborah Knott books, *Killer Market* also paints a humerous portrait of our old and new Southern ways—this is—reading at its best."

—*Independent Reader* (Durham, NC)

By *Margaret Maron*

Deborah Knott novels:

KILLER MARKET
UP JUMPS THE DEVIL
SHOOTING AT LOONS
SOUTHERN DISCOMFORT
BOOTLEGGERS'S DAUGHTER

Sigrid Harald novels:

FUGITIVE COLORS
PAST IMPERFECT
CORPUS CHRISTMAS
BABY DOLL GAMES
THE RIGHT JACK
BLOODY KIN
DEATH IN BLUE FOLDERS
DEATH OF A BUTTERFLY
ONE COFFEE WITH

MARGARET MARON

KILLER MARKET

WARNER BOOKS

A Time Warner Company

WARNER BOOKS EDITION

Copyright © 1997 by Margaret Maron
All rights reserved.

Cover design by Rachel McClain
Cover illustration by Donna Diamond
Hand lettering by Michael Sabanosh

Warner Books, Inc.
1271 Avenue of the Americas
New York, NY 10020

Visit our Web site at
http:warnerbooks.com

 A Time Warner Company

Printed in the United States of America

Originally published in hardcover by Warner Books.
First Paperback Printing: January, 1999

10 9 8 7 6 5 4 3 2 1

For Dorothy, Sarah, Sue, Joan, Charlotte, Sharyn, Barbara, Penny and Sandy—nine of the grouchiest women I've ever had the pleasure of knowing!

All chapter captions are taken from *The Great Industries of the United States,* Hartford: J.B. Burr & Hude, 1872.

ACKNOWLEDGMENTS

Special thanks to Mary Ellen Hiatt, Executive Director of the Southern Home Furnishings Association, who first suggested that Deborah come to High Point and showed me a whole new world. Thanks also to all the men and women of High Point who graciously answered questions and let me look behind the scenes, especially Ann A. Pickering, Director of Operations at Market Square, and her assistant, Ginger Hicks; Susan M. Andrews, formerly of *Furniture/Today*; Yolanda Jackson of The Father's Table; Detective J.L. Grubb of the High Point Police Department; and Dawn Brinson, Executive Director of the Furniture Discovery Center and former proprietor of the sorely missed bookstore, One for the Books.

KILLER MARKET

1

> *"Man, as classified at the head of the organic evolution of intelligence upon this planet, is a measurer, and, as symbols of his true domination of the world, a rule and a pair of scales would be much fitter and more expressive of his glory than a crown and a sceptre."*
> *The Great Industries of the United States, 1872*

I hate child custody cases.

I hate having to choose between two people who clearly love the child they've created together but who now detest each other so thoroughly that there's no way they can share joint custody of that child.

I particularly hate it when I have to make such judgments in an unfamiliar courthouse after less than four hours' sleep on a stranger's lumpy guest room mattress.

I'm not Solomon, full of God-inspired wisdom. I'm just a thirty-six-year-old district court judge, paid by the State of North Carolina to make Solomonic decisions when its citizens can't—or won't—decide for themselves.

Some days I earn my pay; others—like today—I'm not so sure.

Randy J. Verlin versus April Ann Jenner. Unmarried. Both were twenty-three and high school graduates. Both had past records of minor substance abuse and driving violations. He had shoplifted a six-pack of beer when he was seventeen; she bounced two checks around the time of the baby's birth, and they once drove off from a convenience store without paying for a tank of gas. Both were currently employed for the longest sustained periods of their young lives. Both wanted sole custody of twenty-month-old Travis Tritt Verlin.

"Both of you still like country music?" I had asked upon reading the baby's given name.

Each had nodded warily.

"Well, now, that's a starting place," I said, which got me a skeptical smile from April Ann. "What were you going to name her if he'd been a girl?"

"Kathy Mattea Verlin," they answered together.

That would have been a first for me. I've passed judgments affecting two Patsy Clines, several Loretta Lynns and even a Dolly Parton, but never a Kathy Mattea. *Autres temps, autres noms.*

Custody hearings can be as formal or informal as the judge wishes, especially when neither side is represented by an attorney, as was the case today. My style is to let all the parties speak freely. I usually learn a lot more that way.

Randy Verlin told me he worked as a rough carpenter at Mulholland Design Studio here in High Point, just a few blocks from where I was holding court for a week, substituting for a colleague who had flown out to Detroit to welcome the arrival of her first granddaughter.

"What is it you actually do?" I asked.

"It's like building part of a new house inside a warehouse every week," he said. "Like if they're shooting a bedroom, we have to put up two walls, do the sheetrocking, maybe set new windows, hang some doors, then tear it all down again after the photographer finishes and turn it into a den or a dining room. I'm learning how to sheetrock and do a little wallpapering, too."

"Does the studio have a family leave plan?" I asked, trying to ignore the headache that was building in my left temple from too much caffeine and not enough sleep.

"You mean like if Travis gets sick, could I get off?"

I nodded.

"He's on my medical plan and they're pretty good about letting you off if you really need to do something. Like today. 'Course they do, like, dock your pay."

He showed me pay stubs to prove that he'd been employed there for over a year and he had a letter from his supervisor that said he'd been steady and dependable and had already received two merit raises.

April Ann Jenner had been a data entry clerk for a large insurance company over in Greensboro for the past eight months, and she, too, had a glowing letter of commendation. Her salary was less than his, but her company did have a family leave plan.

Neither employer provided day care, though.

Randy had recently moved back to his parents' house so he could save money and have help with Travis on the weekends. If granted full custody, his mother, a youthful fifty, was prepared to keep Travis during the day since she was already tending a neighbor's child and often cared for Travis as well whenever April Ann got in a bind.

At present, April Ann and Travis shared an apartment with another woman and the woman's three-year-old daughter. The roommate kept both children as a rule, but occasionally she took part-time jobs. When that happened, her daughter went to preschool and Randy's mother would come and get Travis.

The housemate was another reason Randy was asking for full custody. According to him, she had a different man there every week, sometimes he could smell alcohol on her breath when he went to pick Travis up after work, and her daughter bullied Travis.

April Ann admitted that her friend had boyfriends, liked her beer, and didn't always control her daughter, "But don't no men sleep over in our apartment, which is more than Randy can say about his women. And I know for a fact that he has a beer or two when he's got Travis."

Living alone was not an option, she said. "My salary just won't do it."

I leaned my head on my hand so that I could unobtrusively massage my throbbing temple and asked, "What about family?"

"My mom, you mean? She's got a new boyfriend and lives in Memphis now. I got a sister in Wilmington, but she's sharing with two other girls herself. I could ask her if she wants to come to High Point or maybe I could get work down there if that's what it takes to keep my baby."

The trouble was, I didn't know what it would take to give either of them full custody. I had read the Social Services report. It said that Travis was healthy and well nurtured and seemed to be happy and sociable. It also said that April Ann appeared to be a warm and loving mother doing the best she could with her limited resources.

Randy also got high marks for being a loving and responsible father who was almost never late when it was his turn to pick up Travis. Too, he had never missed a child support payment, although that was because his parents helped him out before he got taken on at Mulholland. His father was a career lathe operator at one of the furniture factories outside town, the house was large enough for Travis to have his own room and there was a fenced-in backyard where he could safely play.

I looked at Randy's mother, who was seated in the row behind him.

"Mrs. Verlin, do you think that Ms. Jenner is an unfit mother who deserves to lose custody of your grandson?"

I could see on her face the struggle between loyalty to her son and what appeared to be an innate sense of fairness.

"I don't know how to answer that, Your Honor."

"Try," I said gently.

She shook her head. "They were both of 'em too young to be having a baby. April Ann's done what she's had to do, I reckon, and Randy hasn't always been ready to settle down. I just wish they could've worked this out without having to come to court."

"Me, too," I said, leaning back in my chair to think about the situation. I had all the objective facts Randy and April

Ann could give me and, honestly, there didn't seem to be a nickel's worth of difference between them so far as character and dependability went.

If April Ann were a drunk or did drugs, if Randy had been violent with her or the child, my decision would be clear.

As it was—

My concentration broke as the door to the right of me opened and a middle-aged man came in. He was medium height, of slightly more than medium weight and had medium brown hair that had receded almost to the top of his head. A thick brown mustache made up for the loss above.

He took a seat on the side bench where attorneys and law officials usually wait for their cases to be called, and the bailiff who was sitting there nodded and smiled. They had a whispered conference, then the bailiff, a Mr. Tomlinson, caught my eye.

I motioned for him to come up and leaned forward to hear what he wanted to say.

"Ma'am, Detective Underwood wants to know if he could speak to you at recess?"

"Detective?"

"Yes, ma'am. High Point Police."

"Certainly," I said, assuming he wanted me to sign a search warrant or something.

"Ma'am," said Mr. Tomlinson, "could I tell him how much longer that'd be?"

It was only eleven-thirty, but having skipped breakfast, I was more than ready for lunch. I motioned him back to his seat and sat up straight to speak to the courtroom at large.

"At this time, we will take a lunch break and I will render my decision when we return." I gave an authoritative rap of my gavel and said, "This court will be in recess until twelve-thirty."

"All rise," said the bailiff.

Detective David Underwood followed me down the hall to the small office that had been assigned to me for the duration.

"So what would you like me to sign?" I asked.

He looked at me blankly. "Sign?"

"Isn't this about a search warrant or—?"

"Oh, no, ma'am. We need for you to come over to Leonard Street, if you will."

"You've found my purse?"

"You lost one?" he asked, holding the door for me. "Somebody steal it?"

"Well, no, not exactly. Not deliberately anyhow."

"Actually, we did find it," he said hesitantly.

"So why didn't you bring it with you?" I was definitely getting cranky. "And are my keys still there? I need to move my car if y'all haven't already towed it."

He looked a little uncomfortable. "I'm afraid it's part of the evidence, ma'am."

"Evidence?"

"Yes, ma'am. We're treating last night like a homicide and your bag was found near the victim. So what I was wondering was if you could come on over to the Leonard Street building and let us get your fingerprints?"

And to think that when I got up this morning, I had absolutely convinced myself that my second day in High Point couldn't possibly be as bad as the first.

2

*"Falstaff's question, 'Shall I not take mine ease in mine inn?'
is an expression of that complete comfort and entire indepen-
dence which travellers in all ages and in all nations have at
least expected to find in a public house."*
                    The Great Industries of the United States, 1872

Yesterday—Thursday—had started out so nicely, too, a
beautiful sunny day in mid-April. I finished court early, ran
a couple of errands, and by the time I finally left Dobbs, I
knew I was going to be hitting High Point around rush hour,
but hey, there are rush hours and then there are rush hours,
right?

High Point's about a hundred miles west of Dobbs. The
only time I'd actually driven through it was a few summers
back when my friend Kiernan was visiting from California

and was suddenly seized by a desire to see Old Salem. We were talking so hard when we got to the I-85/I-40 split at Greensboro that I took the wrong fork and was on my way to Charlotte before Kiernan, who was supposed to be navigating, caught it. To get over to Winston-Salem, I had to cut back through High Point.

I remembered a sleepy main section though, about six blocks wide and four or five blocks deep, with a lot of furniture stores sitting on broad streets that were mostly one-way. ("There aren't enough cars on these streets to justify stoplights," Kiernan had said, "so why all the one-ways?") With a total population of seventy thousand or so, how bad could its rush hour be?

As soon as I exited off of I-85 onto Main Street, I found out.

Ten minutes past five and judging by the way cars and buses were streaming away from midtown, Pharaoh had just said, "I'll let you people go," and the children of Israel were rushing toward the Red Sea as if pursued by locusts and serpents.

Where were all these people coming from? Too late for basketball, too early for football, and the Greater Greensboro Open wouldn't start for another week or two. Besides, from what I could see of the shirts and ties and conservative suit jackets on the people inching past, they weren't dressed like golf enthusiasts, who tend to favor green blazers or turquoise and coral knits.

At the Atrium Inn, inbound traffic was held up while an outbound bus in the opposite lane disgorged at least a dozen passengers who blithely crossed against the light, heading for the motel. The men mostly wore business suits and wingtips, several of the women wore sneakers with their suits or business dresses. All seemed to carry heavy brief-cases and notebook computer bags.

When I got to the Radisson Hotel, the parking attendant tried to wave me off, but I slid into an Unloading Only space near the front entrance.

"I'm sorry, ma'am," he began, "but you can't—"

"It's Judge," I said firmly. "And I *am* unloading just as soon as I register."

As I headed for the main door, I caught a glimpse of early revelers standing with drinks in hand on a bricked patio that probably connected to a bar. Five-thirty on a Thursday evening? When did sleepy little High Point turn into a party town?

I threaded my way through milling clumps of people to the front desk, where a slender black clerk gave me a slightly frazzled smile when I set my purse on her pink mar-ble counter and told her I wanted to register.

"Your reservation confirmation number, ma'am?"

"Well, actually, I don't have a reservation," I admitted.

"No reservation?"

In retrospect, I can appreciate how very well trained the Radisson staff is. Her jaw didn't drop, she did not tear at her stylish French twist, nor did she break into gales of laughter. Instead, she gave me a look of such commiseration that I al-most expected her to pat my hand. "I'm sorry, ma'am, but we're full. It's Market Week, you know."

"Market Week?" I asked blankly, having heard the capital letters in her tone.

"The International Home Furnishings Market."

Furnishings. As in furniture. As in that large gold-framed

drawing on the wall behind her. It showed, in cutaway detail, how a massive credenza of Italian Renaissance origin had been replicated for mass marketing by a local company.

"Ma'am, this week's been booked solid for months. In fact, most of our rooms were reserved last year."

I read the gold name tag pinned to her neat navy blue blazer.

"Listen, Marilyn," I said, using my best just-us-girls-together tone, "I really do need a room. I'm a district court judge and I'm supposed to hold court here tomorrow morning."

Marilyn was unmoved. "Sorry, ma'am."

"Perhaps you'll get a cancellation?"

The gold hoops in Marilyn's ears swung sympathetically as she shook her head.

"Even if we did, our waiting list is pretty long. Why don't you try the Chamber of Commerce's housing bureau? They might could fix you up with something in a private house." She glanced at the clock. "You'll have to hurry though. I think they close at five-thirty."

It was now 5:35, but she said the housing bureau was only a mile or so further along Main Street. "And sometimes they stay open a little later at the beginning of Market."

She gave me more specific directions, which I took rather reluctantly.

A room in someone's house? A sofa bed in someone's living room? Having to make small talk for the next six or eight days?

I didn't think so.

It was moot anyhow. By the time I got to the housing bureau, it was closed.

No big deal, I thought. So the Radisson was filled. There were other hotels.

"You don't have a reservation?" the clerk at the Holiday Inn asked incredulously. "In *Market* Week?"

The receptionist at the turquoise-and-pink Super 8 Motel suggested that I call the housing bureau. "They can usually come up with something."

I pointed out that the housing bureau was closed for the day.

"Oh, but it'll be open first thing tomorrow," she assured me cheerfully as she bustled away to help guests lucky enough to have confirmed reservations.

The Atrium Inn sports *faux* marble frescoes, a small waterfall, and a wonderfully tacky statue of King Neptune, even though High Point is two hundred miles from the ocean. But I could have been a mermaid with starfish pasties and it wouldn't have helped me one iota, because guess what?

"It's Market Week," said the manager to whom I appealed after the front desk turned me away. He spoke slowly and distinctly, as if I might be four oysters short of a peck. "You'd probably have to go forty miles to find a vacancy this week."

I co-opted a phone book at a second-story food court down the street and carried it over to an empty table, determined to prove him wrong. Several phone calls later, I realized he'd sadly underestimated. Some of the national chains had rooms available in Durham or Charlotte, both at least seventy miles away. Nothing in Greensboro or Winston.

"They must be having a big convention or something in that area," the 1-800 Reservations person for Embassy

Suites apologized. "We're showing full occupancy through next Wednesday."

Now I'm not a complete ignoramus. I do know that High Point is probably the center of the state's enormous furniture industry—that's the main reason I took this assignment. I've finally decided to get a house of my own and I figured I could spend the weekend browsing stores and pick up some ideas about styles, colors and prices.

And yeah, I'd heard of the Southeastern Furniture Market before it went international and changed its name, but it didn't affect me or anybody I knew so I never paid it much attention. I certainly had no idea it was so huge that it could take over the whole Triad.

As I slid my new flip phone back into my purse, I was beginning to have second thoughts about that sofa bed in someone's living room. If there truly was no room at the inn for me, I'd have to scrap the idea of shopping and instead drive back home tomorrow night and see if I could talk Aunt Sister into letting me borrow her RV for the week, assuming I could get away with parking it beside the courthouse for that long.

The food court had filled up while I'd been on the phone. At the next table several women with Iowa accents were regaling each other about their lodging arrangements. From their groans and laughter, I gathered that four of the women and two male co-workers were sharing a private house that their company had rented for the week.

"—just two bathrooms. I had to wash my hair in the kitchen sink this morning while Sam was making coffee."

"Was that Sam snoring last night? I thought I'd never get to sleep."

"—from the Friedman chain, says they lucked out this year. Four bedrooms, three baths and only five people, but one of them—"

More of their friends arrived. My table for four was down to two chairs, and as one of the Iowans started to confiscate the remaining empty, a smaller, oddly dressed woman put out her hand to stop her.

"Excuse me," she said in a deep gravelly voice. She wasn't much taller than five one or five two. Her build was that of a young, sexless child, but her voice could have been Lauren Bacall's had Lauren Bacall been born with a thick Southern accent. "I believe this is my chair?"

The words themselves were courteous enough and even ended on a polite up-tone, the sort of tone that many cultivated women use when pretending they might be mistaken in their understanding of the situation. As with such ladies, there was so much ice beneath the politeness that Iowa backed away, apologizing profusely.

"You *are* alone this evening, are you not?" the woman asked me, seating herself in the disputed chair and settling two canvas tote bags at her feet like one of my aunts after a hard day of shopping. This being High Point though, her bags had the logo of a large furniture company.

It was a week past Easter, the date when it becomes officially permissible in the South to wear white shoes and pastels; and this small-boned woman was dressed like a slightly disheveled Easter egg. Layers of pink, green and lavender chiffon scarves enveloped her body. Her wide-brimmed garden hat was woven from pale lavender straw and had lavender and green ribbons that tied beneath her chin. The hat itself had slipped down onto her shoulders and her wiry gray hair was barely constrained by a chignon that looked dangerously close to exploding. She wore pale blue tights and dirty pink satin ballerina slippers.

I reserved judgment because the South is full of elderly eccentric women who may look like bag ladies but who turn out to be the wealthy blue-blooded widows or spinster daughters of exceedingly prominent men.

"Mrs. Jernigan," she said in that hoarse voice, abruptly extending the tips of her fingers. "Matilda McNeill Jernigan."

"Judge Knott," I replied, extending my own fingers.

She frowned. "What makes you think I would?"

It was a common error.

"That's my name," I explained. "Deborah Knott. I'm a district court judge."

"Really? How fascinating. And is your husband a judge, too?"

Well, of course, she's that generation that still defines a woman by the man in her life.

"Y'all eating?" asked the teenage busboy as he removed a cup and napkin left by a previous diner and gave the table a quick swipe with his cloth. He pointedly straightened a small placard that read, "Please be mindful of others during Market Week and vacate this table when you've finished eating."

Actually, food was beginning to sound like a good idea. I glanced around at the various kiosks. The choices ranged from pan pizzas and fried chicken to alfalfa salads and yogurt.

I glanced inquiringly at my tablemate. "Could I get you something while I'm up?"

"Why, thank you," she said, and inclined her small head so graciously that I realized she thought I had invited her to be my guest. "I do like a little something to take the edge off my appetite before the parties. Perhaps turkey salad on a croissant and hot tea with lemon? Wine will flow, I fear, and a lady should not risk the danger of an empty stomach."

Turkey salad and hot tea sounded as good a choice as any and quicker than waiting on lines at separate stands.

When I returned with two of everything, I found Matilda McNeill Jernigan absorbed by the yellow pages that still lay open on the table.

She lifted the thick book in her little hands and held it out of the way while I set down our tray. I returned it to the telephone stand, and as I got back to the table, Mrs. Jernigan took out a tiny coin purse, carefully extracted two pills, one a green-and-white capsule, the other a white tablet, and laid them beside her plate.

Seeing her pills reminded me that I was due for a pill of my own. I'd had a throat that was raw as freshly ground hamburger last week and the doctor had prescribed ten days of antibiotics—one tablet three times a day. They were supposed to be evenly spaced, but I kept forgetting and instead of one tablet every eight hours, it was apt to be ten hours for one and six hours for the next till I was back on schedule. How on earth people with chronic conditions manage to keep it all straight, I can't begin to imagine. I swallowed the tablet and was thankful that I had only one more day to go.

Between nibbled bites of her croissant, Mrs. Jernigan gave me a concerned look and said, "I could not help but notice that you were calling hotels. Please do not tell me you have no place to stay?"

"Afraid so," I admitted.

She made a cluckling sound of sympathy. "In Market Week, too."

"I had no idea that Market was this big a deal," I said ruefully. "There must be ten thousand people here from all over the country."

"Try seventy thousand." Her tone was dry. "From all over the globe. And it *is* a big deal. This is when the town comes fully to life. Ten days in April, another ten in October."

With a sweep of chiffon, she gestured toward the big windowless buildings that could be seen from our table overlooking Main Street. "Seven million square feet of showrooms in a hundred and fifty places around the area and all the buildings are dark and silent for three hundred days of the year. Then we have a month of hustle—tearing out walls, putting in new ones, laying carpets, painting, hanging wallpaper, installing the furniture—just to get ready for nine days of buyers. Retailers come from all over the world to order the chairs and couches and case goods that will wind up in Mediterranean villas and Manhattan penthouses. Japanese decorators will buy outrageously expensive bibelots to grace a chain of hotels from Nagasaki to Sapporo. And those polyvinyl chaises that a newly famous Hollywood star will buy for her first swimming pool next fall? Someone will sell the line to a California distributor this week."

The Midwesterners at the next table were raising their eyebrows at each other, but Mrs. Jernigan was oblivious. Her voice became throatier, her dark eyes flashed and I abruptly downgraded her age from late sixties to mid-fifties at most. The gray hair had fooled me.

This was no little old dowager.

"Think of the great couturiers who show their spring and fall fashions," she said. "High Point is Paris! New York! The Milano of the furniture industry!"

"No wonder I couldn't find a room." Half-jokingly, I added, "I don't suppose you have a spare couch you could rent me for the night?"

Mrs. Jernigan drew back so sharply that all her layers of pastel chiffon swayed and quivered as if tossed by the wind. "Stay with me? Oh, no, that would not do at all. No, no, no. That is totally out of the question."

Her hat bumped the back of her chair and more wisps of wiry gray hair escaped from her chignon. She was becoming so agitated that I quit feeling offended and urged her to take a sip of tea while it was still hot.

She held the plastic cup to her lips with both hands and took several swallows. When she was calm again, she said, "I cannot extend you hospitality, but perhaps I do know someone who can help. However, she will not be there until later. Would you like to go to a party or two first? Experience the Market for yourself?"

"Sure," I said. What the hell?

Matilda McNeill Jernigan finished her turkey salad croissant, fished around in one of her tote bags and came out with a plastic badge holder which she pinned to a green chiffon scarf on her shoulder. The name on the badge was Louisa Ferncliff, representing Quality Interiors of Seattle, Washington.

She tilted her head closer to mine and I smelled rose cologne and a faint hint of that ubiquitous almond-scented liquid hand soap one finds in most public restrooms these days. Her husky voice dropped to a more confidential level. "Press badges are better."

She eyed the badge on a raincoat that someone at the next table had draped over the back of a chair next to mine and I wondered if I were about to see a minor felony committed. "Press badges get you into any showroom without people trying to sell you a truckload of coffee tables, but a buyer's will do fine too. A word to the wise though—do not try to get into a showroom while wearing an exhibitor's badge. They will think you are a spy."

She fished around in her bag again and frowned. "They all seem to be males and— Ah! Have you a black pen?"

I handed over my favorite Pentel and watched as she artistically changed *Jack Sotelli* of Home-Lite in Newark, New Jersey, to *Jacki Sotelli*.

"Should anyone notice, just flirt your eyes and say that they always misspell your name," she said, adjusting her scarves before gathering up her bags to go.

I pinned the badge to my jacket dubiously. "But I don't know a thing about Newark."

"Then you will have to pretend you have just been transferred, will you not?"

3

"Music is supposed to be good for the dyspepsia, has an excellent influence on torpid livers, and cures melancholy in a moment."

The Great Industries of the United States, 1872

The Global Home Furnishings Market was a block off Main Street and seemed to have started life as a collection of adjacent buildings of different heights and architectural styles. Now they were painted a uniform navy blue and were interconnected by futuristic tubular glass walkways high above the street

In my beige slacks and black jacket, I wasn't exactly dressed for a formal cocktail party, but neither were most of the other people crowding into the elevators that whisked us up to the ninth floor of the huge Global Home Furnishings building. Some of the older women looked as if they'd gone back to their hotel rooms and changed into softer clothes and prettier earrings, but the majority were still in daytime business attire. Male uniformity dictated dark suits and white shirts but an occasional seersucker blazer or outrageously colorful tie broke that lockstep monotony and the aroma of fresh cologne mingled with spritzes of perfume.

Anticipation bubbled like champagne as friends and associates greeted each other each time the doors opened.

Eventually, the elevator deposited us in a wide hallway tiled in polished pearl gray marble and lined with such lavish furniture showrooms that I thought for a moment I was in an upscale mall. Brand names only subliminally known from magazine ads flowed in gold script across gleaming glass windows or were chiseled over pink marble archways. Behind the windows and archways were mahogany chests and beds heaped high with colorful designer linens. Across the hall was a collection of painted furniture with a breezy California look. Next door, a classical Roman atrium contained modern dining furniture wrought from ebony and attenuated iron, with touches of blue-green verdigris.

I was on sensory overload. The shiny surfaces, the heady smell of new leather and plastic and textiles that was like opening the door on your first new car, the excited voices— I wanted to stop and take it all in like a kid in a video store, but Mrs. Jernigan, who was several inches shorter, darted and danced straight ahead and I was forced to keep up or lose her in the crowds.

We entered a glass-enclosed tube and passed high above a clump of dogwoods below into an adjacent building, then onto another elevator for two floors.

Old Home Week parties seemed to be going on everywhere—in the showrooms or in small nondescript rooms down side halls. People wandered past with printed guide maps and blank looks.

"Did they say third turn to the left?"

"This *is* the tenth floor, isn't it?"

"Hey, what happened to Stan?"

On my own, I, too, would have been confused, but Mrs. Jernigan seemed to know every turn and twist through this maze of showrooms and branching hallways.

We passed through an austerely formal marble vestibule where chrome and glass elevators were disgorging more people. Just beyond, a weighted brass stanchion held a placard which pointed the way to the Fitch and Patterson reception.

Even though I've never paid much attention to furniture makers, Fitch and Patterson is a household name in certain households. For years, the company used to give a miniature cedar chest to every girl who graduated from high school in North Carolina. They stopped the practice when I was in second grade, but I've kept the one that my mother used as a jewelry box. Even though the concept of hope chests seems like a hopeless anachronism to me, a lot of aspiring debutantes across this state still own full-sized, cedar-lined Fitch and Patterson chests to which their female relatives will donate lace tablecloths and pieces of heirloom silver every Christmas until the day they marry.

(You don't think someone with pretensions of blue blood ever *buys* her own silver, do you? No, no, no, no. It's always handed down from before the war. The Civil War. Even though a surreptitious glance at the back of a fork may reveal a hallmark that didn't exist before 1940, your hostess will proudly tell you how the Yankees were too dumb to discover that her clever forebears had hidden the family silver in a hollow porch column/on the smoke ledge up inside the open hearth/under great-great-grandmother's hoop skirts as she sat in her rocking chair on the veranda when Sherman's scavengers came riding up. "And there's the dent where she accidentally rocked over this very same tray." Being columnless and hoopless, my dirt-farming Civil War forebears were doing good to have tin forks for their cornbread and collards.)

Two perky young women with big hair and even bigger smiles were working the Fitch and Patterson reception table, trying to match badge names to their guest lists; but with such a crush of people streaming past them toward the open bar inside, they hindered us no more than had the guard on the street doors downstairs.

"As long as we wear badges and act as if we have been invited to these parties, no one will stop us," said Matilda McNeill Jernigan.

We accepted complimentary tote bags and a handful of advertising flyers from more young women and sailed on into the reception amid a group of jovial bald men who seemed to be at least three drinks ahead of us.

The tote was rather attractive: sturdy black canvas with a discreet Fitch and Patterson logo in gold and white on the front. I slipped my purse inside and jammed the flyers in on top as Mrs. Jernigan redistributed some items in her own bags.

My whimsical guide had the build of a ten-year-old child or aging elf, and beneath the soft glow of the crystal chan-

deliers, her—dress? costume? assemblage?—of pink, green
and lavender chiffon lost some of its eccentricity and took
on a festive playfulness. Like a small rainbow-colored
cloud, she drifted through the crowd toward the buffet
where smoked salmon, boiled shrimp, fresh fruits, cheeses
and crisp crackers tempted those who had evidently skipped
dinner. After my turkey croissant, I was no longer hungry,
but I snagged a glass of white Zinfandel and drifted after
her.

"Savannah! How perfectly splendid to see you here," exclaimed an ash-blonde, middle-aged woman in an elegant
black brocade suit that probably cost more than my entire
wardrobe. The diamonds on her finger and ears would have
gone a long way toward reducing the national deficit.

Matilda McNeill Jernigan looked all the way up into the
taller woman's face. "Were you addressing me, madam?"

The woman faltered before those piercing eyes. "It's Elizabeth, Savannah. Elizabeth Patterson."

Mrs. Jernigan turned away. "You are mistaken. We have
never met."

The woman gave an entreating smile. "Of course we
have. You styled our catalogs three years in a row. You men-
tored our daughter Drew."

"Drew?" For a moment her eyes softened.

"Don't you remember, Savannah?"

Mrs. Jernigan stiffened again. "Even were that my name,
your familiarity would not be appreciated."

Her husky voice, so at odds with her small size and wispy
chiffon, cut like a rusty band saw. "For your information,
my name is Melissa Dorcas Poole. *Mrs.* Melissa Dorcas
Poole."

Being accosted by Elizabeth Patterson—as in Fitch and Patterson?—seemed to have made Mrs. Jernigan forget that she was supposed to be Louisa Ferncliff from Seattle.

On the other hand, she had not forgotten my *nom de nuit.* "Come, Miss Sotelli. Let us seek greener pastures where we may browse in peace."

I gave the woman an apologetic smile and turned to follow, but Elizabeth Patterson put out her hand and with a dazzle of diamonds caught me by the sleeve. "Miss—Sotelli, is it? Please tell me—"

"Darlin'?"

A stocky, white-haired man emerged from the crowd and put his arm around her waist with a proprietary air. They were almost exactly the same height, but he wore only one diamond, a large square stone set in a heavy gold ring. His badge told me that he was J.J. Patterson of Fitch and Patterson Furniture Incorporated, headquartered in Lexington, N.C., less than twenty miles away.

"Oh, Jay," said Mrs. Patterson. "Did you see her? That was Savannah."

J.J. Patterson had a broad square face with a bulbous nose that was finely webbed by small broken veins. He looked like one of those hard-working, hard-playing, savvy businessmen you find the world over, ready to cut the cards, cut a deal, or cut a throat (economically speaking) if it would sweeten his bottom line. And he had a wide mouth that would probably broaden into an amiable smile to show you that there was nothing personal in it if he cut you off at the knees.

He wasn't smiling now as he stretched himself to get another look over the heads of the revelers. Matilda McNeill

Jernigan or Melissa Dorcas Poole or whoever she was had disappeared into the crowd.

"Savannah? Really?" asked a stocky young woman who wore a *Furniture/Today* press badge and carried a reporter's narrow notebook. She had straight black hair that hung halfway down her back and swung like a shimmering curtain when she pivoted on her tiptoes and looked eagerly in the same direction.

"You sure, darlin'? Didn't look like the Savannah I remember."

"She's let her hair go gray and she's wearing color, but it's Savannah, all right. Ms. Sotelli here was with her. It *was* Savannah, wasn't it?" she asked me now.

"I'm sorry," I said, "but I just met her and—"

"Home-Lite?" Jay Patterson gave a polite smile as he read my badge. "Newark, New Jersey. That's Paul Schaftlein's outfit, isn't it? Ol' Paul come down this year?"

I had a feeling this man probably had a personal acquaintance with every furniture retailer on the East Coast.

"Excuse me," I said brightly.

And fled.

I let myself go with the flow and soon wound up in the ballroom next door.

The Fitch and Patterson reception had been tasteful and dignified. Taste and dignity did not seem to be considerations of the American Leathergoods Wholesale Association's party. It was a let-down-your-hair romp and stomp. A four-piece combo dressed in blue leather chaps and big white Stetsons was pounding out the latest rockabilly and a large blue ox was leading a group of line dancers in front of the bandstand.

Before I could stop myself, a good-looking guy in a three-piece suit, an open shirt, two gold neck chains and cowboy boots grabbed my hand and pulled me into the line. It took me a couple of awkward steps to catch the pattern, but once I got into the rhythm, I was high-stepping right along with him.

When the set ended, my dancing partner grinned and with an exaggerated drawl said, "I'd be plumb proud to stand you to a drink, ma'am."

Before I could agree, he did a double take. "*Deb'rah? Deb'rah Knott?*"

"I'm afraid you have the advantage of me, sir," I said in my best schoolmarm voice.

But he was serious now. "It's me—Chan. Chandler Nolan. Don't you remember?"

The name rang no bells and I was sure I'd remember if I'd ever met somebody who filled his jeans the way this guy did.

"Frederick, Maryland," he said. "The spring you stayed with your aunt?"

I'd done a pretty good job of erasing that nineteenth spring from my memory, but now it came rushing back, along with the face of a kid who used to mow Aunt Barbara's two-acre lawn, a horny, pimple-faced seventeen-year-old who'd tried to grope me every time I let him take me to a movie or walk with me down to the creek that flowed through the back of Aunt Barbara's meadow.

I was on my way to messing up my life for good that year with sex and drugs and drink. Aunt Barbara took me in, held my hand through the annulment of a disastrous runaway marriage, and pointed out how stupid I was being when she walked up on Chan and me in her gazebo one sunny afternoon.

"Chastity may be highly overrated," she told me after Chan had grabbed his pants and fled, "but so is this so-called free love."

"Sex has nothing to do with love," I'd muttered.

"Nor does corrupting children," she'd said tartly. "Do you know how difficult it is to find someone reliable to cut my grass?"

Put like that, I'd decided it was time to move on. And I hadn't given another thought to Chandler Nolan in all the years since.

"What're you doing down here?" I asked, amazed that he'd turned out so handsome.

Unfortunately, he still had that randy look in his eye, and I saw him checking my left hand for a wedding band. "Let's go get us something wet and I'll tell you."

We snaked our way through laughing, perspiring dancers to the far end of the room where two long serving tables stood draped in blue calico. On one of them, several shiny galvanized washtubs held ice and five or six different brands of beer. The other table featured huge platters of Texas-style ribs, fried chicken, jalapeño cornbread, corn on the cob, and some sinfully rich-looking chocolate brownies. Instead of napkins, the American Leathergoods Wholesale Association had thoughtfully provided blue-checkered washcloths.

Favors were scattered at intervals along the table: bookmarks cut from supple, multicolored leathers and stamped in gold with the ALWA ox-head logo. As I waited for my

Maryland cowboy to push his way up to the beer tubs, two buyers? sellers? designers? in front of me began to rub the bookmarks against one of those washcloths as if to see if the bright clear colors would come off on the white checks.

"Nice hand," said one, flexing the bookmark carefully, "but in this range of color, it has to be naked aniline."

"They swear it's pigmented," said the other. "One-point-five on the gray scale."

"You believe that, I've got a bridge I'll sell you."

"But even if it's only a three," he said as he whipped out a pocket calculator and began punching in some numbers, "we could use it to create a whole new pricing umbrella, elevate points right across the board."

"*If* it comes in at no more than two-fifty a square," his colleague agreed doubtfully. "Sure does have a nice hand, though."

They were talking in tongues as far as I was concerned.

Through an opening in the crowd I caught a glimpse of pastel chiffon, and there was Mrs. Jernigan standing halfway down the food table. She had draped one of her pale green scarves over her head, but strands of gray hair strayed from beneath the edge.

Chandler Nolan, who had a beer in each hand, had been waylaid by a couple of corporate types and he gave me a shrug.

Just as well, I decided, now that I'd had a minute to think it over. I really wasn't in the mood for *Remember when—?* And though I wasn't wearing Kidd Chapin's ring on my finger or through my nose, Chan had a plain gold band on his significant finger and I never mess around with married men.

("Not if you know they're married," came the voice of pragmatism in my head.)

I gave him a cheery wave, warbled, "Good seeing you again," and headed instead toward the woman who'd promised to find me a bed tonight.

As I came up to Mrs. Jernigan, I saw her slip a zip-lock plastic bag filled with fried chicken into the new Fitch and Patterson bag between her feet. From the damp stain spreading across the bottom of her second tote, I could only assume that she had helped herself to a few cans of iced beer as well. She reminded me of my Aunt Sister, who keeps similar plastic bags stashed in her carryall bag because, and I quote, "I just can't stand to see good food go to waste."

(Let her loose at any restaurant with an all-you-can-eat buffet or serve-yourself salad bar and Aunt Sister comes home with enough food to feed her and Uncle Rufus for three meals. "Well, I never eat enough to feed a bird," she rationalizes, "and you know good as me that they're just going to throw out anything that's left over.")

To my surprise, J.J. Patterson was there at her elbow and seemed to be helping her stow away a couple of drumsticks while the reporter with the long dark hair watched in fascination.

One of Mrs. Jernigan's plastic bags had fallen to the floor. I bent to retrieve it and was almost stepped on by some sales rep who'd shoved in to fill his plate. As I straightened up, a soft hand touched my arm and for the second time that night, a surprised voice said, "Deborah? Deborah Knott?"

I turned and saw a familiar face. The shining chestnut hair, slanted feline eyes, and long leggy body were familiar, too, but I was blanking on her name.

"Well, I'll be blessed! It *is* you and you haven't changed an inch since law school. What the L-M-N are you doing here at Market?"

Her law school reference and that L-M-N substitute for blunter language brought her into focus.

Dixie Babcock.

We'd sat next to each other in several classes, shared notes and lunch, and were even in the same study group for contract law. We had liked each other well enough, but she was nearly ten years older and a single mother struggling for a law degree after too many dead-end jobs that barely paid for day care. At that point in her life, she just didn't have enough time to develop any strong new friendships so our tenuous connection stayed tenuous despite splitting an occasional pizza at the Rat on Franklin Street. Then she had to drop out for a semester when her daughter got hit by a car and after that we pretty much lost touch with each other.

I shoved my bag under the edge of the table and gave her a hug.

She hugged me back, then held me at arm's length to assess time's changes. My Jacki Sotelli badge made her laugh. "Newark? You?"

"It's a long story," I said, but my hopes began an upward rise as I did my own assessment: expensive haircut, manicured nails, the blue-enameled gold collar that topped a deceptively simple green shift. This was not Kmart chic.

According to her name tag, she was now the executive director of the Southern Retail Furnishings Alliance. I had never heard of the Southern Retail Furnishings Alliance, but surely its executive director would have an extra bed she could offer to a former classmate?

Dixie shook her head sympathetically as I gave her an ab-breviated version of why I was in town and how I was be-ginning to wonder if I'd have to sleep in my car beside the courthouse.

"Judge? God, I'm so impressed! But I can't believe they'd let you come over here during Market week without a room reservation. I'd invite you to stay with me if I didn't already have a decorina friend from California on my couch. My granddaughter's sharing with me, and my son-in-law has the guest room. When he bothers to come home," she added with a touch of bitterness that made me wonder if said son-in-law had a roving eye.

"Your daughter's not with them?" I asked.

Raw, naked pain shafted across her face and I saw the lines of age and grief that had, till then, been hidden beneath her skillful makeup.

"Evelyn's dead," she said bluntly. "She took a bad fall. A year ago last October. The baby she was carrying died, too."

I was stunned. "Oh, Dixie! How awful!"

"Yeah," she agreed bleakly. Then she took a deep breath, smoothed her gleaming hair, and visibly collected herself. "So you need a bed, huh?" Her voice became bright and cheerful again. "I bet I know where there's one going beg-ging."

"That's okay." Suddenly I was feeling gauche for pre-suming upon what really was a very slender friendship. "Mrs. Jernigan here knows someone."

I turned to that lady, who was adding several large wedges of jalapeño cornbread to her tote bag. The gauzy green scarf had slipped from her hair and now trailed from her shoulders.

"Mrs. Jernigan—"

She completed her raid on the table with a couple of brownies, then looked up at me with a cold eye and in that distinctive, husky voice, said, "My name is Hadley Jones Edminston. I cannot fathom why all of you continue to address me incorrectly when I have never met *any* of you."

With that, she crushed her lavender straw hat down squarely on her head, gathered up her bags and stalked away. The *Furniture/Today* reporter hurried after her and I was left to stare blankly at Dixie Babcock and J.J. Patterson, who seemed to know each other.

Dixie's brown eyes widened as she gazed after Mrs. Jernigan. "That voice—was that *Savannah*?"

Patterson nodded. "I couldn't believe it either at first. I had no idea she was back in town."

But Dixie was still processing what she'd just seen. "Savannah with gray hair? In a dress? Wearing *color*?"

"Who's Savannah?" I asked. "And what's the big deal about color?"

Patterson put out his big hand. "Jay Patterson, Ms. Sotelli. We didn't get a chance to talk before, but—"

I took his hand as Dixie said, "Come on, Jay. Does she sound anything like a Sotelli from Newark?"

"Well—"

"This is Deborah Knott, an old friend from law school. She's a district court judge now. Sitting here for a week."

He grinned. "So where'd you steal that badge, Judge?"

"You accuse a judge of theft?" I bantered. "Actually, Mrs. Jernigan, or whatever her name is, gave it to me."

"Aha!" said Dixie. "Receiving stolen goods. That's even more serious."

"You be serious," I said. "Who's Savannah What's-her-name?"

"Savannah's all I ever heard." She looked at Patterson, who nodded.

"Me, too. Hell, when she did her first catalog for us and our payroll department head kept trying to get a full name for the W-2 forms, she told him to draw her check to S.A. Vannah if it'd make him happy, 'cause that was all he was getting."

"She was the best designer and stylist in the business," said Dixie, "and she did everything with panache. Dressed only in black—black shoes, black stockings, black hats, black mink, onyx cigarette holder. Drove black Porsches."

"Great jewelry though," said Patterson, helping himself to a wedge of the jalapeño cornbread from the sadly depleted platter.

"The only color she wore," agreed Dixie. "If you don't count the bright red lipstick and red nail polish. Splashy necklaces of coral, topazes, turquoise, jade and cinnabar. Unusual cloisonné brooches. I never saw her in a dress either. It was always slacks or leggings or tights. She said skirts made her legs look too short."

"Short? She had great legs," said Patterson.

He took a large bite of the cornbread and nearly choked. His already florid face turned even redder and his broad nose was almost purple.

Alarmed, Dixie thumped him on the back as tears streamed from his eyes while I tried to remember exactly how the Heimlich maneuver goes.

Across the narrow table, a heavyset woman quickly thrust her open can of beer at him and Patterson drained it in three long gulps. When he finally caught his breath, he said, "Thanks, Kay. I owe you one for saving my taste buds."

"I'll take it out in trade tomorrow," the woman said and turned her attention to the platter of ribs that was going fast as more people filled their blue plastic plates.

A look of dismay flashed across Patterson's broad face, a look instantly replaced by his former joviality as he told Dixie and me, "Watch out for those chunks of red. Those aren't pimientos. They're red chiles and hotter'n hell."

"Yummy," said Dixie, reaching for a piece. "I love it hot."

"So what happened to Savannah?" I prodded as Patterson mopped his face and streaming eyes with his handkerchief.

"Nobody knows," said Dixie. "She was at the top of the pile and she just disappeared. One Market she was doing all the high-end projects, next Market, poof! Gone. Nada. She was always temperamental though. It wasn't the first time. She was always popping off to Europe or South America for a few months. Was it five years ago she was gone for so long, Jay?"

"Six," said Patterson. "I remember because it was right after she smashed her car and nearly killed Drew."

"Everyone knows she'll be back when her money runs out, but this time it's been at least eighteen months."

"Ah, here's where you all are," said an easy male voice.

It was Chan Nolan, my erstwhile cowboy. He might have been looking at me, but I had to assume he was speaking to Dixie since he now had his arm around a pretty little blonde who wore a dress cut low enough to be his dancehall queen.

Jay Patterson immediately took my hand. "It's been a pleasure, Judge Knott. See you, Dixie. Drew, your mother could use some help in there."

"Tell her I'll be right back," said the blonde.

Patterson gave a curt nod, then turned on his heel and was gone.

Chan Nolan gave a boyish grin and reached for a piece of cornbread. "Was it something I said?"

"More like something you did," Dixie told him crisply. "Deborah, this is my son-in-law."

4

"Very beautiful enamelled furniture, especially for bedchamber sets, is extensively manufactured."
The Great Industries of the United States, 1872

"We've met before," Chan drawled.

Not wanting to go into all the circumstances of my misspent youth, I hastily said, "He and that blue ox just gave me a line dancing lesson."

Chan raised an eyebrow, but mercifully took the hint. There was a battered tomcat sexiness to the smile that twitched the edge of his lips, a smile that meant he'd pursue the subject later if I knew anything about battered tomcats.

(And yeah, unfortunately, I do, having gone so far as to marry one once.)

The young woman hanging on his arm was Drew Patterson, who had her mother's fair coloring and slender height and her father's wide smile with only the merest hint of his broad nose. As she glanced from his face to mine and back again, I could almost see a hurt suspicion in her blue eyes, but she made a quick recovery.

"Dad's still mad 'cause Jacaranda's stealing the best vice president of sales in the business," she told me after introductions were over.

Chan Nolan took a long pull on his beer. "Fitch and Patterson doesn't have to worry about Jacaranda."

"They're moving into high end, aren't they?"

"So?"

"Don't be coy, Chan. You'll be competing against us directly."

Chan shrugged. "Fitch and Patterson doesn't own high end."

"But that infusion of Hong Kong money *will* make Jacaranda another one of the high rollers," said Dixie.

Chan caught my eye and appealed to me for support. "You see how they gang up on me, Deborah? Like it's my fault? Jacaranda's going offshore and high end whether I'm there or not. So why shouldn't I jump on a moving wagon?"

"What's high end?" I asked. "And who or what is Jacaranda?"

"High end's the luxury market," he explained. "The best quality and most expensive furniture to make and sell."

"And Jacaranda is a Texas company that makes schlock!" said Dixie.

"It might've been schlock years ago," he agreed easily, "but they've been steadily upgrading and now they're poised to get huge. Once they finish tooling up the Malaysia factory, you're going to see hand-carved mahogany case goods that'll set the market on its ear. By this time next year—"

"Coming through, please!"

I grabbed my new tote bag from under the edge of the table and stepped back as waiters removed the nearly empty serving dishes and deposited fresh platters of ribs and chicken.

More dancers surged forward to stoke up. I still wasn't hungry but Drew fixed a plate for Chan with a proprietary air. "Cornbread, hon?"

"Yes, ma'am! And what about a couple of those brownies?" he said hungrily.

"Two?"

"One for me, one to take to Lynnette. She loves nuts and chocolate as good as I do."

"Chan, you idiot!" Drew scolded. "You can't give a seven-year-old chocolate at bedtime. She'll be bouncing off the walls. Tell him, Dixie."

"He's the daddy, honey. I'm just the grandma."

Dixie's tone was light but that lightness didn't quite reach her eyes.

Before Chan could reply, a pudgy middle-aged man tapped him on the shoulder. "We talk to you a minute, Nolan?"

The "we" was the heavyset woman who'd earlier handed Jay Patterson her beer when he was gasping from the jalapeño cornbread.

"Look, Jackson, I told you and Kay both—"

"Just hear what we've got to say, okay? Is that too much to ask after twenty-seven years?"

With an exaggerated sigh, Chan told us, "Be right back," and followed them over to the corner that was probably the quietest place in the overcrowded ballroom at the moment.

"Poor Poppy," said Drew. "He told Dad if Chan gives Muir an exclusive, they might as well close up now."

Dixie frowned. "He's yanking their account?"

I had only the vaguest idea what Drew and Dixie were talking about, but from the half-angry, half-entreating gestures the older man and woman were making, it certainly seemed as if Chan was yanking their chains, if nothing else.

Dixie saw my blank look and laughed. "Are we talking Urdish again?"

"I guess every industry has its shorthand jargon," I said. "Are they buyers?"

Drew nodded, brushing a long blonde tress from her cheek. "Retailers. Here to check out the new designs and see what's going to be hot this fall. Poppy Jackson has a beautiful old store in Green Oaks, Virginia, and Kay Adams has a store down at the beach. They've been selling us since before I was born."

I began to see why those two seemed so hostile. "But why would Fitch and Patterson give another store an exclusive? Isn't the object to sell as much furniture as possible as widely as possible?"

"It is," said Dixie, "but high end has the snob appeal to do that if it's marketed slickly. A lot of the retailers in our Southern Retail Furnishings Alliance are small independents like Poppy and Kay. They run a single-store mom-and-pop operation, maybe gross a million-five a year if they're lucky.

Muir's a chain that's moving into the Southeast. These huge new stores are really starting to hurt my little guys."

Drew chimed in. "Stores like Poppy and Kay's stock too much inventory. They may carry middle to high end but they jumble our pieces in with Lane and Thomasville. A chain like Muir will hire designers like Connie Post or Lynn Hollyn, install a three thousand square foot Fitch and Patterson gallery full of exciting room vignettes, and show a whole line for a synergistic effect."

"And gross two hundred million in the process," said Dixie.

"But they won't do a gallery unless you give them an exclusive for that town," Drew finished. "They don't want to be undercut by a store that doesn't have the same class and image. And I'm sorry, Dixie, but in your heart, you know that most of the independents look like dowdy old maids next to these high-tech chains. Poppy and Kay and retailers like them want to keep on doing what they've done for the last fifty years and that simply won't cut it in today's market."

"But what about loyalty?" I asked. "If these two have been with you for so long— ?"

"I know, I know," said Drew. "It just about breaks my heart, and Dad feels rotten about it, too, but Chan's right. If Fitch and Patterson's going to stay competitive, we have to cooperate with the chains and we couldn't say no to Muir's offer."

She glanced at the tiny jeweled watch that encircled her slender wrist.

"And speaking of cooperating, I'd better get back to our own reception before Mother comes looking for me." She handed Dixie the plate she was holding. "Give this to Chan? Nice meeting you, Deborah. You going to be around all weekend?"

"I hope so," I answered, patting my Home-Lite badge. "As long as I don't run into the real Jack Sotelli."

"Good. Maybe I'll see you again."

She gave Dixie a quick kiss on the cheek and then slipped away through the crowd.

Dixie sighed as she watched Drew go. "She's such a sweetie and Chan's treating her so badly."

"He is? She doesn't act like it."

"Because she probably doesn't fully realize it yet," Dixie said darkly.

She gave me a considering look. "You know something, Deborah? I'm really glad you turned up tonight. I seem to be in need of some up-to-the-minute legal advice."

"Advice? But you probably know as much as I do." Suddenly though, I wondered. "You *did* pass the bar, didn't you?"

"Nope. I went back for a while after Evelyn was out of therapy, but I couldn't seem to stick it. Luckily, a good job opened up here and one thing led to another and here I am—B.A. but no J.D."

Briskly, she checked her watch and swung into what was probably her Executive Director's mode. "We can talk about my problems later though. Right now, let's see. It's only eight-fifteen. I saw Pell—he's the one with the spare room—cruising the halls about twenty minutes ago which means he won't be home yet. Tell you what. Why don't you wander around, enjoy the Market while I mingle and show the flag?

Things'll start winding down in another half hour, so let's meet back at my office around nine?"

She gave me her card and sketched a simple map on the back. "These buildings can be a little confusing if you don't know where you're going. The easiest way is to take the elevator out there in the lobby down to nine, cross over the skywalk into the first building and then take the main elevator down to six. Here's what you do when you get off the elevator."

I was still studying her sketch when she walked over to Chan, handed him the plate Drew had fixed, then began making nice to those two retailers who seemed so upset with Fitch and Patterson's new sales policy.

The sea of people around the table parted briefly, and sitting on the blue tablecloth like a small island was a platter of those moist and chewy brownies, studded with walnuts and dusted in powdered sugar. Their siren voice of chocolate sang to me, tempting me with promises of sensuous pleasure, assuring me that of *course* I was strong enough to take just one tiny bite and throw away the rest. Since there wasn't a mast in sight to which I could lash myself, I launched off in the opposite direction.

Up by the bandstand, the American Leathergoods Wholesale Association's blue ox had grabbed a mike and was belting out "We Are Family."

He didn't sound at all like Sister Sledge.

Out in the vestibule, people were starting to leave both ballrooms and the elevators were as crowded going down as they had been coming up. In the second elevator, after crossing the skywalk, I was pushed against someone wearing such strong perfume that my sinuses began to close up and I got off as quickly as I could even though it was only the eighth floor.

These halls were as brightly lit as the others I'd seen, but most of the showrooms were locked and dark, and there were fewer people wandering around. A set of benches and planter boxes filled with flowering azaleas, irises and buttercups were clustered where four halls intersected. I had to touch the flowers to convince myself that they weren't real. A small sign announced that they were silk creations fabricated in Arizona and that orders could be placed at their showroom around the corner.

A harried-looking man in shirtsleeves and loosened tie had slung his jacket over one arm of a bench and papers spilled from his opened briefcase beside him as he spoke angrily to someone over his cell phone.

"—so they'd only give me one car. No, I do *not* know where Mary is. We lost her at the airport this morning and the fucking rental clerk wouldn't take my word that I was authorized to pick up the car she reserved in her name alone for some fucking reason. She's God knows where and the five of us are stuck with one car. Nothing to be had between here and Durham. So here's what I want you to do and I don't give a damn what it costs: start phoning and get me another fucking car! And if Mary calls in, tell her she's fired and I really mean it this time."

Having been through the same thing with hotel rooms, I could sympathize with his frustration over the shortage of rental cars, only there was nobody I could call up and bully into getting me what I needed.

I walked past him and wandered aimlessly through the

nearly empty halls, pausing here and there as a leather chair or chrome and glass coffee table or a sofa upholstered in a rich tapestry caught my eye. I tried to imagine Kidd Chapin's lanky, six-foot-three body stretched out on that couch, his head in my lap, flipping through the channels by remote control. Antique tapestry fit the picture better than the polished floral chintz in the adjoining showroom. Somehow I couldn't see Kidd amid floral chintz.

The trouble was I really didn't know what my tastes were when it came to furnishing a home.

There was a stretch of several years between the time I stormed away from my father's comfortably shabby farmhouse and the time I moved into the apartment my Aunt Zell and Uncle Ash had carved out for his mother on the second floor of their big white brick house, a few blocks from the courthouse in Dobbs.

In those years, home was wherever I happened to light for ten minutes. Some of the places were furnished in early Salvation Army; some were bare except for futons and sleeping bags and a few rickety tables and chairs.

Old Mrs. Smith had died the summer before I came home to Colleton County, and since Uncle Ash's job required a lot of traveling, Aunt Zell said I'd be doing her a favor if I moved in. Uncle Ash said he'd rest a lot easier on the road, knowing she wasn't alone in the house when he was gone. There was no way I was going to swallow my pride and go back to the farm, so it's worked out fine all around.

I've rearranged the furniture to accommodate some updated audio and video equipment, but otherwise the three-room apartment—bedroom, sitting room, efficiency kitchen—still reflects the late Mrs. Smith's taste for white organdy curtains, pale greens and blues, and dark wood. The place is bland enough not to jar on my nerves and pretty enough that I've never been motivated to redecorate, even though Julia Lee, the wife of my cousin and former law partner, is itching to redo the whole place.

A lot of my sisters-in-law have worried that I've settled in too comfortably at Aunt Zell's, and now that Uncle Ash is talking about retirement, they're pushing me to get a place of my own. Their thinking here is that while I'm acquiring new furniture and curtains and kitchen equipment, I'll get so caught up in domesticity that I may decide to go on and acquire myself a husband at the same time.

Land isn't a problem. Mother left me some and I've bought more of my own over the years. Several of my eleven brothers have offered to cut me off a couple of acres of their land anywhere I want, and Daddy would probably have the deed drawn up in ten minutes if I asked him for a building lot next to him.

Andrew's April knows of a 1920 bungalow in Cotton Grove that's up for sale. "You could move it out by the long pond. Be cheaper than building from scratch."

Zach gave me floor plans for some houses that would use passive solar design to heat and cool.

Herman says never mind about passive solar. He and Annie Sue and Reese will wire a house for me at cost.

My nephew Reese, who's closer to my age than his father is, says I just ought to pull in a double-wide on the back side of that Stephenson land, well away from the rest of the family, and make sure it has a king-sized water bed.

Reese has a point.

Since Kidd's the reason I do finally want a private place

of my own, maybe I should start with the bedroom and branch out from there.

But just looking at the variety of beds along this hallway made my head spin: old-fashioned four-posters or modern versions with posts that were a foot square and eight feet tall? Mahogany Chippendale headboard or oak Moderne? Organdy ruffled canopy or tapestried tester? Or, hmm-m. What had we here?

The showroom was locked, but lights had been left on inside. Above the door hung a wide white board that was lettered in shiny black enamel: *Stanberry Collection.* A leafy green vine with generic purple berries twined through the letters.

Although there were several hand-painted three- and four-panel folding screens scattered around the small showroom and clustered across the rear corner, the Stanberry Collection seemed to consist mainly of headboards, headboards of a design I'd never seen before. These were like upright wooden boxes that slanted back at a slight pitch and had a wide ledge at the top. With a few pillows, you could lean back at a comfortable angle to read or watch television and the ledge would still be a few inches higher than your head so that your pillows wouldn't bump into your books or pictures or whatever personal knick-knacks you wanted to display. The slanted headboard was hinged at the bottom and magnetic latches at the top allowed access to a concealed space that could store extra pillows or hide the family silver. The box extended around on either side of the mattress where it jutted forward to become built-in bedside tables wide enough to hold reading lamps, radios, and bedtime snacks. Some were a series of open shelves, others had a couple of drawers built in below. Some were constructed of fine-grained natural woods, but most were painted and then stenciled in sophisticated colors and patterns.

They really were quite striking and extremely practical and I was not the only one drawn to the Stanberry Collection. Another man had left his briefcase on the floor beside me and was roaming up and down the long windows, occasionally pressing his face right up against the glass and cupping his hands around his eyes as if to see past any reflected glare.

All of a sudden, I heard a muted roar from inside the showroom and saw a man, his face contorted with fury, dart out from behind those screens at the rear and rush toward the door.

Instantly, my fellow viewer jerked back from the window and hurried over to collect his briefcase, which was now behind me.

I tried to zig as he zagged and we wound up in that embarrassing tango of two strangers trying to pass each other, until he quit trying and barreled right into me. I went flying into the projecting corner of the hall with such force that my shoulder hit the sharp edge and I gasped in pain. In his haste, he stumbled over his briefcase and sprawled full length on the floor. He scrambled up almost immediately but that slight delay was just enough to let the second man fling open the door and pounce on him.

"Okay, asshole! Gimme the film," he snarled.

The first man tried to bluster, but even though he was a couple of inches taller and several pounds heavier, the showroom proprietor wasn't intimidated.

"Give me the film or I'll stomp your camera."

Defeated, the man took a tiny camera out of his pocket, snapped it open, and extracted the film.

"I see you or anybody from your company back here again, I'll stomp your camera *and* smash your face. You got it?"

"Yeah, yeah," muttered the other man as he slunk away.

The second man finished exposing the roll of film and turned to me with a big smile. "Hey, you okay?"

"I guess so," I said, rubbing my bruised shoulder. "What was all that about?"

"Bastard was trying to steal our designs."

"Jeff?"

The woman who came out to join us was about my age and height, but her almond-shaped eyes and straight black hair showed an Asian heritage even though she spoke with no discernible accent. She carried a battery-operated vacuum cleaner and gave me a friendly smile as her husband explained why he'd rushed out like that. "And if this lady hadn't been there to slow him down, he'd have got away."

"We're Mai and Jeff Stanberry," the woman said. "If you're interested, we'll be glad to show you our line."

According to the clock on the wall behind her, I had enough time and soon I was happily wandering through the Stanberry Collection, opening drawers, admiring the capacious storage space in each headboard, and picturing my mother's *Made in Occupied Japan* porcelain shepherdess and a few other personal treasures clustered on the top ledge of a painted headboard while the Stanberrys proudly explained that theirs was a fairly new company.

"Originally, we were just going to build screens. I'm an artist and Jeff's an engineer. He knows about hinges and strapping and ratios of board feet to finished product, and I know decoupage and stenciling. We brought two dozen to our first show three years ago and sold out, but there's not much profit in them."

Their line of headboards grew out of a lack of finances to buy a ready-made one, coupled with their fondness for reading in bed.

"So Jeff started out with a slanted backrest."

"And Mai realized that a piano hinge at the bottom would let us utilize the empty space behind for storage."

"Then Jeff wanted a place for his cassette player—"

"I like to listen to old Nichols and May routines when I'm going to sleep."

"—and I wanted my clock radio and a box of Kleenex."

"And that was the first prototype of these."

"Last year we brought three-dozen screens and a dozen headboards and went home with enough orders to hire two people to help us," Mai said proudly. "A carpenter and a painter."

"And if we do good this year," said Jeff, "we can maybe move out of the garage and get a real workshop."

They told me that this was the first time they'd rented an official showroom.

"Before, we've had open booth spaces across the street at Market Square. This year we can afford a real showroom. We may be small, but our quality is high and we don't make promises we can't deliver on."

They gave me their brochure and an order form and I found the model number of the headboard I was sure would be perfect for my new house, whatever that house turned out to be.

"This is my first Market," I said, circling the model number, "so I don't quite understand why you think that guy was stealing your designs. Don't you have a patent?"

They laughed and Jeff Stanberry said, "You *are* new, aren't you? We do what we can to protect ourselves, but if a big company wants to do a knockoff of our designs, their pockets are a lot deeper than ours if we tried to sue."

"All we can do," said Mai Stanberry, "is try to land as many new accounts as we can before the big boys notice us." She gave a winsome smile. "So! Does Home-Lite do a large volume in sleep products?"

Guiltily, I realized that my badge had misled them into thinking I was a buyer. "I'm afraid I'm not exactly a commercial customer."

Jeff Stanberry gave me a wary look. "Hey, you're not another exhibitor looking to knock us off, are you?"

"Nothing to do with the Market at all," I assured him. "Someone gave me this badge so I could get into one of the parties upstairs. I'm actually a district court judge. And I really do like that headboard. Does anybody in the Raleigh area carry it?"

"Not yet," said Mai. "But we've had nibbles."

"If you land one, would you please have the store drop me a note? Or can I order from you directly?"

"Tell you what," said Jeff. "If you're going to be around till the end of the show next week, we'll be selling these samples at wholesale so we don't have to cart them back to the mountains with us. If you like, I'll red dot the one you want and you can pick it up then."

Before one of us could change our mind, I sent Reese a mental thank-you and reached into my tote bag for my checkbook.

Instead of my purse, though, my hand closed around a plastic bag of fried chicken.

5

"Among the marvelous accomplishments of human study and genius, nothing, all facts considered, can well be regarded as more important than man's triumph over space and time in the matter of the intercommunication of widely separated individuals."

The Great Industries of the United States, 1872

The Stanberrys stared while I slapped at my pockets in mild panic. All I needed to make this day complete was having to spend half the night on the phone trying to cancel all my credit cards.

My wallet is nothing more than a flat nylon-and-Velcro folder made to hold driver's license, the usual set of cards and whatever paper money I happen to have on hand. When I travel, I usually stick it in an inside jacket pocket so that I don't have to dig through my purse at the gas station or ATM.

Happily, my wallet was still there.

Unhappily, my car keys were with my purse and checkbook. Not to mention my cellular phone, lipstick, hairbrush and God knows what else.

"Something wrong?" asked Mai Stanberry.

"This isn't my tote bag."

Of course it had to be Savannah, the erstwhile Matilda McNeill Jernigan alias Louisa May Ferncliff alias Melissa Dorcas Pond or whatever that last alias was, who had taken my bag by mistake.

At least I *hoped* it was by mistake.

"Of course it was," said the preacher who lives in the back of my head (and who always gives everyone the benefit of the doubt).

"Humph!" snorted the pragmatist (who doesn't).

The Stanberrys were sympathetic once I convinced them that this wasn't some sort of con game. They weren't set up to take plastic, but they did agree to take my business card and a fifty-dollar deposit, which was all the cash I thought I could spare without hunting for an ATM.

By then it was two minutes till nine, and now I had to worry that Dixie might leave without me.

"Hey!" called Mai as I hurried down the hall. "I thought you wanted to get to the main elevators."

"I do."

"Then you're going in the wrong direction. It's this way. Come on, I'd better show you."

I hadn't realized how many branchings I had taken, but

eventually we turned a final corner and there were the elevators.

"See you next week," said Mai as I pushed the Down button.

Nice woman. And tactful, too, to pretend she believed that I could actually find my way back to their showroom in only a week.

Two cars went past—one with a blue ox—then a third, and each time there was no room for me.

An exit sign over a doorway at the end of a short hall finally convinced me that it would be quicker to walk down.

Inside the stairwell I found a world removed from polished tile and gleaming glass. Here were grungy walls, concrete steps, utilitarian steel railings and low-wattage lightbulbs. Here also was an institutional smell that was one part disinfectant and the other part damp cement with just a dash of machine oil for pungency. No windows, of course, no markings on the doors, and utter silence except for the sound of my echoing steps.

After several flights, I lost track of the floors and pulled open a door hoping to see someone to ask. Instead, I seemed to be standing at the back of a dark and deserted showroom filled with wicker chairs and couches.

"Careful you don't set off a burglar alarm," whispered the preacher.

"Better try Door Number Two," advised the pragmatist.

As I closed the door and stepped back into the dimly lit stairwell, I heard another door swoosh open below me. Great! Someone I could ask for directions.

But when I reached the next landing, there was no one in sight and no sound of other footsteps. Puzzled, I tried the door. It didn't budge.

I began to get uneasy. And just a tad claustrophobic. Surely I was on the sixth floor by now? But what if all the rest of the doors were locked? Should I go back up or keep going down?

I compromised and continued on down. One more door, I told myself. If it didn't open, then I would go back up and take my chances with the wicker. A banner headline flashed across my mind: JUDGE NABBED IN MARKET BREAK-IN.

As I paused on the landing, I heard the door I'd just tried slowly open on the landing above. I shrank back in the corner shadows directly below and froze.

A long silence, then the door gently closed and footsteps started down.

I hadn't checked to see what else was under the fried chicken, but that tote bag had a certain heft and I wound the straps around my hand, prepared to slug my way past whoever was playing cat and mouse with me.

The steps came closer, closer. They had nearly reached the foot of the flight when I stepped out of the shadows and with tote bag poised to strike, rasped, "What are you—?" before I recognized the woman.

She gave a terrified moan and all the color drained from her face as she half fell, half scrambled back up the stairs.

"Wait!" I called, running after her. "I won't hurt you. I thought you were chasing *me*! Please stop."

She turned and faced me warily, a stocky young woman with long black hair. Color crept back into her face as she recognized me. "You're the one who was with Savannah at the reception upstairs."

It was the reporter from *Furniture/Today*.

"And you followed her out of the Leathergoods party," I said.

"You scared the bloody hell out of me," she said, taking deep breaths as she pushed her heavy hair away from her face.

I realized I was breathing just as deeply. "How do you think *I* felt hearing someone sneaking in and out of the same door?"

"God! When you pushed against it, I thought I was going to pass out."

"We are Woman," I said wryly. "Hear us whimper."

She gave a shaky smile. Her face was too broad and her nose was a little too big for prettiness, but her smile was engaging and intelligence shone in her dark eyes.

"Do you have any idea where we are?"

"I think that was the fifth floor," she said in an accent I couldn't quite place.

"Hallway or showroom?"

"Hallway. All the elevator cars were full so I thought I'd walk down, but when I heard your footsteps, I got nervous for some reason."

"I think I'll see if I can get one going up," I said.

"Maybe I'll come with you. I've had enough of creepy stairwells for one night."

"I thought you said you just got here."

"But I've been pretty well lost for the last half hour," she said, following me up the steps. "I went after Savannah, hoping for an interview. I want to write an article on her."

"Did you get it?"

"She never let me get close. I was going to wait till she left the elevator, but she didn't get off till the ground floor and it was so damn crowded I had trouble keeping up. That woman can move when she wants to."

"Tell me about it," I said, remembering how I'd had to rush to stay with her earlier in the evening.

"I saw her go through a door at the far end of the corridor and I didn't think to see if I could get out again until it latched tight. But I could hear her rushing on down the steps as if she were late for an appointment and I figured she must know a shortcut out. It was like Alice following the White Rabbit. I don't know how far down I went, but I think I must have wound up in a sub-sub-basement—really dark and creepy. I called, but she never answered and I started thinking maybe it was pretty dumb to go wandering around the bowels of a deserted building. Except that I knew it wasn't deserted. That's what's so weird about this place. Parts of it are jammed to the gills while other parts are like this."

I reached the landing, pushed open the door, and we were back in civilization again. Around the corner, a cluster of laughing and chattering sales reps were waiting for a Down elevator. I mashed the Up button and was almost immediately rewarded with an empty car.

"Hey, great idea!" said one of the men. "If we ride up, we can then ride down."

So many of them piled in with us that we were separated and when I got off at the sixth floor, I expected that she would continue on up. Instead, she pushed her way through and looked at me like a happy, long-haired puppy.

"You know, we didn't actually get introduced before. I'm Heather McKenzie."

"Deborah Knott," I said, as I studied Dixie's diagram.

Her office wasn't hard to find. Straight down the hall past Vittorio E's, Dixie had said.

Vittorio E's was a large showroom filled with what, for lack of a better term, I would call Italian Provincial. The pieces would have been right at home in the first Victor Emmanuel's palace. All the rococo couches and tables and chairs had bent—cabriole?—legs and all the exposed wood was either painted an antique ivory or ornately encrusted in gleaming gilt.

What stopped me in my tracks though was a lamp that sat atop a bow-fronted ivory-and-gold chest: the base was a three-foot-long porcelain piece cast in the image and likeness of an eighteenth-century open carriage pulled by four white horses with pink plumes on their heads. The carriage held four porcelain Barbie types in period bouffant wigs and colorful, low-cut dresses. The whole improbable contrivance was topped by a pink silk lampshade shaped like Aunt Zell's oval roasting pan if you turned it upside down and put a pink fringe around the bottom.

Heather McKenzie giggled. "How would you like to have something like that in your living room?"

I shook my head. "I don't think there's a single house in North Carolina that could live up to that lamp, but I've got a sister-in-law who would just love it to death."

On the corner beyond Vittorio E's was an open gallery that featured what I was learning to call motion furniture, i.e., anything that rocked, reclined, swiveled, tilted, popped up or swung. As we approached, several people seemed to be rocking and swinging, but as we got closer, I saw that Dixie Babcock and another woman were the only real people. The rest of the figures were stuffed dummies that looked like large Cabbage Patch dolls.

"There you are," said Dixie. She stood up and smoothed the wrinkles from her chic green linen dress. "I was beginning to wonder if I needed to send out a Saint Bernard."

The other woman stood up, too, and began carrying the dummies inside a lockable area of the gallery.

"Aw, they looked comfortable," said Heather.

The woman laughed. "We left one of them out last year and somebody carted him off to a party at the Longhorn."

"No one steals the chairs?" I asked.

She pointed to inconspicuous bolts and chains. "Not yet." She held out her hand. "Kelly Crisco."

"Oh, I'm sorry," said Dixie and hastily introduced me as an old friend and Market first-timer.

"And this is Heather McKenzie from *Furniture/Today*."

"Oh, yes," said Dixie. "You were with Jay Patterson."

She leaned forward to look at Heather's badge more closely. "Are you new to the paper?"

"Actually, I'm a freelancer from the Massachusetts office," she said, which explained the accent. "They asked me to do some profiles on some of the legends of the Market, and Savannah's my first choice. They say she originated so many design concepts that have become standard practice. Do you know her?"

"I thought I did, but tonight's the first time I've seen her in ages and I barely recognized her." Dixie glanced at her watch. "Sorry to break this up, but I've got a rough day tomorrow. Pell said he'd be glad to put you up as long as you need, Deborah. Where're you parked?"

"That's going to be a bit of a problem," I said and explained about the mix-up with the totes. "I've got Savannah's fried chicken and she has my purse, car keys, checkbook, cell phone—hey! Wait a minute. You don't suppose—?"

Dixie grinned. "Worth a try. Wasn't there a guy last year who had his car stolen and he called up his car phone—"

"Yeah," said Heather. "And he talked the thief into bringing it back for what the insurance company would have paid him."

We said goodnight to Ms. Crisco and walked down to Dixie's phone in the Southern Retail Furnishings Alliance office where I dialed my cell phone.

It took two tries and eight rings before a husky Lauren Bacall voice said, "Hello?"

6

"*The general good sense of the people is superior to their philosophy, even though the latter be clothed in the dignified solemnity of the Puritan, or wear the soft graces of the purely religious enthusiast.*"
The Great Industries of the United States, 1872

Trying to sound like a friendly non-threatening airhead with no ulterior reasons for calling except to get my own bag back, I said, "Ma'am? This is Deborah Knott. We had supper together at the food court this evening?"

Silence.

"Ma'am?" (No way was I going to risk offending her with any of the names she'd used in my hearing.) "I don't know how I made such a silly mistake, but you remember those

Fitch and Patterson tote bags they gave us? Well, we seem to have gotten them mixed up."

More silence, but at least she hadn't cut me off.

"So what I was wondering was if I could come and bring you yours and get mine because I left my car keys in it?"

"No, no, no!" Her husky voice held the same vehement withdrawal as when I'd suggested earlier that she might let me crash on her sofa.

Hastily, I amended, "Or maybe we could meet somewhere? I'm at Dixie Babcock's office on the sixth floor of the Global Home Furnishings Market and she could bring me anywhere you say."

I raised my eyebrows inquiringly at Dixie and she nodded.

"Please? I really do need my things tonight and I'm sure you want yours?"

"Go to the open door," she said at last.

I looked around wildly. The Southern Retail Furnishings Alliance suite consisted of Dixie's office and two smaller ones, a generous reception area and an overcrowded work/storage area that housed the basic machines without which no modern office can function: fax, communal printer, copier, microwave and coffee maker. From where I stood, every door in sight was already wide open.

"*Which* open door?" I asked.

There was a barking sound at her end of the connection. It took me a moment to recognize that the sound was laughter.

"On North Centennial," she said. "I will leave your bag with Yolanda and you may do the same with mine."

"Yolanda who? And when will you be there?"

Too late. The connection was broken. I tried to call her back, but after three rings, an operator came on the line to inform me that the person I was calling was unavailable at that time.

Savannah must have found the Off switch.

"Not to worry," Dixie told me. "North Centennial? She probably means the Open Door Ministry. It's a shelter for the homeless and Yolanda Jackson runs the soup kitchen for the hungry. The Father's Table. I've volunteered there a few times. It's not far."

"May I come with you?" asked Heather McKenzie.

"Only if you promise not to spook her before I get my purse back," I said.

Dixie picked up her own purse and keys. As she began switching off lights, the phone rang.

"That's either Pell or the baby-sitter wondering where we are," she said and picked up the receiver. "Dixie Babcock . . . Oh, Mr. Sherrin." Her voice flattened and then became artificially bright. "Good to hear your voice, too. When did you get in?"

She gave us a pained look and her free fingers pantomimed a ponderous male mouth opening and closing with pompous authority. After a couple of minutes in which her side of the conversation seemed limited to "Yes, I see, yes," she put her hand over the mouthpiece and whispered, "One of the directors. He's liable to talk another twenty minutes. Why don't you two go on ahead and I'll catch up with you at the shelter—yes, Mr. Sherrin, yes I *do* see, but—"

She tore a sheet off her scratch pad and drew us a rough map of where to go.

"We can take my car," Heather McKenzie said. "It's just over in the Holiday Inn parking lot."

As we left, Dixie's voice followed us down the now-deserted hall, "Yes . . . I see . . . yes . . ."

After nearly three hours of new-furniture smells, it felt good to get outside to a spring night in North Carolina. Despite dew-dampened streets, car exhausts, and occasional whiffs of fried food, there was an overarching sweet freshness to the April air. Cars and shuttle buses had melted away for the evening and now High Point's Main Street was almost as traffic-free as I remembered.

Just as Dixie Babcock was probably ten years older than me—"Than *I*," came Aunt Zell's schoolteacher voice in my head—Heather McKenzie was probably ten years younger. She was also several inches shorter yet her stride matched mine as we crossed Main Street to the Holiday Inn, and she seemed to be enjoying the cool air, too. Her camel slacks and teal blue blazer looked expensive and fit her compact body stylishly but they weren't exactly designed for April in North Carolina.

"Wasn't that jacket hot today?"

"If it stays this warm, I'll have to buy something cotton," she admitted. "I wasn't thinking clearly when I packed nothing but wool and corduroy."

"This your first time in the South?"

"First time to really look around and enjoy."

"Oh?"

"Actually, I was born in Georgia, but my parents took me North when I was only ten days old. It's so different down here, isn't it? Everything's already in bloom. Up there, buds are barely starting to swell."

Her car was a white Lexus and the passenger seat was littered with maps and folders and a couple of empty fast-food bags.

"Sorry about the mess," Heather said. "Just throw all that stuff on the backseat."

As I gathered up a handful, a glossy eight-by-ten sienna-toned photograph slid out of one folder. It showed three people in a workroom or studio. Sketches of furniture groupings covered the bulletin board behind the tilt-top drawing table. The central figure was a small, dark-haired woman, who'd half turned on her swivel stool and had one high-heeled foot extended as if she were about to stand. She wore black slacks, a short-sleeved black turtleneck, and what looked like an authentic Navajo squash blossom necklace of turquoise and silver.

She was laughing at the two men, who looked as if they could eat her with a spoon. The first was casually dressed and unfamiliar to me, but the man in a sports jacket and tie was a much younger Jay Patterson, unmistakable with his broad face, square jaw and bulbous nose. It took me half a minute longer to realize that the small stylish woman in this photograph was the same chiffon-draped Matilda McNeill Jernigan that we were on our way to meet at a homeless shelter.

"Dear Lord above!" I exclaimed. "If this is what Savannah looked like when she left, no wonder people didn't immediately recognize her tonight."

Heather took the photograph and slid it back into the folder. "I just hope she'll talk to me. You were with her tonight. What's she like?"

"Nothing like the reactions I've heard from people who knew her. I thought she was someone's eccentric mother or grandmother. She talked about the Market, but anyone who lives in High Point could probably tell you the same things she told me. Do you specialize in furniture people up there in Massachusetts?"

"Not really," she answered vaguely.

We had turned off Main and were now driving east on Kivett Drive. Heather, who'd been in town long enough to get her bearings, pointed out various buildings: "The Hamilton Square showrooms are over there and Hamilton Wrenn's here, and down that way's a building shaped like the world's largest bureau if you're into that sort of thing."

"I'm more interested in shopping than doing the tourist bit," I told her.

"All the same, you really ought to go by the Discovery Center and see how a furniture factory works if you've never been inside one," she said. "It's amazing to see how they set the knives for cutting legs and spindles when a piece is in production."

She turned left on North Centennial Street and soon pulled into the parking lot beside a red brick building. Open stairs mounted to the second floor and several men lounged there under the security light to smoke their cigarettes, a mix of black and white, drably dressed, an air of defeat on most of them. And even though I'd never seen them before, they were familiar to me. I'd probably see some of these very men in court next week.

Their eyes sized us up as we approached and when I said, "Yolanda Jackson? The Father's Table?" a couple of them

gestured to the short flight of steps that led down to a metal
door beneath the stairs.

The basement was built of cement blocks. Beyond a small
vestibule were double glass doors that led into a large and
surprisingly cheerful dining area. Although the ceiling was
low, there was nothing cavelike about the room. Its block
walls had been painted off-white and someone had done
fool-the-eye paintings which gave the illusion of looking out
wide windows into a vaguely Biblical landscape of calm
green hills. Painted geraniums bloomed on the "window
ledges" and green vines seemed to twine along the top.

The fifteen or twenty bleached-oak tables had matching
chairs stacked upon them and an elderly white man was
mopping the floor.

He gave us a smile as we came in, but kept mopping. Instead, we were greeted by a small, energetic woman of late
middle age with flashing brown eyes, beautiful olive skin
and short black hair that had a heavy dusting of gray. Her
smile was warm and welcoming but with a touch of regret.
"I'm sorry, but we've finished serving for the evening. If
you're hungry though, I could give you some bananas and
maybe a peanut butter sandwich."

"We're not here to eat," I said. "We're just looking for
Yolanda Jackson."

If possible, her smile became even warmer. "I'm Yolanda.
How can I help you?"

I introduced myself and Heather, then said, "A woman
asked us to meet her here tonight. She's wearing a dress that
looks as if it's made out of chiffon scarves. A Matilda Mc-
Neill Jernigan or maybe Louisa May Fern—"

"Savannah," the woman interrupted.

"You know her?" asked Heather, surprised.

"Sure. She's been coming to us since the end of January."

"No, I mean, do you know who she really was?"

"I know who she *is*," said Yolanda firmly. "But I've lived in High Point long enough that if you're asking if I know she used to be an important designer, yes, I know that, too."

"Does she ever talk about it?" Heather asked eagerly.

The woman's friendly smile faded.

"Why are you really here?" she asked us sharply. "What is Savannah to you?"

I explained about the mix-up in tote bags and Heather described the series of profiles she wanted to do on Market innovators.

"She may come. She may even bring back your bag. But talk about herself?" Yolanda Jackson gave a Latin shrug. "She doesn't speak of her past life once. Not about the furniture part anyhow."

"About other things?" asked Heather.

Yolanda gave her a slow, appraising look and her lively brown eyes narrowed. "That's not for me to say. When people come here, I give them dignity and respect. What they tell me in confidence, I keep in confidence. And now I must leave you. You may wait until we lock up if you want to, but I have work to do."

She crossed the room and disappeared into a corridor beyond the kitchen.

The old man finished mopping and courteously lifted down two chairs from a nearby table and set them on the damp floor for us.

I checked my watch. It was now nearly twenty-five minutes since I'd spoken to Savannah, almost twenty since we left Dixie, and no sign of either woman.

"Maybe there's something in her bag that could tell us where she lives," said Heather when another five minutes passed and conversation dwindled to nothingness.

I pulled the Fitch and Patterson brochures from the bag, then the packets of fried chicken and another of ribs. Beneath that was a mahogany doorstop carved in the shape of a frog sitting on a lily pad, a flashlight, several chiffon scarves, and a much-folded page torn from an issue of *Furniture/Today*. The date at the bottom was last December. One side carried a full-page story about a cooperative venture between a Chinese particle-board manufacturer and an American-based company. On the other side was a picture of Jay and Elizabeth Patterson with their daughter Drew and Dixie's son-in-law Chan at a party somewhere.

A little black book with her own address circled in red would have been nice, but the bag held nothing that helpful.

As we sat there, an occasional man or woman, one with three young children, came in for bananas, and Heather watched each one with covert distaste.

"You know what must be the worst thing about being poor?" she said suddenly. "The clothes you have to wear. Old clothes are so—so *gray*. No bright clear colors."

Beneath her own rich blue jacket, she wore a white silk shirt. A purple and red silk scarf was tucked into the open neckline. Her nails were short, but neatly manicured and painted a pink that matched her lipstick. Clearly color was important to her, but— "Believe me," I said. "Drab, faded clothing is not the worst thing about being poor."

"Savannah must feel the same way," she said, ignoring my remark. "You have to admire her for that. Even if her mind's a little scrambled right now, she hasn't been defeated. She still finds a way to wear colors."

"Which is odd, if you think about it," I said idly. "I heard that she never wore color before. Just black."

We were abruptly joined at our end of the table by a belligerent man who hunched and mumbled over his banana as if afraid we were going to try to snatch it from him—another manifestation of the Law of Unintended Results.

Civil rights for the mentally handicapped and the mainstreaming of psychotics back into the community are commendable goals, but when Reaganites emptied out our federally funded institutions, they sent federal patients home without compensatory federal funding. I've had a lot of these unfortunates in my court, and I've seen the despair of their families, who've been pushed to the end of their financial and emotional limits. When I say that I'll ask to have a relative put on a waiting list, we both know that our county facilities can't begin to service the number of seriously disturbed people who need help.

This man who guarded his banana from us probably wasn't violent, but you can never be sure. I'd have felt more comfortable if I'd had my usual bailiff near at hand.

After thirty minutes, it seemed clear to me that Savannah wasn't going to show. Heather would have waited longer but Yolanda Jackson was ready to lock up, so I gave her the tote bag and asked her to please hang on to my purse if Savannah should happen to bring it in. "And if Dixie Babcock comes looking for us, would you tell her I'll be sitting on the sidewalk in front of her building if she's not in her office?"

Yolanda looked at the man who'd been sharing our table. Where I saw latent paranoia, she seemed to see an ordinary human being who had no reason not to be helpful. "Hey, George? You gonna be sitting on the steps for a while? If this lady's friend comes looking for her, tell her she's gone back to the office building, okay?"

She gave his arm a squeeze.

"Yeah, okay," he mumbled, and as we drove away, I looked back. He was sitting on the very top step, watching, and he gave me a thumbs-up gesture.

A few exhibitors were still straggling out of the GHFM building when Heather dropped me off a few minutes past ten. Inside the lobby, the guard gave me a dubious look as I passed, but I flashed my badge and kept going to the elevators.

Everything was silent on the sixth floor and the tap of my heels echoed loudly on the polished tile as I hurried past Vittorio E's gold-and-ivory display and turned the corner past the motion furniture's archway.

Dixie's door was closed and the office looked dark. I could see a note taped to the door, but I didn't go down the hall to read it because I suddenly noticed that Kelly Crisco had left one of those large dummies face down in the swing.

Except that he was clutching the cushions in a way no dummy could.

The cowboy boots looked familiar.

"Chan?"

He didn't move and his breathing seemed shallow and irregular.

I touched a pulse point on his neck and the heartbeat was

almost undetectable. An odor of alcohol, chocolate and sour vomit emanated from the cushion beneath his head, and he didn't respond when I shook his shoulder.

I flew back down the hall to the elevator and cursed its slow descent every inch of the way.

As the door opened to the ground floor, I was startled to see Dixie talking to the guard. She smiled and said, "Perfect timing. Ready to go?"

"Call an ambulance," I gasped. "It's Chan. Up at the Swingtyme place. I think he's dying!"

7

"*Even in our own times, with all the industrial appliances and the more extended knowledge which characterizes this epoch of modern civilization, a satisfactory bed has been realized only within the last few years.*"

The Great Industries of the United States, 1872

For the rest of the night, without car keys or hotel room, I was a helpless participant in someone else's drama.

Later I was glad that I'd been there for Dixie when she had no one else, but she hadn't immediately needed my shoulder and I felt like an intruder.

While the guard summoned help, she left a message on her friend Pell's machine, asking him to send the baby-sitter home and to hold the fort till she got there. Then we followed the ambulance over to the hospital and sat outside the ER while the trauma team worked to stabilize Chan's breathing.

As a nurse took down his history and questioned Dixie about his allergies, I remembered that I'd seen a gold medic alert on one of his neck chains.

"He's allergic to several things," Dixie said, "especially bee and wasp stings. He almost went into shock the last time he was stung."

Allergies? Could allergies have been the reason for his heavy breathing that spring in Maryland and not my fallen-woman status?

Dixie looked at me guiltily when the nurse was gone. "I must have just missed him. He knows I keep a stash of anti-histamines in my office for my own hay fever, especially with pine pollen so bad right now. Maybe he felt an attack coming on and came looking for me."

"If he's that allergic, he must carry his own supply," I argued.

"Maybe. Thank God Lynnette inherited Evelyn's constitution and not his."

Here in the ER waiting room with us were a black mother and an obviously feverish child who leaned against her mother's comforting bulk with listless apathy.

A defeated looking middle-aged white couple—he in overalls, she in a faded print housedress—waited for someone to see them. The wife's eyes were pools of anxiety and she kept asking him in low tones how he felt. He merely grunted and sat hunched over with his crossed hands pushing against his abdomen as if to hold back the pain that left him gray-faced and sweating.

Two shabbily dressed white teenagers whispered together on a corner couch and a large black woman with a dazed expression kept going up to the receptionist every few minutes to ask, "He's gonna be okay, ain't he?"

The black receptionist was patient, but obviously harried. "They still haven't told me anything, Ms. Robinson. I promise I'll let you know the minute they do."

Two very bloody and very drunk white adolescent boys came rushing through the door, propelled by a white High Point policeman. They yelled that they were the victims of police brutality, probably maimed for life, and that their fathers would have his badge. The trouble was not that they really believed it but that their fathers probably believed it, too.

They alternated their belligerent threats with whining complaints and rather than sit there and listen to them, I went out to hunt up some coffee. It took a while but what I finally found smelled delicious and when I got back, Dixie sipped hers appreciatively.

"What happened to the Hardy boys?" I asked, but she looked at me blankly and I realized that very little about this waiting room was registering.

To take her mind off Chan, I said, "You mentioned earlier you wanted some legal advice?"

She sighed. "It seems so petty now with Chan like this."

"It concerns him?"

She nodded. "I wanted an update on grandparents' rights. You heard him earlier. Jacaranda's merging with a company in Malaysia and he's going to take that job. Uproot Lynnette and haul her off to Kuala Lumpur halfway around the world where I'll never see her except in the summer. If I'm lucky."

Tears filled her eyes. "She's all I have left of Evelyn. What if he finds someone out there and remarries? What if she's jealous of his first marriage with Evelyn and won't let me visit Lynnette? Don't I have any rights at all?"

"Well . . ." I said cautiously, "as a judge, I'm not allowed to give legal advice, but if you want to hear what a friend thinks—"

Dixie slumped back in the ugly plastic chair, discouraged. "I know, I know. As long as he's a good father, I have no real rights, just what he chooses to give me."

"*Is* he a good father?" I asked.

"Materially, yes."

"But not emotionally?"

"How do I know, Deborah?"

"Don't you?"

She gave a reluctant grin. "You really haven't changed, have you? Okay. You're right. He dotes on her and she adores him right back. But then, most females *do* adore Chan."

"Like Drew Patterson?"

"Exactly like Drew. She'd marry him tomorrow and don't I wish! She's crazy about Lynnette, too, and even if they did move to Malaysia, she'd see to it that I stayed part of their life. But Chan—"

She broke off as a nurse came out and asked if we'd come with her. She led us into a small room furnished with only a few chairs and benches. A doctor in green scrubs was waiting for us. His face was young but his weary eyes were ancient.

"Mrs. Babcock?" There was pity in his voice. "I'm truly sorry to have to tell you this . . . We did everything we could. Unfortunately, Mr. Nolan didn't make it."

"Didn't make it?" Dixie looked at him blankly, as if his words held no meaning.

I was just as uncomprehending. "He's dead?"

That laughing, dancing, sexy hunk of manhood?

"I'm truly sorry," the doctor said again. "He was already in anaphylaxis when he got here and we just couldn't reverse it. Were you with him earlier? Was he stung or did he accidentally eat something he's allergic to?"

"Not that I know of." Her chestnut hair swirled around her face as she shook her head.

"Those chocolate brownies?" I offered, trying to be helpful. "Nuts?"

She shook her head even more vigorously. "Foods never seem to bother him all that much. It's the histamines and pollen, of course."

She looked at the doctor. "Pine pollen's so bad this time of year, but he was taking something for it. Could he have taken too much?"

The doctor looked dubious. "His condition didn't quite present that way, but I'll check. Who was his allergist?"

"I'm not sure. Is there a Dr. Harrison over in Winston?"

"Amos Harrison. Right. I'll give him a call." He patted Dixie's hand, murmured more apologies, then left us with a nurse to finish filling in the forms.

"You're Mr. Nolan's next of kin, right?" the nurse asked.

"Next of kin? No, not really. He's my son-in-law. I guess my granddaughter? But she's only six. She couldn't possibly—"

"Oh, no, ma'am. It would have to be an adult. What about his parents?"

"They're both dead, but his sister's in Maryland. I don't have her number with me though."

Dixie looked at me in grief and dismay and I told the nurse, "Let me take her home now and she'll call you in the morning with that information."

The nurse nodded sympathetically. "Certainly."

More than ever I felt the loss of my purse and keys and the lack of a hotel room. I realized now that Yolanda Jackson at the shelter must have been the "she" that Savannah had thought could help me with a bed. I offered to try to call her, but Dixie wouldn't hear of it, so I followed her out into the parking lot and again the cool night air felt like spring and new beginnings.

As we drove to her house on the north side of town, Dixie spoke of Chan and her daughter Evelyn, of how she had never been able to trust his salesman's charm, his smoothness, his easy way with women.

"He even flirted with me, for God's sake. His own mother-in-law! I knew he wouldn't be faithful, but you couldn't tell Evelyn. Not that I ever tried to, once she was married to him. She had to have known though. Women couldn't keep their hands off him. They throw themselves at him and he doesn't—*didn't*—always dodge. After Evelyn died, poor little Drew almost made herself sick before he started seeing her."

Fairness made her admit that at least Chan kept up appearances and hadn't flaunted his unfaithfulness to Evelyn. "I honestly think he loved her as much as he could love any one woman and he did make her happy most of the time."

As her thoughts turned from the past to the future, she sighed and worried aloud about telling Lynnette. "She'll probably be asleep when we get home, but even if she isn't, I think I'll wait till tomorrow so she doesn't lie awake all night grieving." She sighed again. "I guess I'd better go ahead and call Chan's sister tonight, though. It's going to be rough. They have one of those big-brother/little-sister relationships and she still idolizes him."

I tried to remember a little sister, but truth to tell, I'd been in such a self-destructive haze that year after my mother died that I could barely conjure up any real sense of Chan's teenage personality beyond his groping hands and pimply face. What he talked about, whether he sneezed much, who his people were—what little I did remember was rapidly being overlaid and replaced by the vividness of the man he had become.

A few blocks east of Main Street, Dixie turned into an alleyway that formed a cul-de-sac between two old bungalows. From what I could see by the streetlights, they had been restored to prewar beauty and looked both trendy and solid at the same time.

A slender, loose-limbed man appeared in the doorway of one and came on out to the car.

Until that moment, Dixie had seemed fairly controlled, but when he opened her car door and asked, "How's Chan?" she leaned against his thin chest and fell apart.

He held her quietly until her sobs subsided, then put out his hand to me and said, "Deborah Knott? I'm Pell Austin. Sorry we have to meet under these circumstances."

*   *   *

It was almost three o'clock before Dixie was ready to call it a night. Lynnette was sound asleep, Pell told her, but as soon as we stepped inside, Dixie still had to tiptoe down the hall to her bedroom and check for herself.

As we passed the darkened living room, a woman who was lying there on the sofa bed roused up, the "decorina friend from California," no doubt. A blanket slid off her bare shoulders as she propped herself on one elbow and I had an impression of long yellow hair that fell over full breasts.

"Dixie? Where the heck were you, girl?" Her voice was slurred with either sleep or alcohol. "I snagged you one of the cutest guys at the whole damn party. And I'd've brought him and his friend home with me 'cept I'm still lagged out from that red-eye special. Sorry."

"Go back to sleep, Cheryl," said Dixie. "We'll talk in the morning."

Out in the kitchen, she shook her head wearily. "I can't deal with Chan's death and Cheryl's annual party-girl syndrome at the same time. I feel old, Pell."

"Not you, love," he assured her gallantly.

Here beneath the bright kitchen lights, I saw that Pell Austin was probably no older than Dixie, who no doubt owed the lack of gray in her gleaming chestnut tresses to the skills of an expensive beautician.

Pell's thick straight hair was more salt than pepper. It was cut short in back but had been left long enough in front to brush across his eyes.

His face was long and narrow but his plainness was more than offset by level blue eyes and a humorous quirk to his small mouth. There was something oddly familiar about him that I couldn't immediately place, but I am always drawn to faces that seem to look on human folly with compassion and amusement and I could understand why Dixie might be fond of him.

At first I wondered if they were old lovers, but as he puttered around her kitchen, brewing fresh coffee and toasting English muffins, I realized that theirs was a deep and long-standing friendship, much like mine with Dwight Bryant back in Dobbs: more brother and sister than man and woman.

Eventually, of course, the penny dropped all the way. Not that he was effeminate of manner or prissy of speech or any of the other stereotypes. Quite the contrary. But with most men—whether they're twenty or sixty, and even if I'm not on the prowl and neither are they—there's usually an initial sexual awareness when we first meet, the old primeval "you man/me woman" thing. There was no answering awareness from Pell, only a certain sweet gentleness.

"Pell's head designer at Mulholland Studio, two blocks over from the GHFM building," Dixie told me. "He handles the national print campaigns for Start SMart, Coley Bridge, and Kindlehoff."

"Coley Bridge makes mattresses, right?"

He nodded.

"And I gave one of my nieces a Start SMart lamp at her baby shower because she wanted everything in the nursery to be from their—Fairyland, was it?"

"The Elfhome Collection," Pell murmured.

"But what's Kindlehoff?"

Dixie grinned and her tone was teasing. "Remember when Tammy Faye and Jim Bakker got into trouble with their gold-plated bathroom faucets?"

"Don't you listen to her. That was *not* Kindlehoff," Pell told me. "But they are the Cadillac of high-quality plumbing fixtures for bath and kitchen."

"God don't say his preachers got to use junk," Dixie deadpanned.

Like Dixie, Pell Austin seemed to know everyone in the industry and, as is often the case after the sudden death of someone not exactly beloved, the conversation in Dixie's kitchen that night swerved from stunned bewilderment to a certain cynical assessment of Chan's life as it affected them, Lynnette, and people like Poppy Jackson, Kay Adams, and Fitch and Patterson. Not to mention Drew Patterson.

"Jay won't be sorry Chan's dead," said Dixie.

"Because of Drew?" I asked.

"Because of Jacaranda. He accused Chan of planning to take proprietary sales data with him."

Pell's lips crooked ironically. "Jay Patterson's no one to grumble if his pet bulldog bites him in the ankle. You hear about Hickory-Dock? It was all over the Market tonight."

"No, what?"

"What's Hickory-Dock?" I asked.

"Children's furniture. Like Start SMart, only higher end," Pell told me. To Dixie, he said, "They're claiming that Fitch and Patterson—more specifically, that Chan, as Fitch and Patterson's VP of Sales—got hold of their preview catalog. They're saying Fitch and Patterson's new children's line is a direct knockoff. They don't know who's to blame precisely, but rumor has it that Lavelle Trocchi's head is on the chopping block."

For my benefit, they explained that Lavelle Trocchi was one of Hickory-Dock's top sales representatives.

"She was the one I was talking to when I saw you at the ALWA party, Deborah," Dixie said. "She seemed a little down, but I thought that was because Chan—dear God! I can't believe he's really gone. What am I going to tell Lynnette? How could an allergy kill him so quickly?"

Pell squeezed her shoulder.

To divert her from dwelling on it, I said, "I don't remember who you were talking to at the party. Was she involved with Chan?"

"Somebody saw her coming out of his hotel room early one morning up at the Fitchburg Market last month," said Pell.

I was puzzled. "So what difference does it make if he saw their catalog a little early? Doesn't it take three or four months to put a new piece of furniture into production?"

Dixie said grimly, "Honey, Fitch and Patterson has an engineering department that can look at a photograph or line drawing, then spec out the proportions and have a good knockoff on the floor in twenty-four hours."

I was impressed and said so.

"Some companies are so brazen," said Pell, "that they openly brag that they don't bother to fund a design department. They just send their engineers to spy on what Stanley or Wesley Allen or Thomasville are doing. Look at how Lexington sued Vaughan-Bassett. Somma Mattress got hit last year with a ninety-five million judgment for stealing a water mattress design from General Bedding. John Charles Design just won a patent information infringement against Queen International over a curl-arm design. Things like that go on all the time."

"I had a run-in—literally and physically—with some guy who was trying to steal headboard designs tonight," I said.

As I described my adventure at the Stanberry Collection, Pell poured coffee, a rich dark roast, and smeared a stack of hot toasted muffins with cream cheese and a drizzle of honey. It was a perfect snack for that time of night and I bit into it gratefully as conversation looped from Chan, to the Market, back to how to tell Lynnette that her daddy had died.

"The exhibit next to Swingtyme had potted azaleas around their doorway," Dixie said. "Maybe a bee stung him. Or a spider. If only I hadn't left!"

"Or if I'd come back a few minutes earlier," I said, knowing I'd forever wonder if those few minutes would have made much difference.

We told Pell how I'd lost my purse and keys and he seemed interested in every detail of my bizarre encounter with the legendary Savannah.

"That's where I've seen you!" I exclaimed. "I've been trying to think why you look so familiar. I saw a picture tonight of you with Savannah and Jay Patterson."

"I know the picture," he said. "Taken down at Mulholland. She's had studio and office space there from the beginning even though she's always worked freelance. We were on several projects together and she taught me a lot. Brilliant lady. Unstable, of course, but brilliant as hell. Right up to the time she smashed her car."

"Jay Patterson said something about that tonight—that Drew was nearly killed? They were in a car wreck?"

"No wreck," he answered sardonically. "Drew was driving and dented the fender or something and Savannah took a sledgehammer out of Mulholland's toolroom and smashed forty thousand dollars of chrome and steel to Porsche hell."

"But why?"

He shrugged. "Probably for the same reason she flushed a ruby solitaire down a toilet or dumped the Zavala account just when they were going to launch a new national campaign based on her ideas."

"Poor Drew. She must have felt awful."

"Maybe. It was nothing to do with her though. Not really. I think Savannah was mad at her insurance company."

While we talked, Dixie toyed with her toasted muffin until it lay in a hundred crumbs on her plate. Occasionally she would turn another leaf in her address book as she searched through the slips of paper and miscellaneous business cards she had jammed in helter-skelter without any consideration of alphabetizing. Eventually she found Chan's sister's phone number.

"It's awfully late. Maybe I should wait till morning? But what if she's gone to work when I call? I don't have a clue where that is."

Pell picked up the phone that was hanging on the wall beside her. "You're procrastinating, Dix."

"But a phone call at this hour of the night? She'll think it's bad news."

"It *is* bad news," he reminded her.

Reluctantly, she took the phone he held out and began to dial. We heard one ring and then an answering machine clicked in and Dixie immediately hung up.

"How the L-M-N can I leave her a message like that?"

"So ask her to call you back," he said inexorably.

It wasn't long after she'd done so that I began suppressing one yawn after another.

"I've got a spare toothbrush if Dix will lend you a gown," said Pell, and soon I was trailing him out the back door, across the narrow cul-de-sac and into his own kitchen, an eclectic space that mixed antique utensils with high-tech equipment. When I remarked on the display, he pointed to a cast-iron apple corer and said, "Savannah gave me the first piece. It's nineteenth-century."

The cabinets were painted a rich dark red and the leaded glass doors were beveled and then etched with art deco designs.

The rest of the house was dark and I was too sleepy to want a tour, especially since his guest room was right next to the kitchen.

I accepted towels, availed myself of the toothbrush, thanked him again for his kindness and had just switched off the lamp (two large white glass calla lilies held in the arms of a bronze woodland nymph) when I heard the back door open again. The window blinds weren't quite closed and I saw Pell cross the cul-de-sac and again enter Dixie's house.

I supposed this meant that they wanted to talk without a semi-stranger like me around but I was too tired to get my feelings hurt.

The bed was too soft and tended to lump in the middle. Nevertheless, I fit my body around the lumps and slept until bright headlights raked the room sometime later.

I sat up groggily, urgently needing to use the bathroom after so much coffee but too disoriented at first to remember exactly where it was.

Through the half-opened blind, I saw the headlights of a van go dark, then Pell and Dixie were silhouetted against the lights of her house. He put his arms around her and she briefly laid her head on his shoulder before they moved apart.

A moment later, she entered her house and I heard Pell quietly open and close the kitchen door before passing down the hall outside my room.

I tiptoed to the bathroom and back and was still so sleep-drugged that the lumpy mattress could have been a Coley Bridge Deluxe Air Foam for all I noticed.

8

"Household furniture, of a rude description, dates back to the time when men began to build houses to live in."
The Great Industries of the United States, 1872

I couldn't have been asleep more than five minutes when I heard a pleasant, if annoyingly persistent, voice in my ear, a masculine voice that told me that this was Friday and that I was listening to National Public Radio's *Morning Edition*. To my utter disbelief Bob Edwards also told me that it was fifteen minutes past the hour. Groggily, I checked the digital numbers on the clock radio beside the bed and saw that the hour in question was seven A.M.

I didn't remember setting the alarm, but the radio was a model so like my own that I must have automatically flipped the switch. Sheer dumb luck that it was set for seven-fifteen. Otherwise, I'd have slept till noon. Even though I only had one custody case scheduled for ten o'clock, missing it would not endear me to the Guilford County Clerk of Court.

My head throbbed, my eyeballs felt as if they'd been dipped in sand, and it took a conscious act of will to push my stiff and aching body off the lumpy mattress and stagger to the bathroom when every muscle whimpered for another five hours' sleep.

Ten minutes under a hot, pulsating shower head washed away some of the sand and part of the headache. Another ten minutes of stretching exercises got rid of most of the kinks in my body. The kinks in my wet hair were another matter. I toweled it dry, gave it an inadequate finger comb and put back on the clothes I'd worn last night.

There was moisturizer in the bathroom but no lipstick and I looked like Death's grandmother.

Morning sunlight streamed through Pell Austin's front windows when I stepped out into the hallway and I did a startled double take as I came nose to nose with a wall full of faces from floor to ceiling. Some were animal, some human, some other-worldly, but all were carved in realistic detail from various dark woods and they peered out through a trompe l'oeil jungle that was part painted background and part three-dimensional vines covered with green silk leaves.

Through the open archway was a living room far removed from anything I'd ever seen in Colleton County. Or in New York City, for that matter. The jungle motif continued in the dark green walls and leafy prints on the loveseat and chaise.

Pride of place, though, went to a life-size stuffed lion who stood frozen in mid-pace in front of the windows. Instead of a swag of drapery fabric, a well-preserved boa constrictor was looped over a hunting spear that acted as curtain rod. The snake's head curved upward and seemed to have its eyes fixed on a porcelain monkey that gibbered from the top of a decoupaged chest, but I couldn't be sure since it was wearing dark wraparound sunglasses.

The end tables came in the guise of two life-size ebony native boys who knelt in slightly different poses with thick squares of clear glass in their hands. Both were buck-naked except for matching white plastic sunglasses. (The boa constrictor's sunglasses had red frames.)

"So what do you think?" asked Pell Austin from the kitchen doorway.

"Well, it's certainly different," I said.

"It's all that's left of my *faux* fey period," he said in his gentle voice as I followed the aroma of fresh coffee back down the hall. "I keep it for sentimental reasons."

His blue chambray shirt had mother-of-pearl snap buttons and looked freshly ironed, his red-and-blue neckerchief was crisply knotted, and his thick gray hair had been neatly combed, but from his bloodshot eyes and the lines of fatigue in his long thin face, I wondered if he'd made it to bed at all.

"People expect designers like me to live in larger-than-life settings. It's part of the window dressing. Besides, Dix's granddaughter likes to ride on the lion."

He stepped aside to let me enter the tastefully designed kitchen and I glanced around with even more appreciation than I had given it last night, taking mental notes for my own future kitchen. "This room certainly doesn't—"

I suddenly saw we were not alone. Seated at Pell's breakfast table in front of a bowl of cereal was a young child who wore pink sneakers, jeans, and a Bugs Bunny T-shirt. Her hair was as thick and straight as Pell's, the color of beach sand, and it was plaited into a single braid that hung halfway down her thin back. The shorter side wisps were held back by two plastic barrettes shaped like little yellow ducks.

"Well, hello," I said.

Her two front baby teeth were missing and so far, only the leading edge of one adult tooth had emerged to fill the gap. She gave me an appealing lopsided smile. "Hello."

"I just bet that you're Lynnette."

The child giggled at my unconscious rhymes and glanced at Pell. "She makes poems, too."

"Judge Knott, may I present Miss Lynnette Nolan?" said Pell.

"Judge Knott/ got a lot/ of hot—" She ran out of rhyming words. "A lot of hot what, Uncle Pelly-Jelly?"

"Fudge?" I suggested.

"Judge Fudge?" She considered and then nodded. "That would work." She cut her eyes mischievously at Pell. " 'Specially since I'm not supposed to say snot."

He ignored the bait and she grinned at me again.

I am always fascinated by the genetic repackaging of children. Whenever a new baby is born into our family, we can spend inordinate time deciding where he got his hair and eye coloring, skin tone, bones, the shape of his chin, the crook of his little finger and whether that sleepy burp indicates Knott patience, a Stephenson sense of humor, or merely the Carroll appetite.

The only time I'd seen Lynnette's mother was when I

once stopped past Dixie's boarding house in Chapel Hill to drop off some study notes. Back then, Evelyn would have been a few years older than Lynnette was now, but I recalled a similar slender build and fair coloring. Something of Chan's forehead was in her brow, and her eyes were blue like his even though hers had the same feline tilt as Dixie's. There was something familiar about the way her small lips quirked that I couldn't quite place until I remembered that Evelyn's smile had also been delightfully asymmetrical.

"Judge/fudge/budge/grudge—if you're a judge, do you have one of those little hammers?"

I nodded.

"Did you ever hit anybody with it?"

"No, I just bang it to make people be quiet."

"You probably wish you had one now," said Pell with mock severity.

Lynnette laughed and chattered brightly as she spooned Cheerios from a dark red cereal bowl. I gingerly sipped the orange juice Pell handed me. My stomach considered rebellion, then decided it wasn't worth the effort.

"Grandmama's talking to Aunt Millie and Uncle Quentin and Shirley Jane," she told me. "They're maybe going to come see us soon."

I glanced at Pell and a slight shake of his head let me know that Lynnette had not yet been told of Chan's death. I couldn't fault Dixie for putting it off as long as possible, but it did limit conversation at the breakfast table. Instead, we discussed how much money Lynnette could expect to make off the Tooth Fairy in the next year or so, we heard how her cousin Shirley Jane was half a year younger but none of her teeth were loose yet, and we were given a demonstration of how nicely she could print our names.

"Next year we'll write cursive. Daddy already showed me how to do a capital L. See?"

I learned that the school she attended was out this way from Lexington and close enough that she'd been staying with Dixie most of the spring because of Chan's frequent trips to Texas and Malaysia. Normally, a baby-sitter drove her back and forth, "But Grandmama said I could stay home today."

She doodled a wiry creature with four legs and a long tail on her paper. "Does this look like a monkey, Uncle Pell?"

Before he could answer, she said abruptly, "I wish Daddy wasn't going to make us move so far away. Malaysia is even farther than Aunt Millie's house and we have to drive all day to go see her."

"To Frederick, Maryland?" Pell scoffed. "Four and a half hours tops."

"Well, it *seems* like all day," said Lynnette as she finished off her cereal and carried the empty bowl over to the dishwasher.

From their easy familiar manner toward each other, I guessed that Lynnette must have run in and out of Pell's house since birth.

Pell offered to fix me toast and scrambled eggs, but my stomach still felt too queasy for anything except coffee and juice. He thought that the soup kitchen wouldn't open its door before noon, but he knew the number of a locksmith who agreed to meet me at my car so I could pick up my suitcase and the garment bag that held my judicial robe. At least, we agreed to meet where I'd left my car the day before. My back bumper carries a small shield that identifies me as an officer of the court plus stickers for temporary parking at several courthouses around the state, but that was no guarantee that some overly zealous traffic officer hadn't had it towed.

"Take my van," Pell said. "I don't keep any set schedule during Market Week and if you're not due in court till ten, you can come back here and change and I'll drop you at the courthouse."

I started to demur but then Dixie let herself in the back door. She looked almost as haggard as I felt, and after I'd hugged her and heard that Chan's sister was on her way, I accepted the keys to Pell's blue Ford Aerostar and took myself off so that they could tell Lynnette in private.

My car had a parking ticket tucked under the wiper blade; otherwise my rendezvous with the locksmith—"Jimmy's my name, and jimmying's my game"—went off smoothly. Ol' Jimmy had a door open before I finished writing a note of explanation on the back of the ticket in case that officer came back, then he put my suitcase and garment bag in Pell's car and offered to get me a new set of keys for a price.

I told him I'd let him know.

The morning paper had a little box on the front page: *Fitch-Patterson Exec Dies* and a few sketchy details.

"Lynnette took it as well as could be expected, I suppose," said Pell as he drove me over to the courthouse an hour later after I was freshly dressed, combed and lipsticked. "Cried a little and then said she didn't mean that she really didn't want to go to Kuala Lumpur."

"Oh Lord."

"Yeah. We both told her that wasn't why her Daddy died, but I'm afraid we're going to have to get her some counseling to make her believe it. Dix, too, for that matter."

"Oh?"

"It was tearing her to pieces that Chan was moving Lynnette halfway around the globe." That long lank of straight gray hair fell boyishly across his eye and he pushed it aside with a heavy sigh. "She's going to have a hard time making herself believe she's not glad he's dead."

"Dixie's lucky to have you next door," I said as we headed downtown.

Rush hour was past, but the Market vans and buses that shuttled between downtown and satellite parking areas were out in full force.

"Have you two known each other long?"

"Since first grade at Sedgefield School over in Greensboro. She was in the third grade and the bus stop was in front of her house. About the fourth day, some big kid—big to me anyhow—tried to take my lunch bag and she sailed in and bloodied his nose."

I smiled, remembering a few noses I'd bloodied in school myself.

"Both our fathers had taken off before we could walk, but Mrs. Babcock and—"

"Dixie's *mother*?"

He raised his eyebrow at the surprise in my voice.

Disconcerted, I said, "I guess it didn't occur to me back then that Dixie had kept her maiden name."

His half-smile made me realize what else I hadn't picked up on and I could feel myself turning red.

"Evelyn would be what now?" I asked defensively. "Twenty-four?"

"Twenty-five. Almost twenty-six."

"Whatever. The point is, twenty-six years ago, nice middle-class Southern girls like Dixie didn't openly raise a child born out of wedlock."

"Who said we came from a nice middle-class neighborhood?" he asked sardonically as he slowed for a long white stretch limo that was hogging both lanes.

I didn't have an answer to that one.

"Actually, it was worse than middle-class," he said, taking pity on my embarrassment. "It was poor-white respectable, and Dix didn't hang around to be preached at. She took off to someplace down East before anybody here knew she was pregnant."

"What about the father?"

"He never knew. He was just someone she met down at the beach the Easter before she graduated. A gang of senior girls went down for spring break, met some guys from the Citadel. You know how it goes."

I did. Too much Carolina moon, too much warm spring nights, too much beer and pot. Been there, done that, but only bought the T-shirt, luckily—not a baby.

"Close as we were, Dixie didn't even tell me. Just dropped out of sight. First I knew about Evelyn was when I found her again, when she was going for that law degree."

"At Chapel Hill?"

"Yeah. I was over there helping Savannah design and decorate a funky place on Franklin Street—the owner had more money than taste—and there was Dix, working the afternoon shift at a coffee bar next door. I hadn't seen her since high school and even then, I don't think she'd have told me about Evelyn except that she was pouring me an espresso when the phone call came that some drunk had plowed through a school crossing. I rushed Dix over to the hospital and I was still there when the doctors came out of surgery and said Evelyn was going to be fine. And she was, but it took a lot of nursing and physical therapy and Dix had to quit law school."

"Surely there was insurance money?"

"From the drunk? Yeah. They got a nice settlement. Eventually. After the guy's parents dragged it through court for two years trying to keep it off his record."

He edged the van around the limo and took a left over to North Centennial. Several blocks ahead, the new courthouse rose white and gleaming at the top of a hill, in contrast to the huge navy-blue cluster of windowless GHFM buildings off to the right.

"She had it rough, didn't she? I never knew how rough." Even though Dixie and I hadn't been particularly close, learning what she'd gone through back then made me feel callous and self-centered in retrospect.

"You were younger then," Pell said, reading my mind. "You probably had your own problems."

Well, yes, there was that.

He pulled up to a side door of the courthouse.

"But everything worked out great after they came to High Point." His voice turned suddenly venomous. "Until Evelyn married that prick."

I wanted to ask what he meant, but a uniformed guard was motioning for us to move it.

Pell handed me a house key. "I don't know when I'll be back, but make yourself at home."

I thanked him and hurried inside. Only ten minutes to do the professional courtesies and find the courtroom for Randy J. Verlin vs. April Ann Jenner for the custody of Travis Tritt Verlin, minor.

Which was where Detective David Underwood found me.

9

"Chair manufacturing is carried on by contract in several of the prisons and penal establishments in the country, and it is a very important American industry."
The Great Industries of the United States, 1872

"Chan Nolan's death was a homicide?" I was bewildered as I followed Detective Underwood out to his car. "But the doctor said it was an allergic reaction. Anaphylactic shock."

"Yes, ma'am." He held the door open for me on a car ankle-deep in empty foam coffee cups and crumpled hamburger wrappers—"Just kick 'em out of your way," he murmured—and we drove the short distance to police headquarters on Leonard Street. "We have a little problem with how he ingested the agent."

Here at lunchtime, the streets were clogged again with shuttle vans, cars with license plates from a dozen different states, and a couple of black limos of ordinary length.

"I can't get over the difference," I said, telling Detective Underwood how deserted the streets seemed the day my friend and I drove through.

"Most of the year, we're just another Piedmont mill town. But during Market, we—oh damn and blast and expletive deleted!" he muttered as a shuttle van stopped in our lane to let someone out.

Detective David Underwood was an impatient driver and he squeezed his car through nonexistent openings and narrow alleyways.

The brick and concrete block building on Leonard Street was a remodeled school, he told me, and once we were inside, he took me into a small room that could have been the school nurse's office. A uniformed officer quickly and efficiently rolled my fingertips, one at a time, from ink pad to a card that could be scanned by the computer.

I cleaned my hands with a packaged towelette, then followed Underwood as he stopped by the squad room to pick up a legal pad and a bulky manila envelope from a desk that was even messier than his car.

A few steps farther down the hall was a tiny interview room no bigger than six foot square and bare of all furnishings save two straight-backed chairs that faced each other across a small metal table.

Underwood rummaged in his manila envelope and pulled out a clear plastic bag with a brown plastic prescription bottle inside.

"This yours?"

The label was still intact. If I could clearly read my name and my doctor's, surely he could as well.

"Do we really have to play games, Detective Underwood?" I asked. "Of course it's mine. Penicillin. And it's hours past my time for another dose."

I reached for the bag, but Underwood continued to hold it.

"How many tablets are supposed to be here?"

"Six? Or is it four?"

"That's what I'm asking you, ma'am."

His tone wasn't threatening, just mildly inquisitive, and I knew he was just doing his job, but lack of food and sleep was starting to make me cranky. Nevertheless I tried to hold on to my temper as I worked it out on my fingers.

"I started with thirty. Three tablets a day for ten days . . . breakfast, mid-afternoon and bedtime . . . But I didn't take last night's and I still have today's to go. . . . Four?"

He handed me the baggie. "Shake it."

Empty.

The bottom fell out of my stomach.

"That's what put Chan Nolan into anaphylactic shock? My penicillin?"

"According to his allergist, even one tablet would be dangerous for him. Didn't you see his Medic Alert medallion when you were dancing with him last night?"

"I remember two gold chains, but if there was a medallion, it must have been tucked inside his shirt. I certainly didn't read it."

"No?" He twisted one end of his thick brown mustache into a sharp point and regarded me with those warm brown eyes.

"And I certainly wasn't his only dancing partner."

"So far though, you're the only one with missing penicillin tablets," he pointed out.

"The only one you know about," I snapped.

"A soft answer turneth away wrath," warned the preacher deep inside my head.

"Losing your temper is not the way to go," agreed the pragmatist who shares the same space. *"He's not Dwight."*

"Half the medicine cabinets in America must be stocked with half-empty bottles of penicillin," I said as calmly as I could. "Besides, from early in the evening, I didn't even have mine."

I described the mix-up with tote bags and he wanted to know who'd been where from the minute I set my tote under the table. He wrote down all the names, beginning with Savannah, continuing through Dixie Babcock, Drew Patterson and her father Jay, Kay Adams and her colleague Poppy Jackson, Heather McKenzie, Mai and Jeff Stanberry, and, even though I didn't know her, that Lavelle Trocchi who was supposed to have given Chan the Hickory-Dock catalog last month and who, according to Dixie, had been next to the table.

He was particularly interested in the plate of food Drew had fixed for Chan and which Dixie had actually handed to him, "although Dr. Harrison says that with that much penicillin, Nolan would have started to react immediately. You sure you didn't see him again after you left that ballroom?"

As he wrote down my denial, the officer who'd taken my fingerprints tapped on the door, stuck his head in and said, "Two hits on the baggie, Dave."

"What baggie?" I asked apprehensively.

"The tablets were crushed and stuck into some brownies. We found a baggie in his jacket pocket with brownie crumbs and some of the penicillin residue. Your prints are on the baggie."

"That's impossible!" I snapped. And then I remembered the zip-lock bag that Savannah had dropped.

My sudden recollection and hasty account of picking up the bag sounded limp and guilty even to my ears. With as much dignity as I could muster, I said, "Dwight Bryant's the deputy sheriff over in Colleton County and he's known me since I was born. He'll tell you I don't make a habit of going around killing perfect strangers."

(Okay, so maybe that was a slight fudging of the facts, but *I* knew our brief acquaintance in Maryland wasn't relevant. For all practical purposes, Chan *had* been a stranger and I really didn't want to talk about that time.)

"I'll give you his phone number."

Underwood's shaggy brown mustache quivered and I realized he was grinning. "I already talked to Major Bryant this morning before I went over to the courthouse."

"Well, then," I said.

"Always a first time." His grin faded as he asked me again about the people I'd seen in Chan Nolan's company.

He particularly concentrated on Savannah's movements. "You're positive she'd already left the table and the room with your bag before Nolan joined your group?"

"If you don't believe me, ask Heather McKenzie. She followed the woman out."

His legal pad lay on the narrow table between us and he made no attempt to conceal it as he drew a heavy black arrow on his notepad from Heather's name to Savannah's. "Now, Judge, what makes you think I don't believe you?"

"The question marks you're drawing around that arrow, maybe?"

He smiled. "And you're staying with Nolan's mother-in-law, right?"

"She found me the place, but it's actually with her neighbor next door."

He took down Pell Austin's address and telephone number, then gave me back my tote bag and purse. The empty penicillin bottle he kept. So far as I could tell, nearly everything else seemed present and accounted for, right down to my cell phone, checkbook and car keys. I usually had three tubes of lipstick. The darkest one was gone. Gone, too, were my nail clippers. And I was in the habit of dropping in my loose change. Sometimes there would be five or six dollars' worth of coins rattling around at the bottom. At the moment, there were only a nickel and three pennies.

Underwood made a note of it even though I considered them a small enough payment for getting my other things back.

"I'll have someone drive you to your car," he said, "and, Judge?"

"Yes?"

"Major Bryant also told me that you're bad for sticking your nose in where it doesn't belong—his words, not mine." His half-teasing tone became wholly serious. "Do us all a favor while you're in High Point, Judge? Don't."

10

As a uniformed officer escorted me out of the building, I met Dixie coming in.

She gave me a wan smile. "They found your bag?"

"Yeah."

Her drawn features and the dark circles under her eyes let me know that she hadn't caught a nap this morning. What I didn't know was if she'd been told yet that Chan's death was a homicide. "You okay?"

"Hanging in," she said gamely.

"Court should adjourn by one-thirty," I told her. "Want me to take Lynnette for a drive or something?"

She brightened. "Could you? That'd be great. Cheryl's with her right now but she's hyped for Market and there's so much I need to do before Chan's sister gets here."

I suborned my escort to drive through Hardee's before taking me on to my car. I tried to buy him a burger, too, but he swore he wasn't hungry yet. Tasted like ambrosia to me though, and I had my daily dose of grease and red meat half-eaten before we pulled up beside my car, still parked where I'd left it.

No second ticket on the windshield either.

Licking ketchup off my fingers, I drove back to the courthouse, parked in a judge's slot, and made it up to my courtroom where I reconvened Verlin vs. Jenner only eight minutes late.

Travis Tritt Verlin's young parents sat almost exactly where I'd left them on opposite sides of the room, and each eyed me anxiously as I leafed through all the documents looking for answers that weren't there.

I tried to focus on what was right for this toddler at this time and to keep my mind clear of preconceptions and outside influences.

When I finally came down on the side of the father, I truly do not think it was because I'd let myself be influenced by Dixie's fierce love for her granddaughter and her despair at the thought of Lynnette leaving for Malaysia.

But how can we ever say for sure what tips the balance?

The tension went out of Mrs. Verlin's shoulders, April Ann Jenner sat with tears spilling down her thin cheeks, and a big smile split Randy Verlin's face.

Holding up my hand for silence, I forced him to look me straight in the eye and said sternly, "Even though I'm giving you custody of Travis, Mr. Verlin, that does not mean that I think Ms. Jenner is unfit or a bad mother."

I gentled my voice as I spoke to that unhappy young woman. "Nothing that I've read in these documents, nor heard here today, has made me think that. We'll set up a visitation schedule and if your situation changes radically or if Mr. Verlin moves out of his parents' house, then you can come back to court and ask for a new judgment. I'll put that in my written decision. But I think we all want what's best for Travis, and right now, it's my opinion that he can have a more secure and stable life in the Verlin household since his grandmother can care for him full-time."

Now my eyes moved to the older woman. I told her that her fairness toward April Ann this morning had impressed me. "And I think you can be trusted not to try to turn your grandson against Ms. Jenner."

"She's his mother," Mrs. Verlin said softly.

"Exactly," I said and turned back to the parents of her only grandchild.

"What both of you need to remember is that the two of you are going to be Travis's mother and father for the rest of your natural lives. For his sake, I urge you to try to get along. Don't tear him apart and make him have to choose between you. If you can't say something nice about each other, at least don't say anything hurtful, okay?"

Both of them promised they wouldn't and we worked out

a schedule that gave Travis to April Ann every weekend. We also agreed on the amount of child support she would pay each month.

By the time I adjourned, she may not have been smiling, but at least she no longer wept.

Before I left the courthouse, I got through to my doctor's assistant in Raleigh and explained how I hadn't taken a penicillin tablet since around six the day before. "And your throat hasn't bothered you in four days? Then she'll probably say it's okay to stop."

I gave her Dixie's office number and told her to leave a message there if it wasn't okay.

Road workers with jackhammers and dump trucks were tearing up Johnson Street and I had to maneuver a maze of one-way streets in this older part of town before I finally found my way back to the cul-de-sac a half-block off Johnson.

No sign of Pell's van nor of Dixie's car nor even the California decorina's bright red rental that had been parked on the street when I left this morning. Instead, I found Drew Patterson pacing up and down the walk. Last night she'd been soft and feminine in her loose hair and low-cut dancing dress, but today she was all business in a crisp black linen miniskirt and matching jacket over a soft white shirt. Her black patent leather shoes had Cuban heels and flat silver buckles, and her blonde hair was gathered off her face in a French braid.

"Hello again," she said sadly, as I got out of my car.

Up close, I could see that her eyes were bloodshot beneath a light coat of mascara.

"Drew, I'm so sorry," I said, taking her hand. "Are you okay? I guess you knew him for a long time."

"Half my life." Her blue eyes glazed with tears, but her chin came up as she reined in her emotions. "Ever since I was thirteen and he came to work for us. Before he married Evelyn. Before Lynnette was born."

I made comforting noises and she tried to shrug.

"It's not like we were lovers or anything—he always acted like I was thirteen and still in braces—but he was so much fun to play with. We were dancing together just last night and now he's gone. Just like that! I can't believe—"

She broke off and took a deep breath.

"Chan was okay when you last saw him, wasn't he?" I asked as curiosity got the best of me.

Drew nodded. "He came back to our party and was schmoozing buyers just like always until Jacob Collier grabbed him and tried to pick a fight."

"Did I meet Collier?" I wondered aloud.

"Probably not. You didn't come back to our party after you left ALWA's, did you?"

"No."

"It got a little awkward for a minute there. But Jacob should have retired years ago. He's seventy-eight, for Pete's sake. And the Pinecroft account should've been converted *years* ago."

"You've lost me," I said.

"See, some accounts take a lot of hard work. There's no loyalty or they're extra fussy or you just can't count on them to do the same amount of business with you each time. But some accounts are going to be with you forever. They're comfortable, pleased with the new lines, predictable. You don't have to stroke them. When that happens, Sales will often convert it to a house account."

"So why would that anger this Jacob Collier?"

"Because it means that instead of getting a five percent commission on those sales, he'll now be getting one percent to service the account and *that* means he'll have to hustle up some new business if he wants to make up the four percent he's losing."

"But surely a man who's seventy-eight is ready to retire?"

"He is. But his son and granddaughter are taking over the territory and it means less money for them." Drew shook her head. "It's not as if they couldn't see it coming. That's business."

Less for Collier's family, more for hers, I thought as I gathered up my purse, tote bag and robe from the car.

"And probably more for a sharp sales director like Chan?" asked my internal pragmatist.

"Not your business," the preacher said, sternly reminding me of Detective Underwood's request to keep my nose out of his investigation.

"Dixie's not back yet?"

Concern crossed her lovely face. "No, and I'm starting to get worried. I stopped by an hour ago to see how she and Lynnette were doing and her friend Cheryl asked me to stay till Dixie got back. She forgot she had an appointment with the marketing head of a sleep chain. Or so she said."

Drew's smile was rueful. "I myself think she saw a way to cut out early. The thing is, she said Dixie would be back by two and I'm supposed to be at the String and Splinter at two-thirty."

I glanced at my watch and made shooing motions with my hands. "It's five after. Go. I saw Dixie at the police station and—"

"Police station? Cheryl said she had to go sign some papers or something. I thought it was the hospital. What would she be doing at the police station?"

If Chan's death were indeed a homicide, it wasn't my place to tell her.

(The preacher gave a nod of approval.)

I made a dismissing motion with my hand. "It's probably because he died without his own doctor around."

"But his doctor's right over in Lexington," said Drew, looking confused.

"There's always bureaucracy and red tape," I said. "Anyhow, I told Dixie I'd stay with Lynnette. Speaking of whom, where is she?"

She pointed and I walked over to Pell's back porch and looked up. There sat Lynnette about twenty feet off the ground, half hidden in the branches of a tall oak tree that had almost finished leafing out.

"Hi there," I said.

She gave me a solemn nod, then looked away.

I was learning that her plaited pigtail was a barometer of her mood. At the moment, it hung limply over her left shoulder and she twisted the end aimlessly through her small fingers.

Drew touched my arm and we walked out of earshot. "She's been up in that tree ever since I got here and I can't get her to come down. She's always been so sweet and precious to me and now I can't even get her to talk. Poor little thing must be grieving her heart out."

"Don't worry," I said. "It's like cats. She'll come down when she's hungry or thirsty or needs the bathroom. You go ahead. I'll watch her till Dixie comes."

"There's just one hitch," said Drew, adjusting the cuffs of her black linen jacket. "I have my car out front, but there's no time now to hunt for a parking space over there. I was going to get Dixie to drop me off."

"I can do that," I said. "I'll put my stuff in my room and you write Dixie a note so she'll know I've got Lynnette."

When I got back, the child was still up in the oak.

While Drew stuck the note on Dixie's screen door, I called up,

"Hey, Lynnette,
Want to get
In my Corvette?"

"That's not a Corvette," she said scornfully.

"Well, Lynnette doesn't rhyme with Firebird."

She didn't move. "I'm waiting for Aunt Millie and Shirley Jane."

"I don't think they'll get here much before dark and Drew really needs us to drive her somewhere right now," I told her. "Besides, I was hoping you'd show me through the Discovery Center this afternoon."

"With the dolls?"

"Dolls?" It was my understanding that the Center was devoted to a history of furniture making. Where did dolls come in?

"They've got a bajillion. Wait'll you see. Don't budge, Miss Deborah Judge. I'm coming."

"You must have children," Drew said as she tucked herself into my passenger seat.

"Nope. Just lots of nieces and nephews."

Lynnette dropped like a feather from the lowest limb and scrambled into the backseat. If her braid didn't exactly float, neither did it droop.

"Click it or ticket," she chanted as we buckled up and hit the road.

The resiliency of childhood.

Having grown up in the area, Drew Patterson knew every inch of High Point and she knew how to thread the one-way streets to get us over to the west side of town and eventually cross the railroad tracks without having to double back.

The String and Splinter, I was told, was in Market Square, a complex of interconnected buildings that looked like an old antiques mall grafted on a modern high rise.

"So what is it?" I asked as we waited through a second cycle of lights while trying to cross Main Street. "A restaurant?"

"Dining club. Most members are either in furniture or hosiery. They should have called it Fabric and Wood, but I guess that wouldn't have been cute enough."

"Are you a member?"

"Dad is. My grandfather was one of the original members." She gave a small laugh. "Now *that* could be the furniture industry's motto: I'm Following in My Grandfather's Footsteps. It's almost like medieval Europe. Your grandfather worked on the line, you work on the line. Your grandfather was sales rep for this territory, you work the same territory fifty years later. Your grandfather owned a furniture company and joined the String and Splinter, you do, too."

"You serious?" I asked as the light finally stayed green long enough for me to get through the intersection. "You actually inherit a spot in a factory or a sales territory?"

"Absolutely. That's why Jacob Collier was so furious with Ch—"

She broke off as she suddenly remembered that Lynnette was sitting quietly in the backseat.

"So now you go on around the hospital and just keep straight till we cross over the railroad tracks, then take the first left."

I did as she said and fetched up in front of a charming black iron gate that led to the String and Splinter Club's heavy oak door. The facade was brick and boxwood and frosted glass for privacy.

"Very British-looking from out here," I observed.

"Inside's full of Sheraton and Queen Anne reproductions. Queen Victoria would feel right at home."

She might poke fun at it, but I could hear the affection in her voice.

"Dad and Mother love it and the chef is wonderful. Maybe you could join us for lunch one day next week?"

Spoken with the graciousness of a hereditary princess.

"I'll have to look at my schedule," I said.

Drew thanked me for the lift, told me how to get to the Discovery Center, and reached back to squeeze Lynnette's knee. " 'Bye, punkin. I'll see you tonight, okay?"

"Okay."

11

> *"The ancient Egyptians had in their houses, not only such articles of use as tables, chairs, and couches, but in the residences of the rich, these pieces of furniture were made of the rarest woods, with costly carvings, and inlaid work of gold and ivory."*
> *The Great Industries of the United States, 1872*

The Furniture Discovery Center is back of the Convention Bureau's tourist information office and only a short walk from many showrooms, but most Market people must have been heeding the *Museum Visitors Only* sign in the parking area because I actually found a spot on the first try.

"Do you come here much?" I asked Lynnette as we crossed the graveled lot.

"Uh-huh." She headed directly for the correct door and her sand-colored braid swung jauntily across her narrow back.

I paid our admission fee to the attractive brown-haired woman at the desk and followed Lynnette, who knew exactly what she wanted to see and it wasn't how tree logs get turned into Queen Anne armoires, which was the main focus of the museum.

"First come see the model bedrooms," she said, leading me off to the left, past the gift shop and into a small room devoted to dioramas of fifteen famous bedrooms through the ages. The sleep furniture, as I was learning to call it, ranged from King Tut's bull-shaped gold bed and Queen Elizabeth the First's massive four-poster to the moon bed of Kublai Khan and Queen Liliuokalani's ebony bed with its horsehair mattress, each reproduced in delicious detail on a one-inch to one-foot scale and commissioned, I was amused to discover, by the Serta Mattress Company.

From there, Lynnette took me up a short ramp, past some dollhouses, including a little house trailer furnished in Fifties decor, and into a display area that truly seemed to hold a bajillion dolls. The floor-to-ceiling shelves and cases were jammed with dolls of all sizes, all materials, all nationalities, all time periods, and all collected by one Angela Peterson.

Lynnette showed me her favorites; then, while she wandered from case to case discovering new faces, I went back to the entrance to read about the woman who had built the collection. The placard was chatty and informative and told me that Mrs. Peterson had joined the military after the early death of her husband and had been stationed in Korea during that war. Later she was in Turkey for several years and used it as a jumping-off place to travel and collect. By the time she settled down in High Point, she had visited forty-four different countries and had brought back dolls from every one of them—some sixteen hundred dolls in all.

I spent more time on the placard than I normally would because two equally chatty women with Market badges were standing in the gift shop a few feet away and my ears pricked up as soon as I heard one of them say, "—just surprised nobody killed him before this."

"Like Tracy Collier?"

"Yeah. The way he was sleeping with her, getting kickbacks from her father and jerking her grandfather around by the nose—"

"Poor old Jacob." The younger woman's voice held youthful pity.

"Humph," said her friend. " 'Poor old Jacob' is so past it he couldn't sell ice cubes in Hell if it wasn't part of the golden egg. I heard that the real reason Chan converted them to house accounts was because he was so ticked at Jacob's heavy dating."

Golden egg? Heavy dates?

They moved on over to the cutaway upholstered couch on the main floor of the museum and I drifted after them, pretending to read the explanatory cards about eight-way hand-tied cone coils, kiln-dried wood frames, and flow-matched custom upholstery as I strained my ears to hear more about Chan Nolan and the Collier family. The news of his death must be all over the Market and I wondered if the woman's choice of words was accidental or if it were already known that someone really had killed him.

Unfortunately, I had come in on the tail end of their gossip about Chan. A third buyer joined them burbling about

"Alexander Julian's color seminar" and how Vanna White, there to promote a mattress line, had planted a lipsticked kiss on a fabric mogul's polished bald dome at lunch today, which, for some reason, made the first two laugh so hard that they had to head for the exit before one of the docents could ask them to leave.

I walked back toward the doll exhibit wondering about the animosity between Chan Nolan and Jacob Collier. How sexually active could a seventy-eight-year-old man be? And who was Chan Nolan to object to the grandfather's randiness if he himself was getting it on with the man's granddaughter?

It was, as the King of Siam once said, a puzzlement.

"And none of your business," the preacher reminded me.

By three o'clock, Lynnette and I had exhausted the dolls. It was too early to take her back to Dixie's but she was clearly ready to move on.

"Is there a playground nearby?" I asked as we walked out into the warm spring sunlight. An hour on the monkey bars or swings would probably ensure an early bedtime.

But Lynnette was to the industry born and had her own idea of how to spend the rest of the afternoon, an idea spurred by three huge helium balloons in the shape of a ewe and two lambs that floated against the bright blue sky, mascots for a line of designer sheets and spreads.

"Could we go to Market Square?" She tugged me toward the street, her braid swinging from side to side. Like Dorothy yearning toward Oz, she was lured by the balloons and by the cluster of mismatched buildings built into the hillside beneath them. "Please?"

I hesitated for a moment, wondering if Lynnette would be recognized. Unlikely, I decided. Fitch and Patterson was quartered in the Global Home Furnishings Market, a full three or four blocks from Market Square, and while we might pass business acquaintances who had known Chan and heard about his death, how likely was it that they'd ever met his daughter? Almost none of them knew me, so who was going to notice my Munchkin companion or give her a second glance at a trade show like this?

Besides, by the time we walked over, wandered around for an hour or so and then walked back, Lynnette would be as tired as if we'd gone to a playground, right?

Okay, okay. So I wanted to go look around as much as she did. After all, furniture was why I'd come to High Point in the first place, so why not throw a rock at both birds and check out the latest fashions?

We stopped by the car to pick up my Jacki Sotelli badge and I stuck a legal pad in my shoulder bag so I could make notes in case I found a perfect table or couch or chair.

"Parking until five o'clock is for Museum Visitors Only," the preacher said priggishly.

"So?" argued the pragmatist. *"You visited, didn't you? I see at least two empty spots and it's not as if there's going to be a rush on the place before it closes, is there?"*

Made sense to me.

According to Pell Austin and Dixie, who had talked about it the night before, the original Market Square building was an old chair factory that had been gutted down to its brick walls and turned into showroom space. A system of escalators and skywalks connected it to buildings on the west side of Main

Street so that buyers could avoid April showers and October winds.

Through the years, the old factory seemed to have sprouted brick wings and annexes all down the hillside, and one tall building towered above the rest. The domed high rise looked like any modern office building in Raleigh or Durham, but Dixie had said that the top of the building was devoted to luxurious penthouse suites for the Market's high rollers.

Just inside the doorway stood two lovely young women who looked like spring buttercups in huge cartwheel garden hats with yellow streamers, wide yellow hoopskirts and low-cut bodices. They were passing out green nylon tote bags imprinted with the name of a waterbed company. I didn't quite get the link between waterbeds and sexy Southern belles, but people were grabbing for them.

After last night's fiasco I was off tote bags, but Lynnette seized one, slid an arm through each handle and wore it like a backpack, "'Cause sometimes you can get a lot of neat stuff," she told me.

Her braid bounced in and out of the tote and her snaggle-toothed smile was electric.

If the Global Home Furnishings Market—GHFM—was an upscale furniture mall, Market Square was a modern version of an Arabian Nights bazaar.

Here on the lowest level, it was hard to tell where one display ended and another began. Hand-tufted velvet cushions and gold tasseled pillows spilled like a silken fountain onto lacquered tables and boxes that edged up against stair runners and area rugs next to Tiffany lamps and porcelain jardinieres big enough for Lynnette to hide inside. Live angelfish swam in a five-foot-tall Plexiglas column that was topped by a traditional clock face with Roman numerals: the grandfather clock as aquarium?

I tried to picture Kidd's reaction to finding something like that in my living room.

(*"Not even if you replaced the tropical fish with bluegills and crappies," the pragmatist said sardonically.*)

There were designer picture frames of inlaid woods, whimsical kitchen stools stenciled with fruits and vegetables, coffee tables topped by real sewer grates that had been buffed to a steely sheen, decorative folding screens that reminded me of the Stanberrys', wrought-iron coatracks and candelabras, handblown glass of an airy delicacy, twig birdhouses and pebbled fountains designed for indoor sunrooms.

Almost every display area had a brass or crystal bowl filled with peppermints, chocolate-covered peanuts or hard candies and Lynnette's grubby little hands dipped into every bowl we passed.

"Daddy always lets me," she said when I suggested she might have collected enough. She dropped some foil-wrapped chocolates into her tote bag. "He says it's like Halloween. I can bring it home, I'm just not allowed to eat it all at once. Besides, Shirley Jane's coming and I can share."

Remembering why Shirley Jane was coming, I didn't have the heart to stop her, especially since she was still referring to Chan in the present tense.

A display of bed linens at the end of a long gallery had drawn a small crowd and as we drew nearer, we saw the attraction. The company's logo was a sheep and two lambs jumping over a fence, just like the balloons tethered outside. Here in a straw-filled pen were the balloons come to life—a mother sheep and two woolly lambs.

A company rep was stationed there with an instant camera and enchanted customers lined up to have their pictures taken with the mascots. When it was her turn, Lynnette dropped down into the hay, put an arm around each lamb and smiled for the camera. She sat on a nearby hay bale to watch it finish developing, then gave it to me for safekeeping in my purse since she was afraid it would get candy smears if she put it in her tote.

"Well, hello," said a friendly voice.

I turned around and saw Heather McKenzie smiling at me.

"I see you got your purse back. Did you find Savannah?"

"No. Sorry. The police found it—"

I broke off, not wanting to say where. Not with Lynnette only a few feet away.

Oblivious to the child, Heather stared at me wide-eyed. "I just realized. You were the one who found him, weren't you?"

I tried to shush her, but her eyes widened even further as she gazed at something in the distance behind me.

"Look!" said Heather. "On the escalator. Isn't that Savannah?"

Lynnette followed Heather's pointing finger and stood atop the hay bale so that she could see over our heads.

"It *is* Savannah-Nana!" she squealed, and before I could stop her, she jumped off the bale of hay and squirmed through the line of people waiting to have their pictures taken.

"Lynnette! Wait!" I called, but she was gone, swallowed up by the crowds.

12

"The couches upon which the old Romans reposed at table were
often inlaid with silver, gold, ivory, tortoise-shell, and precious
woods, with carved ivory or metal feet; and the furniture of a
rich man's house represented in itself an enormous fortune."
    The Great Industries of the United States, 1872

I charged after Lynnette with Heather McKenzie close behind me, but the child was half my size and able to dart
through openings in the crowd that got me a glare or an icy
"Do you mind?" when I tried to slip through the same
spaces.

By the time we finally elbowed our way over to the escalator in the middle of the floor, there was no sign of the child
nor of Savannah in the solid flow of people jammed onto the

moving stairs. Nevertheless, we stepped on and I shoved Heather in front of me since she was several inches shorter.

"You keep looking up there for Savannah," I ordered. "I'll check out the floor."

We rose steadily while I anxiously scanned the area for a small pink T-shirt and a long bouncy pigtail. If there were any children at all on the first floor, I didn't see them. A flash of rainbow pastels entering Arte de Mexico raised my hopes till I saw it wasn't Savannah.

Going with the flow, we crossed a glass-enclosed walkway and reached the mezzanine. Hallways crowded with people branched off in different directions from a central reception desk where more crowds waited for the two elevators. There was a glass door that led outside and I recognized the street where I'd dropped Drew Patterson an hour or so earlier, which meant that this part of Market Square connected with the String and Splinter.

For a panicky moment I considered trying to see if Drew was still inside the club and could help us hunt for Lynnette, but then I recognized a familiar face standing near the elevators. "Mr.—Tomlinson, is it?"

He had switched uniforms and now wore a patch on his sleeve that identified him as an employee of a private security company, but it was my bailiff from the courthouse all right.

"Oh, hiya, Judge," he beamed at me. "Enjoying Market?"

"Not at the moment," I answered. "I'm missing a little girl. Did one pass through here a few minutes ago?"

"Bugs Bunny shirt?" he asked. "Blonde hair in a braid?"

"Yes! Where did she go?"

"She took the elevator up to five. You just missed them."

"Them?" asked Heather.

"Kid with her grandma, right? Gray-haired lady in a fancy spring dress? She asked me where the Century showroom is. On five, I told her."

Unlike the elevators over in GHFM, the elevators at Market Square were built to hold more than six people at a time. And since they serviced five floors instead of GHFM's eleven, we only had to wait six very long minutes instead of twenty.

Of course, it might have been a bit longer if we hadn't had a chatty Mr. Tomlinson to part the waters for us and escort us to the front of the crowd.

"Who'd you wind up giving the baby to?" he asked as we waited, and I remembered that there'd been a different bailiff in my courtroom after lunch.

"The father."

"On account of he's moved back in with his folks?"

I nodded. "That tipped it."

"Figured it would," he said sagely.

"So which is your real job?" I asked.

"Oh, this here's just temporary," he confided to me as we waited. "Normally, see, I take vacation days to work the Market, but the guy who was supposed to be working your courtroom today—Sam Dow? He had to take some personal leave 'cause a water pipe in his camper van sprang a leak and he had to wait in for the plumber, so I took Sam's place till he could get back."

"He lives in a camper van?" Heather asked.

"Oh, no, Sam's bunking in with a bunch of us Market

bachelors for the week, but he didn't just rent out his house this year, he's rented out his camper, too."

Since the elevators seemed to be taking their own sweet time, I said, "Market bachelors?"

"Yeah. There's six of us with houses over near Oak Hollow. Three or four bedrooms from when our kids were growing up. During Market, we can rent 'em to the buyers for three thousand apiece. Our wives go to the beach or go visit relatives and five of us guys squeeze in with whoever's turn it is to put us all up. Normally, see, Sam sleeps in his camper, but this year, what with him renting it, too, there's seven of us bunched up at Marvin's. That many makes it a little hard."

"Crowded bathrooms?" I asked sympathetically.

"Oh, that don't bother guys. No, ma'am, it's the poker. See, poker's best with five guys. Six is stretching it, and seven? Takes too long to go around the table with bets and if you try anything fancier than five-card stud, you run out of cards. Okey-dokey, here's your elevator."

While the car emptied out, I asked Tomlinson to hang around the area for a while. "The little girl's name is Lynnette and I'm supposed to be baby-sitting. If she comes down before we do, would you hold on to her for me?"

"What about her grandmother?"

"That's not her grandmother."

"But yes, please hold on to her, too," Heather said as we entered the elevator.

Amiably, Tomlinson promised that he'd do what he could.

*   *   *

The car stopped at each floor but for every two that got off, three more wanted on and we were still quite crowded when we finally reached five.

Century Furniture Industries seemed to take up most of the fifth floor.

"I'm sorry," said a company employee at the entrance when confronted by this new deluge of potential customers, most of whom seemed to be decorators and interior designers, "but there's a half-hour wait for a representative if you wish to view our galleries."

While others drifted over to hear the mini-lecture on how Century's state-of-the-art robotics could turn out a perfect copy of a fifteenth-century refectory table from a Spanish monastery, I asked the employee if he'd noticed a small girl and an eccentrically dressed woman.

The man shook his head with a rueful smile. "We've been so swamped today I might not have noticed an ostrich in a tutu if it was wearing a buyer's badge."

But he took pity on my obvious anxiety and waved me in.

I left Heather by the entrance to keep an eye out for them.

"Take your time," she said, scribbling on her notepad. "This is really sort of neat. They buy an antique table for five thousand, use a robot to reproduce every wormhole, scratch, or gouge mark and then sell the reproductions for eighteen hundred a pop. You know something? I may actually get a real article here after all."

I cautioned her not to get so caught up in robotically reproduced wormholes that she would miss Lynnette and Savannah.

*   *   *

Despite my admonition to Heather McKenzie, the Century collection was so stunning that I was in danger of forgetting why I was there myself. There was dignity with touches of whimsy, there was an impeccable attention to detail that shrieked quality, and there were so many people in the long galleries that it was easier to look at furniture than scan for Savannah—especially since a lot of the upholstery was in muted spring neutrals that would camouflage her layers of pastel chiffon.

I found myself coveting a massive couch, a solid cherry serpentine sideboard, a bombé-based armoire, an eight-foot-tall highboy.

And then it hit me: these pieces were proportioned for ten-foot ceilings and rooms with twenty-foot-long walls.

Everything was too upscale and too scaled up for me. Even if I could afford to buy a few pieces, they'd look squashed in any house of mine.

A few feet away, as if to underline how hopelessly I was out of it, a high-powered blonde dressed in brown linen and shiny gold cuff bracelets imperiously waved away the fabric swatches that a Century representative was trying to show her.

"I'm sorry," she said in a voice which held no regret, "but as far as *my* clients are concerned, chenille is last week. Over. Finished. *Dead!*"

The representative immediately laid those swatches aside and reached for another set, and for a silly moment I pictured flocks of amorphous little puffy chenilles keeling over in mortification before the interior decorator's scornful pronouncement.

With my furniture envy now in check, I skimmed through the galleries that, altogether, must have covered several thousand square feet. I turned a corner and there ahead of me was a head of blonde hair pulled back in a French braid. I quickened my pace till I was sure it was Drew Patterson, then called her name.

She glanced around and seemed surprised to see me. "Hey, Deborah. Enjoying the Market? Where's Lynnette?"

"I was hoping maybe you'd seen her," I said and quickly explained how I'd lost her. "I just don't understand how she even knows Savannah well enough to go running after her like that. Dixie sounded as if last night was the first time anybody had seen Savannah in years, so how would Lynnette—?"

"My fault, I'm afraid," said Drew. "She was here with Chan last week and I took her for ice cream. Savannah saw us and came over to our table and wound up charming her. Even on Prozac and lithium or whatever she's supposed to be taking, Savannah is magical the way she can relate on any level to anybody, old or young."

I might be curious as to why Drew was the only person who seemed to know current details about Savannah, but the mention of those mind-calming drugs made me more uneasy than ever for Lynnette's safety and I said as much.

Drew smiled. "Don't worry. For some reason she's convinced that Lynnette's my daughter. She'd never hurt her."

Nevertheless, she joined the search and minutes later we found them seated side by side on an overstuffed loveseat in a corner gallery. Lynnette was almost as big as Savannah and she had leaned her head on the woman's shoulder to see the sketchpad Savannah held on her lap and to watch the pencil that flashed and darted as ladybugs and hummingbirds flowed across the sheet of paper chased by a little girl whose braided pigtail seemed to float on the breeze.

Savannah's small face broke into a genuine smile when Drew spoke to her and she even seemed to remember me, but whether as Ms. Sotelli from Newark or Judge Knott from Colleton County wasn't quite clear.

Drew cupped Lynnette's chin in her hand and gently scolded her. "You really scared Miss Deborah running off like that, punkin."

"I'm sorry," said the child, "but Savannah-Nana said she'd draw me again next time and I was afraid she wouldn't see me."

"We knew you would find us," Savannah told Drew. "A mother always knows where to find her daughter."

Drew touched the older woman's hand. "No, Savannah. I told you before. Lynnette's my friend, not my daughter."

"You do not want to talk about it." Savannah nodded knowingly. "Never mind, my darling. No one cares about such things these days."

Bewildered, I looked at Drew, who gave a tiny shrug of exasperation.

Savannah tore off the two sheets of sketches she'd made, handed them to Lynnette, and said to me with kindly courtesy, "It was very nice of you to call. I hope you will visit us again."

I was dying to ask her how my tote bag wound up next to Chan last night and whether my penicillin tablets were still inside my purse when she left it, but my internal preacher was yammering about little pitchers.

Instead, I said an equally formal goodbye and held out my hand to Lynnette. She started to protest, but Drew forestalled her. "You need to let Miss Deborah take you back to your grandmama before she starts worrying about you, too. I'll see you in a little while, okay?"

"Okay." She slid down off the loveseat, stuffed Savannah's drawings into her green tote, slipped her arms through the straps, and reached for my hand. A sudden thought made her smile. "Maybe Shirley Jane'll be there."

"Maybe," I agreed, not looking forward to the emotional scene that was bound to play out when Chan's sister arrived.

Drew remained behind and Heather McKenzie was disappointed when I returned to the entrance with Lynnette in tow, but no Savannah.

"She's back in a far gallery with Drew Patterson," I said and pointed in the general direction. "She seems to be in a good mood, too, so maybe you'll luck out if you approach her now."

"She doesn't like to talk to people," Lynnette piped up. "Just me and Drew. That's all she likes."

Heather wasn't much taller than Lynnette and she gave the child a humoring smile. "And why do you suppose that is?"

" 'Cause she's Drew's other mother," said Lynnette.

13

"The firm have in their employ several designers or artists who occupy separate rooms, in different parts of the building, and who do not intercommunicate, each depending upon his own unaided genius in devising sketches for the models."
The Great Industries of the United States, 1872

"Other mother?"

Drew smiled when I repeated Lynnette's words later that night. "I guess it probably sounds like that to a child. I've known Savannah since I was a baby and she took me under her wing when I was a bratty kid not much older than Lynnette. She was doing a catalog for Fitch and Patterson and she let me help dress the sets. She was really more like a mentor or a fairy godmother and I absolutely worshiped her to the point that it made my mother a little jealous. When I thought I wanted to become a freelance designer, Savannah let me hang out at Mulholland and taught me some of the basics."

"That's what you do now?"

"Except that I design exclusively for Fitch and Patterson."

A cynical thought crossed my mind and she must have seen it on my face.

"I may be a Patterson, Deborah, but that doesn't mean I'm a dilettante. I work pretty damn hard and I have a good eye for fabrics." She said it as a matter of fact, not conceit. "There are only so many designs for a chair or a couch. It takes fabric and color to keep the product fresh. I was one of the first in the industry to recognize how popular chenille could be. Because of me, we were ahead of the curve, not following it."

Again, an absurd image of fuzzy chenilles romped through my mind. "I heard someone today say that chenille's dead."

"Fading perhaps in the premium market, but it'll hold strong in the upper- to mid-range for at least another year or two. Longer in the low end, but by then we'll be into something else."

The April night was so mild that my light sweater was warmth enough. We were sitting in white wicker rocking chairs on Pell Austin's screened side porch where we could see the steady stream of people coming and going from Dixie's house. Market people, Fitch and Patterson people, people who had known Chan and who cared about Dixie—it looked as if half of High Point had come to pay their respects to Chan's mother-in-law and sister tonight.

A local TV van had been there earlier, in time for the 5:30

news. Dixie had made a statement. So far, my name had been kept out of it. Since she was Chan's mother-in-law and the one who called 911, the reporters seemed to assume she was the one who found him. So far, everyone who'd spoken on-camera—including Jay Patterson, Kay Adams and Jacob Collier—was profoundly shocked and everyone was just devastated by his death.

At least that's what they were saying for publication.

Lynnette and her cousin Shirley Jane were sound asleep on my bed in Pell's guest room and I wasn't quite sure where I myself would wind up sleeping, but for the moment, it was my job to keep an ear out for them. Drew, probably at Dixie's suggestion, had come over to bring me a plate of chicken salad and some iced tea, and she seemed grateful to get away from the grief and gloom that wrapped Dixie's house now that Chan's sister was here.

Upon arriving this afternoon, Millie Ragsdale had immediately announced that there would be no traditional funeral.

Despite her misgivings, Dixie was deferring to her wishes.

"Not *my* wishes," Millie Ragsdale said. "*Chan's* wishes. He wrote them down and sent them to me the same time he sent me a copy of his will. Right after Evelyn died."

I had no memory of Chan's sister, but there was no mistaking the family resemblance. Nor her determination to carry out her brother's instructions.

"Chan *hated* funerals," she said. "He always said, 'Millie, don't let them stick me in a box and then stand around looking at me for three days,' and I promised him I wouldn't."

That's why tonight would be the closest thing to a real wake that Chan would have. The Medical Examiner had released his body this afternoon and as soon as she heard that, Millie had asked her husband Quentin to make arrangements with a crematorium.

"Next month, when the worst of our pain is over," she'd said tremulously, "we'll have a memorial service in Frederick and scatter his ashes somewhere along the river."

By this time, for all I knew, Chan's body had already been committed to the flames. Even now, all that was corporeal of him might be cooling somewhere in Guilford County.

"Did Savannah kill him?" I asked Drew abruptly.

"*Savannah!*" Drew sat upright and turned so quickly in her chair to face me that the rockers scraped the wooden porch floor. "What makes you think Savannah had anything to do with Chan's death?"

Dixie had been told that penicillin had brought on Chan's anaphylactic shock and I assumed Drew knew, too.

She nodded. "That's what David told me."

"David?"

"Detective Underwood. His daughter works for us in our billing department. I've known him since he used to direct Market traffic in uniform."

I should have realized that there'd be a connection. Everybody in High Point seemed to have direct links to the furniture industry.

"Did you tell him where Savannah's staying?"

"But I don't know! She won't say. She just suddenly appears when I least expect her."

"But you did tell him you could put him in touch with her?"

"I said I'd try," she answered patiently. "But I still don't see the point of it."

"But didn't Underwood ask about my tote bag?"

"He asked if I saw Savannah take it. He didn't say why."

"So *did* you see her?"

"With one of our tote bags? Sure. And everybody else, too. We're giving out three hundred a day. Every time I turn around I see one. What difference does it make anyhow?"

"Because the one she walked out with was mine. It had my purse in it and in my purse was a bottle of penicillin tablets. Detective Underwood found my tote near Chan last night but the pill bottle was empty. If Savannah didn't take them, who did?"

"It was *your* penicillin?"

For some reason, her tone made me defensive. "I had a strep throat last week."

"Perhaps she left your bag there before Chan came. Perhaps someone else found your tablets."

I took a sip of iced tea and thought it over. "I don't see how there'd be enough time. She was wandering around High Point with my cell phone a little after nine and I found Chan less than an hour later. Someone would have had to take my bag away from her, see the tablets, know Chan was allergic, crush them into the brownies and then somehow lure him down to Dixie's floor and get him to eat them. All that in fifty minutes? I don't think so."

"Someone who knew he was that allergic . . ." Drew's chair rocked back and forth with gentle creaks. "I wonder how many people did know. I certainly didn't."

"No?"

She shook her head. "I mean I knew he couldn't take penicillin like everyone else, but not that it could kill him.

And I knew him about as well as anybody at Market. He never wanted to talk about any kind of health problem."

Out in the street, car doors slammed and engines cranked up as people came and went from Dixie's house.

"So I guess the first question is did Savannah know and the next is would Chan have taken food from her?"

"Chan would have taken anything from any woman," Drew sighed. "Especially chocolate."

She gave me a speculative glance. "It's a good thing you didn't have time to get to know him or David would probably have you in handcuffs since they were your tablets. But to answer your other question, yes, he'd take brownies from Savannah because he knew her from before. His wife Evelyn—Lynnette's mother? Did you know her?"

"Not really."

"She worked at Mulholland, too. Not with Savannah. With Pell Austin's group."

There was a touch of condescension in her voice and for a moment I saw a hint of the pecking order that must have existed in the design studio where the brilliant Savannah had overshadowed her colleagues. Drew might have been a couple of years younger than Evelyn, but as Savannah's protégé, she would have ranked higher than Dixie's daughter even without her wealthy background.

A tall, patrician-looking man was caught in a car's headlights as he crossed the street, and Drew sat up sharply. "Well, bless his heart!"

"Who is it?" Even in the headlights, all I could make out were silver hair and erect carriage.

"Jacob Collier. Good for him," she said approvingly. "He may not cut it in the field anymore, but he still has style."

"I thought you said he got in a fight with Chan last night."

"He did. That's what I mean. He was furious at Chan for taking away some of the accounts he was hoping to give Tracy and Vic, but he's man enough to forget about last night and remember all the good years."

"He's alone," I observed.

"Well, I'm not saying Tracy Collier's got her grandfather's style," Drew drawled.

She said it with enough bitchiness in her tone to remind me that Dixie had considered Drew in the running for Chan's affections even though Drew herself kept saying that they were only good pals. On the other hand, good pals can care enough to keep a wary eye on a pal's romantic entanglements. Dwight Bryant's always treated me like a younger sister, but he doesn't miss an opportunity to snipe at Kidd.

"What about Savannah, though?" I asked, returning to my first question. "If she thinks you're her daughter and that Lynnette's *your* daughter, then maybe she saw Chan with Tracy Collier or that Trocchi woman from Hickory-Dock—"

"Lavelle Trocchi."

"—and thought he was being unfaithful to you."

"And being a good mother, poisoned him so I'd never have to hear he was unfaithful?" she asked sardonically.

Put like that, it did sound absurd.

"I'm not saying it's sane, but then neither is Savannah, is she? What about the time she smashed her car?"

"What about it?" she asked cautiously.

"You think it's sane to smash an expensive car just because you're mad at your insurance company?"

In the dim light, Drew looked uncomfortable. "She has extreme mood swings—what she calls episodes. When she's up, she's brilliant. Nobody comes close to her style. But when she's down? For years, everyone thought she went off on glamorous junkets between projects. Wrong. Her money's gone to pay for stays at a psychiatric facility somewhere in Georgia where they get her medications balanced."

I thought of Savannah's pills, neatly lined up beside the turkey croissant I'd bought her yesterday. From my mental-health hearings, I know how difficult it is to keep the medications balanced in delusional manic-depressives, or bipolars, or whatever the correct term is these days. If indeed she's any of them.

"Does she have family down there?"

"A father maybe? I'm not sure. Pell knows."

"He does?" That surprised me.

"The last time she flipped, Pell was the one who got to her first. He called down there and somebody came and got her."

We rocked in silence for a moment, then she observed, "A lot of gay men have women friends, but I think Pell *really* likes women. After Evelyn got hit by that car and had to have all that therapy, he got Dixie that house, got her that job. When Evelyn died, it hurt him just about as bad as it did Dixie and he loves Lynnette better than anything else in the world. He was absolutely furious that Chan was going to take her off to Malaysia."

"Pell wouldn't be the first gay person who wanted to link himself to the future. It's human nature," I said.

Yet I couldn't help wondering just how furious Pell really had been.

Enough to kill?

14

"Such industry tends towards introducing union and the mutual sympathy of a common destiny among mankind in the place of the jealousies and isolations which have hitherto marked the progress of humanity upon this planet."
The Great Industries of the United States, 1872

It was nearly eleven before the last visitor left and I was still on the shadowy porch, by then half drowsing beneath a Peruvian shawl on Pell's wicker swing.

Drew had gone back over to Dixie's and must have left from there because she wasn't with the others when they came to see about the girls.

"You might as well let Shirley Jane stay over," Dixie told the Ragsdales as they settled wearily into wicker chairs. "Lynnette's spent the night here before so it wouldn't feel strange to her if she should wake up. You don't mind, do you, Pell?"

Pell made a murmur of assent from the other end of the swing.

"He's very good with children," said Dixie.

"I'm sure," said Millie's husband.

Two clipped syllables, but they told me everything I needed to hear about Quentin Ragsdale's opinion of homosexuals.

"We'll go on to Chan's house," said Millie. "It's not all that far and I have a key."

"Don't be silly," Dixie protested. "It's fifteen miles. You and Quentin can have the guest room, Shirley Jane and Lynnette can sleep in my room if you want her near you and I'll take the couch."

I gathered by this that the California decorina had probably found a bed somewhere with a more partylike atmosphere.

"Thank you," said Millie, "but I really think we'd all be more comfortable if Quentin and I took the girls and went over there. Besides, I'll need to look through Chan's papers and see about transferring Lynnie's school records."

"School records?" asked Pell.

"I know it's late in the year, but the quicker we can get her settled into her new school, the easier it'll be on her."

"Wait a minute!" said Dixie. "What the L-M-N are you talking about? You're not taking Lynnette anywhere."

"But surely you know that Chan asked me to be her guardian if anything happened to him?"

Pell turned to Dixie. "I thought you said Chan tore up that will."

"He did. Last week when he applied for passports. He was going through the papers in his lockbox, looking for Lynnette's birth certificate. He saw how hard this move was on me and asked if I'd feel better about things if he made me her guardian. And then he took out the envelope that had his will in it and tore it in half."

"Did he make a new will?" Quentin Ragsdale asked sharply.

"I don't know," Dixie said. "All I know is that he tore up the old one. I saw him."

"But if he didn't make a new one, I still have the copy he sent me and he definitely named me executor and guardian." Millie gazed at Dixie with tearful defiance. "It's what my brother wanted."

"Excuse me, Mrs. Ragsdale," I said, "but is your copy signed and witnessed or notarized?"

She wiped away her tears with the back of her hand. "No."

"Then I suggest you hire an attorney. Without a signed will, it'll be up to the court to decide who'll administer your brother's estate and have guardianship of his child."

"Who *are* you?" she asked peevishly, not remembering which one I was of the many that she'd met in the past few hours. "Do we know you?"

"No," I said.

"She's my friend," Dixie told her. "Deborah Knott. *Judge* Deborah Knott."

Quentin Ragsdale gave me an angry look. "I thought judges weren't allowed to practice law or give legal advice."

I shrugged. "That wasn't legal advice. That was just common sense."

"Look," Pell said in a reasonable voice. "You people don't want to get into a fight over Lynnette tonight, do you? You're tired and unhappy and—"

"And we don't need any of your pansy platitudes," said Ragsdale.

"Now just a minute," Dixie said, jumping to her feet.

"Grandmama?" Lynnette stood at the porch door in her nightgown, barefooted, her braid half undone, sleepy-eyed and troubled. "How come everybody's yelling?"

"Oh, sweetie, we're not yelling," said Millie before Dixie could answer. She held out her arms to the child. "Not really. We're just upset 'cause we're missing your daddy."

"Me, too," said Lynnette, who went to her and crawled willingly into her lap. Her aunt smoothed her tousled hair away from her face and rocked back and forth until everyone calmed down. Quentin, as well.

The mild spring night worked its magic and when Pell brought a jug of rosé out to the porch, Quentin Ragsdale even accepted a glass without any homophobic hostility.

Millie began to tell Dixie, Pell and Lynnette about some incident from Chan's childhood and Quentin turned to me. "Judge, eh?"

He was about my age and he cited the names of three or four attorneys or judges he had known over the years. I recognized only one, but that was evidently the right one, and I heard more about Baxter Haynes' fraternity days at Duke than I really wanted—although it might give me some ammunition the next time we crossed paths. (Haynes is almost as ardent a Republican as I am a Democrat.)

"You know," he confided, "we named Evelyn and Chan in our wills as Shirley Jane's guardians. And we told them sure when they asked if we'd take Lynnie. But none of us ever thought it'd really happen. It's a big step, taking somebody else's kid into your own household."

"Yes, it is," I agreed.

"Of course, she and Shirley Jane get along like sisters."

"But still—?"

"Exactly!" he said and held his glass out for more wine when Pell offered it around again.

The mild night air, the dim light, the wine—we were starting to mellow out when Detective David Underwood appeared in the alley, having deduced from Dixie's brilliantly lit and unlocked house that she couldn't have gone far.

"Miss Dixie?" he called from the edge of Pell's walk.

"Over here, David," she called back.

(And why was I not surprised that she, too, was on a first-name basis with a homicide detective? Yeah, yeah. Directed Market traffic when he was in uniform. Daughter in the industry. Probably brothers and sisters and eighteen cousins, too.)

He accepted a chair, refused wine, and pronounced himself pleased to meet the Ragsdales.

"I'm real sorry about your brother," he told Millie, "but we're going to do everything we can to—"

Dixie turned to Millie in wordless communication.

"Come on, honey," she said to Lynnette. "Let's get you some milk and then back to bed, okay?"

"Okay," the little girl said sleepily and allowed herself to be led back to my bed where her cousin slept undisturbed.

"Sorry," said Detective Underwood when they had gone inside. "Guess I wasn't thinking. It's been a long day."

"Do you know who fed my brother penicillin?" Millie asked bluntly.

"Not yet, ma'am. But don't you worry. We've got the newspaper, radio and television asking folks to get in touch with us if they know anything. As many people as were in that building last night, somebody's bound to've seen him."

Underwood was good. Despite the deep shadows here on the porch, I could see him becoming folksier and warmer by the minute and the Ragsdales were responding in kind.

"If there's anything we can do," said Millie.

"Well, now, you were real close to him, weren't you?" Underwood paused to let her nod vigorously. "Y'all see each other much?"

"He and Lynnie drove up every couple of months and we talked on the phone every week. Before Evelyn died, we'd come here for Thanksgiving and they'd come to us for Christmas, or vice versa. We wanted Shirley Jane and Lynnie to love each other and be friends. I can't have any more children and he didn't plan to either after Evelyn died, so we wanted them to grow up like sisters."

"I see. And did he talk to you about his work? The people he worked with?"

"Not really. Just that he loved it and made a good living from it."

"So he never mentioned any enemies?" asked Underwood as Dixie reappeared in the doorway.

"Never. He got along good with everyone, so far as I know."

Neither Pell nor Dixie was rude enough to snort at that, but I saw Millie looking at me suspiciously, as if she could hear my eyebrows lift in the darkness.

"Of course, there might have been girlfriends. Before he married Evelyn, he used to have three or four at a time fighting over him." She said it admiringly, as if vicariously proud of her brother's affairs.

"So he was one of those," sniffed *my internal preacher.* *"A man who bragged about his sexual conquests."*

The pragmatist shrugged. "Human nature, and what else is new?"

"Since Evelyn died—"

She broke off abruptly and stared at me with wide eyes. "Deborah Knott! Now I remember. You're Miss Barbara's niece. Well, I'll be darned. I always used to wonder and of course, I couldn't ask her."

"I beg your pardon?"

"About the baby. Did you have it or did you get an abortion?"

15

I was so stunned I could only sit there in the half-darkness looking as guilty as a yard dog slinking out of the henhouse.

"What baby?" I asked dumbly. "I don't know what you're talking about."

"Aren't you the same Deborah Knott that's Miss Barbara Peabody's niece?"

"Well, yes." No point in denying something so easily checked.

"Chan told me all about you that summer," said Millie

Ragsdale. "And he told me why you left when you did—because he got you pregnant."

"There's only been one immaculate conception," I said hotly, "and I wasn't there for that one, either. I don't know why he'd tell you such a thing, but he was lying."

"He said you wouldn't leave him alone. Couldn't keep your hands off him."

"Oh, please. Your brother was a horny teenager with overactive glands and what was obviously an overactive imagination. He was at least two years younger than me and I certainly didn't go to bed with him."

This was the truth, technically speaking, but only because Aunt Barbara had walked up on us in the gazebo at the crucial moment and I had split for New York soon afterwards. However, this was *not* something I felt compelled to say with everyone—including Detective David Underwood—staring at me as if my nose was growing longer with every word I spoke.

"When I introduced you," Dixie said suddenly, "Chan *did* say y'all had met before."

I held up my hands in mock surrender. "Hey, wait a minute here. This is getting blown way out of proportion. Yes, I met a kid named Chandler Nolan a hundred years ago and yes, I went with him to a couple of movies and let him kiss me a few times and maybe there was even some heavy breathing. But that was all. I don't care what kind of bragging he did, Mrs. Ragsdale, that was *all*. And as for me leaving because I was pregnant? In his dreams."

"Wet, no doubt," Pell murmured wickedly from the shadows beside me.

Millie Ragsdale glared at him.

"I left because he was a ruddy nuisance. He was supposed to be there to cut my aunt's grass and weed her rose garden. Instead, I couldn't step out the door without him being all over me like flypaper."

"You were after *him*," his sister insisted.

"He was a kid," I told her gently. "A pimply-faced, gangly kid with too much imagination. Think back to when you were nineteen. Think about the enormous gulf between a nineteen-year-old woman and a seventeen-year-old boy. At that age, would you have had sex with a boy two years younger than you?"

At first, I thought she was going to deny the thought of sex with anyone before marriage. Instead, she said stubbornly, "Chan was never pimply-faced."

For some reason, Quentin Ragsdale couldn't let that pass. "Yes, he was, Mill. I remember how he always had Noxzema and Clearasil in his gym bag. And he did like to brag about girls he never really had."

Millie looked at him, suddenly tearful. "Whose side are you on, Quentin?"

He reached out and touched her hand. "There aren't any sides here, hon, and you're tired."

His words seemed to diffuse the tension that hers had built up and there was a general stirring as everyone suddenly realized that yes, it was getting late. Long day today. And longer tomorrow, no doubt.

It was quickly decided that the Ragsdales and Shirley Jane would drive on over to Lexington, that Lynnette would finish the night in my bed and that I could move into Dixie's guest room.

As the others went inside the house, David Underwood drew me to one side.

"You got anything planned for tomorrow morning, Judge?"

"Not really," I answered. "Why?"

"Then how about you come down to my office around ten o'clock?"

The invitation did not sound optional, so I smiled a smile of as much pure innocence as I could muster and told him I'd be happy to meet him then.

"Why on earth didn't you tell me?" Dixie asked later as I was making up her guest bed with clean sheets.

She had packed Chan's overnight case, zipped his extra shirts and jackets into his garment bag, and was now clearing his toiletries from the half bath next door.

"When did I have a chance?"

"At the hospital?"

"Right. While you were worried and feeling guilty because you weren't there when Chan got to your floor, I was supposed to say 'And by the way, your son-in-law tried to get in my pants when I was going through a rough time in my life'? I wasn't being secretive, Dixie. Honest. It just seemed so irrelevant."

She paused with Chan's toothbrush, dental floss and razor in her hand. "But after he died—?"

"It was still irrelevant. And a complication I don't need." I smoothed the sheets and reached for a fresh pillowcase. "Now I've got to go down to Underwood's office tomorrow and spend a couple of hours convincing him that I didn't bear Chan's love child and then murder him twenty years after the non-fact."

"Serves you right," she said tartly, and I knew that at least one person believed me.

She cut those slanted, catlike eyes at me. "Heavy breathing, huh?"

I threw the pillow at her.

We were both tired, but too wound up for sleep, so Dixie found an open bottle of white wine in her refrigerator and we carried our glasses into the living room, a room that was warm and inviting and personalized with family photographs, keepsakes and a shelf full of bulging scrapbooks. We curled up at either end of the long couch and played "Whatever Happened to What's Her Name?" for a while until talk drifted into more personal channels.

I told her about Kidd. She told me about an intense affair that had ended in rancor shortly before Evelyn's death and how she thought she'd maybe just quit trying. "But I met someone down at the Tupelo Market in February. Tom's not handsome, but he's awfully nice. He acts as if I'm special—"

"As well he should," I murmured.

"—and he makes me laugh."

We agreed that laughter was important.

"What about Pell?" I asked when we'd thoroughly dissected Dixie's love life. "I don't see any signs that he's sharing his house with anyone."

She sighed and shook her head. "You don't know what a hellish two years it's been. First we lost Evelyn and then we lost James."

"He and Pell?"

She nodded. "He was an investment broker. Knew the stock market like I know High Point. Thanks to him, Pell and I both have solid investment programs."

She half knelt on the couch to pluck a small framed photograph from the collection on the table behind us. It showed Pell and another man head-to-head in an affectionately clowning pose.

"To look at James, you'd think he was gray tweed, button-down collars and all business. You've seen Pell's living room?"

I smiled.

"Yeah. Well, James was the one who found the boa constrictor and he was the one who put sunglasses on the Nubian slave boys. They were together for eight years."

"Why did they break up?"

"They didn't. He died last summer."

"Oh, Dixie!" Apprehension touched my heart as I asked the inevitable question. "AIDS?"

She shook her head. "Pancreatic cancer. Thirty-nine days after he was diagnosed, he was dead."

We had another glass of wine and eventually our talk wound back to Savannah, and I described for Dixie my impression of the picture in Heather McKenzie's car. "She really looked like a dynamo. I would imagine *her* love life was pretty active."

Dixie sipped her wine reflectively. "At one time or another, I've heard her linked with everybody from Mack Keehbler and Jay Patterson to Jacob Collier and—"

"Jacob Collier?"

"Oh yes. Jacob may be pushing eighty but the man's a billy goat with monkey glands."

I had to laugh at the image that conjured up, and remembering the snippet of gossip I'd overheard at the Discovery Center, I said, "I guess Chan thought his sex life undercut his effectiveness as a salesman."

"Come again?"

"I heard someone say Chan was annoyed about Collier's heavy dating."

Dixie leaned back against the burgundy velvet cushions and laughed so hard that her eyes disappeared into slanted crinkles.

"What?" I said, kicking her with my stockinged feet. "What's so funny?"

"You. You don't have a clue as to what heavy dating is, do you?"

"If it's that funny, I guess I don't."

"Actually," she said, sobering up, "it's not all that funny. Not for Jacob Collier. Heavy dating got him in trouble all right, but it has nothing to do with his sexual proclivities. See, dating is the number of days a sales rep will give a retailer to pay off the sale, usually in increments of thirty: thirty, sixty, ninety, a hundred and twenty, or two-forty. Chan was going over some of Jacob's accounts and saw that he'd given Kay Adams and Poppy Jackson datings of two hundred and forty days on a half-million of goods. That's incredible these days. It's like turning Fitch and Patterson into a personal loan banker, which is another reason why Chan was going to pull their business. They keep too much inventory on hand and they rely too much on heavy dating instead of turning the merchandise over. More aggressive businesses depend on smaller inventories, better management, jazzier sales techniques, et cetera for quick turnarounds. *And* they pay up in a thirty-sixty-ninety-day time frame."

That I could understand. "And what's the Golden Egg?"

Dixie smiled. "It's what sales people call this territory. North Carolina not only has some of the biggest retailers in the country, we also have the transshippers here. Very lucrative pickings."

"Drew says that Tracy Collier and her dad would normally inherit her grandfather's sales territory."

"Was Chan going to cut into her Golden Egg?" Dixie asked maliciously. "You'd better believe it!"

"I gather you don't like her. Because she's ambitious?"

"I don't mind legitimate ambition. Jacob's made a lot of money over the years here, but he genuinely cares about my small retailers. I don't know his son, but I do know that Tracy only cares about the money. And the power. She's bright, she's pretty, and she went after Chan with everything in her arsenal, including messing with Evelyn's head. She asked Evelyn to give him a divorce. And that's where she cut her throat with Chan. As I told you before, he might flirt around, but he loved Evelyn, wanted the marriage to work and he was so happy about the baby. After what Tracy did, her days were numbered. Chan'd already taken some of Jacob's best accounts for the house and he planned to convert most of the rest before he went to Jacaranda. Tracy would have been lucky to have enough egg left for Sunday brunch."

"Sounds like a motive for murder to me," I observed.

Dixie's feline eyes narrowed. "It does, doesn't it? Too bad she wasn't there when Savannah walked out with your bag."

"But did she know Chan was that allergic to penicillin? Drew said she didn't and she must have known him for years."

"Allergies didn't go with his macho image," Dixie said. "He thought allergies were for wimps and always down-played his. I remember last summer when we were all up at the Pattersons' camp on Hidden Lake for the company's an-nual outing. Chan was in the middle of a course of antibi-otics for a root canal and he forgot to bring his pills that day. Elizabeth Patterson offered him some penicillin tablets she had left over from some minor infection or other and he said maybe it wouldn't hurt to skip a couple of doses. She in-sisted until he finally admitted he had a problem with peni-cillin but he really didn't like having to tell her."

Dixie may have understood why I hadn't mentioned know-ing Chan, but by noon the next day, I began to feel that she was a distinct minority.

Before I'd even had my first cup of coffee, she called me to the telephone and there was Dwight Bryant fuming in my ear.

"What the hell's going on up there, Deb'rah?" he asked. "I've just got off the phone with David Underwood for the second time in two days about you. How come you're lying to him about that guy that got himself killed? With your penicillin tablets, too?"

"I didn't lie," I said stiffly.

"He sure thinks you did."

"Okay, maybe I didn't tell the whole truth, but I certainly didn't lie."

"Yeah, I know you and your maybe-I-didn't-tell-the-whole-truth. Listen, Deb'rah. This is no joke. Yesterday morning, Underwood thought you had means and opportunity. Today, he thinks you've got motive, too. I've calmed him down a little, but quit playing games with him, okay?"

Indignation rose within me. "I'm not playing games."

"Want me to call John Claude for you?"

"Oh, Lord, no! Don't you dare." That's all I'd need. Having to explain all this to my very proper cousin, John Claude Lee, who happens to be my former law partner and current attorney? "And don't you breathe a word about this to my daddy or Aunt Zell either, you hear?"

"Then behave yourself, okay?"

"Okay," I said meekly.

And I really meant to.

"You told me Chan Nolan was a perfect stranger," said Detective Underwood.

"I believe my exact words were that I didn't go around killing perfect strangers," I said.

"Implying that Nolan was."

We were once again seated across from each other in one of the department's featureless interrogation rooms, with Underwood's well-doodled yellow legal pad between us once more. His mustache seemed shorter and neater than it had last evening and I realized that he'd had a haircut and trim this morning.

"I'm sorry you took it that way," I apologized, resisting the temptation to smartmouth. "But for all intents and purposes, he *was* a stranger. It was so long ago and so insignificant that I honestly did think it was irrelevant."

"If it was so insignificant, why didn't you mention it when you had the chance?" he growled.

"For this very reason. You think I don't know how suspicious this looks? My bag taken, my tablets used? If I told you that I'd once known Chan, this is exactly how I thought you'd react."

He leaned back in his chair and fingered his mustache as he thought about it.

"I talked to the Stanberrys," he said finally.

"Oh?"

"They say if you were faking your surprise when you pulled out that fried chicken instead of your checkbook, you ought to be on TV instead of wasting that talent on the bench."

I felt a small trickle of relief. "Thanks . . . I think."

"'Course, your Major Bryant tells me you're pretty active in your local little theater down there in Dobbs."

"Oh, for Pete's sake," I started to fume. And then I realized that he was laughing at me beneath that thick clump of brown hair on his upper lip.

"I see Dwight also told you which of my chains to yank."

His grin broadened. "He did say you were real easy to rile."

"Joking aside," I said earnestly. "I did not sleep with Chan Nolan, I did not carry his baby, and I most certainly did not know that he was allergic to penicillin. Have you talked with Savannah yet?"

He shook his head. "She's a hard one to catch, what with Market in full swing. We staked out the soup kitchen and the design studio where she used to work—she's still got office space over there, you know that?—but so far we've come up empty. She's not sleeping in any of the shelters that we can tell."

"Did you talk to Drew Patterson?"

"She swears she doesn't know. Says the woman won't take any money from her, just wants to be with her."

"Then couldn't she—?"

"Get her to light long enough to call us?"

I nodded.

"She's going to try, but who knows? Since you seem to keep running into her, let me give you my pager number just in case."

He scribbled down the number on the end of the sheet, tore it off and handed it to me. There were nine digits on the paper, not seven.

"What's this three-five at the end?"

"So I'll know it's you calling. That *is* how old you are, isn't it?"

"Close enough," I said dryly.

He picked up his pencil again, turned to a fresh sheet in his notepad and said, "Tell me again what you saw and heard Thursday evening, from the first minute Savannah sat down at your table in the food court."

So I told it once more, right up to when the doctor came and told us Chan was dead.

"And you never once caught a glimpse of Savannah during the time you were wandering the halls at GHFM or driving over to the soup kitchen with this reporter, this—" He riffled through the messy pages looking for her name.

"Heather McKenzie. No."

"And no sign of Chan Nolan?"

"No."

"The Pattersons? The Trocchi woman? The Colliers? Dixie Babcock? Or what about those dealers that cornered Nolan at the Leathergoods party?"

"No, no, and no," I said wearily. "I've told you. I didn't see a single familiar face from the time I left the party till I met Ms. McKenzie in the stairwell. And she was it till we got back to Ms. Babcock's floor. I can't swear that I didn't pass Ms. Trocchi or Ms. Collier because I don't know them. Dixie said she was talking to the Trocchi woman when she spotted me, but I didn't notice her."

David Underwood made a notation on his notepad and I almost had to smile. He had turned to that sheet only moments earlier, yet it was already dog-eared and smudged and had begun to tear along the perforations at the top. Two scraps of paper had fallen on the floor and a pencil with a broken lead lay at the edge of the table ready to join them. Amazing. The man himself was immaculately groomed and neatly dressed in a fresh beige pin-striped shirt, crisp green and blue tie, and sharply creased brown slacks, but I had seen his car, his desk and now even this bare room: everything he touched became chaotic and messy.

I couldn't help wondering what his clearance rate was on his caseload.

He tapped the pencil against the pad, making random scratch marks. "Now when you got back to Dixie's—Ms. Babcock's?"

"Pell Austin was there. He fixed us a snack. We ate, we talked. Dixie called Chan's sister and left a message on her machine, then we talked some more and finally called it a night and went to bed around three in the morning."

"In Mr. Austin's guest room."

"Right."

"And Mr. Austin and Ms. Babcock also called it a night?"

"Well, no. After I turned out my light, I heard him go out the back door and saw him cross the alley to Dixie's. Her light was still on."

"You didn't go with him?"

"Of course not. I assumed they wanted to discuss Chan's death without a relative stranger sitting there and besides, I was exhausted. I don't think I turned over once before I fell sound asleep."

"So you don't know when Mr. Austin returned?"

I shook my head. "Sorry. I did hear him come in, and there's a clock radio beside the bed, but I was too tired to notice. Is it important?"

"Possibly. Mrs. Ragsdale called me this morning. One of Nolan's neighbors over there in Lexington saw lights on in the house early Friday morning. She didn't think anything about it till she heard he'd died and then she started wondering. Mrs. Ragsdale says there's no sign of break-in so whoever was there probably had a key to the house."

"And you think that's Dixie or Pell?"

"Well, now, I don't think anything just yet. Both of 'em told me that Mr. Austin went back to Ms. Babcock's for a book he'd left there and that they talked a few minutes and then he went home and she went to bed."

"Tell the truth and shame the devil," whispered the preacher.

"But what if they only ran out for doughnuts or to pick up a carton of milk?" argued the pragmatist.

"Then they should have told him, not lied. Look at the mess you got yourself in by not telling the whole truth the

162   MARGARET MARON

first time around," said the preacher. *"You going to do it again? That's wrong."*

"And stupid," said the pragmatist.

Okay, maybe it *was* stupid, but it didn't feel wrong. I simply couldn't bring myself to tell Detective Underwood that I'd seen Dixie and Pell returning in his van early yesterday morning. If they hadn't taken me in Thursday night, I might have had to sleep on the street. How could I repay their hospitality by ratting on them?

"I really don't have a clue as to what time it was," I said truthfully. "It could have been ten minutes, it could have been two hours for all I know. Was anything missing from the house?"

"Mrs. Ragsdale says the cleaning lady was there on Thursday after Nolan and the little girl left for High Point. Everything was tidy when she and her husband got there last night. She can't tell if anything's gone."

When you play cards with a bunch of older brothers, you learn to keep a poker face real quick if you don't want to keep losing your allowance as soon as you get it, so I doubt if Underwood saw any change of expression other than polite interest.

But if Dixie and Pell *had* gone to Chan's house and if anything had been taken, I had a feeling that I knew what it was.

16

"*The pieces of mechanism used to measure time, and kept in motion by gravity through the medium of weights, or by the elastic force of a spring, are called time pieces, or clocks.*"
The Great Industries of the United States, 1872

I drove back to Dixie's house with as much ambivalence about facing her as I'd had about facing Underwood earlier.

Golden-bell forsythias and borders of bright tulips marched along the residential streets. Each yard seemed massed in red, pink and white azaleas and dogwoods spread their graceful branches of white blossoms everywhere I turned.

The blue-sky morning was so beautiful that I was filled with a sudden longing for Kidd. It was a day made for horse-back riding or canoeing or for just taking a rambling walk through a spring landscape of newly leafed maples, oaks and flowering Judas trees. Not that Kidd was even in North Carolina this weekend, having gone down to the Georgia sea islands for something to do with sea turtles, but it was pleasant to daydream about alternatives to furniture and murder.

Evidently, the Ragsdales felt the same way, for when I got back to the cul-de-sac off Johnson Street, they were there to pick up Lynnette for the day.

"Try to guess who/ is going to the zoo?" she chanted as I walked up.

"What a great idea," I said, half wishing the Ragsdales were friends who would invite me along.

Our state zoo is state of the art, the first natural-habitat zoo in the country, with restraints on human visitors but few visible ones on the wild animals. Located in Asheboro, at the northern tip of the Uwharrie National Forest, the zoo sits very close to the geographical center of the state, which means that it's only about a half hour or so southeast of High Point.

"Say hello/ to the buffalo," I told Lynnette as she and Shirley Jane, who seemed like a nice kid, buckled up in the backseat.

"But don't say boo/ to the kangaroo," Dixie called from the doorway.

The car pulled slowly away from the curb and we heard the girls' alternating giggles as they tried to stump each other:

"Grizzly bear?"

"Please don't stare. Antelope?"

"You're a dope!"

It was just as well I hadn't been invited, I decided. Not even the zoo was worth thirty minutes of nonstop nonsense rhymes by a pair of wound-up monkeys.

Inside Dixie's kitchen—surprisingly plain-vanilla, I realized now, with nothing but purple floor tiles to break the monotony of white cabinets and fixtures—Pell Austin was loading her dishwasher with dirty dishes from the late brunch they had just eaten.

"Did you eat?"

He held out a box of Krispy-Kreme doughnuts, the most delicately delicious doughnuts in the whole world. They're made fresh at least twice a day and when you bite into one so hot that the glaze hasn't yet set, you think you've died and gone to heaven.

"Just coffee and a banana from Dixie's fruit bowl," I said, and yielded to temptation. Even cold, a Krispy-Kreme doughnut is like eating yeasty ambrosia.

"I heard they opened a shop in Manhattan last year," Pell said, as he poured coffee for me in a mug sprigged with violets. "Maybe we ought to buy stock in it."

He and Dixie both seemed more relaxed this morning and in better spirits.

"Did you work it out with your sister-in-law about Lynnette?" I asked.

"For the moment," Dixie said. "Thanks for speaking up last night. I've agreed to let her act as Chan's executor and she's agreed not to try to take Lynnette before the end of school. We're both going to speak to an attorney. I just wish you could advise me."

"I did," I grinned. "I told you to get a lawyer."

"So how'd it go with David?" she asked casually. Her back was to me as she wiped down the stove.

"Fine."

"He decide your teenage fling with Chan wasn't relevant after all?"

She rinsed out the dishcloth, hung it to dry beneath the sink, and sat down at the white table with a tall amethyst glass of water. At least her glassware had color.

I shrugged. "Who knows? Lucky for me, he's still looking at alternatives. Did your sister-in-law tell you that someone was over at Chan's house Thursday night? Or rather sometime before dawn yesterday morning?"

"Chan's been known to lend his key to out-of-town friends looking for a little privacy," said Dixie, a little too quickly. "Millie knows that."

"But she told Detective Underwood that nothing was out of place and nothing seems to be missing."

Pell closed the dishwasher, turned it on, then came and joined us at the table. "Maybe they changed their minds before they got to the bedroom."

"He made a point of asking me if you two went out again after I went to bed."

They looked at me mutely.

"I told him the truth," I said to Pell. "That I knew you came back over here—"

"—to get a book I'd left," he interjected. "I told him that myself."

"—and that I woke up when you returned but that I didn't look at the clock and I couldn't begin to guess what time it was."

I could see them visibly relax.

"Well," said Dixie.

She started to rise, but I motioned for her to stay.

"I did *not* tell him that what woke me up was Pell's van lights when you two drove in."

Instant tension.

"You knew that Chan's will named his sister as Lynnette's guardian, so you drove over there, rifled his lockbox and took the will, right? Please tell me you didn't destroy it?"

"Actually," Pell began hesitantly.

"No, Pell!" said Dixie. Her tip-tilted eyes flashed brown sparks.

I held up my hand. "On second thought, forget about it. I don't want to know. In fact, I don't want to hear a word about anything that happened after I went to bed over at Pell's. I'm an officer of the court. As far as I'm concerned, you drove out for orange juice and were back in ten minutes."

Dixie started to speak, but I shook my head. "I mean it, Dixie. Don't tell me, okay?"

"Okay," she said. "Thanks."

"Me, too," Pell said softly.

"Don't thank me too soon. If I knew for a fact what time it was when you drove into the alley, I'd tell Underwood in a New York minute. And I'd still tell him if I thought either of you had anything to do with Chan's death."

"I didn't," Dixie told me solemnly. "Neither of us did. I swear it, Deborah."

"Where were you Thursday night when Chan came downstairs?"

"After I finally got off the phone with Mr. Sherrin? It was around nine-thirty. I locked up, stuck a note on the door to tell you I'd be back at ten and then ran up the street to talk to Mary Ellen Hiatt, my opposite number at SHFA. We're going to join forces with some other retail associations to lobby against lifting restrictions on selling furniture on military bases. I had just got back and was asking the guard if he'd seen you when you came charging out of the elevator."

"So sometime between nine-thirty and ten, Chan came down and someone poisoned him with my penicillin tablets. Could Savannah know he was allergic to them?"

"Evelyn might have mentioned it to her, but I told you last night—he thought allergies were nerdy. Most people that knew him knew he had some, but I doubt if many people knew specifically what would set him off. Or how serious it was."

"And Savannah might do crazy things," said Pell, "but violence isn't part of her makeup."

"What *is* her makeup?" I asked. "Drew said you know what happens to her when she flips out."

"Just the outlines, not the specifics," he said. "They call it bipolar disorder these days, but it used to be manic-depressive psychosis. I didn't know what the hell it was—just that there were weeks, months even, when she seemed to be flying. You would swear that she was dropping acid—she used to say that she could hear color and feel design, as if electricity flowed from her fingertips—but it wasn't drugs. It was the way her brain was wired."

"And when she crashed?"

"That's when she'd disappear. I used to think she got burned out and went off on cruises or to a spa or something to recharge. I remember the first time I saw it happen, it was like watching a lightbulb on a dimmer switch, until one day

I realized that she was sitting at her drawing table staring at nothing, with tears running down her face over the meaninglessness of the universe. Two days later, she disappeared."

The memory seemed to sadden him.

"That was pretty much the pattern. She'd finish a major project; then would come a letdown, and she'd go off for a month or two. We never knew where. Eighteen months ago, though, she crashed big-time. She was so far gone, I had to violate her privacy and go through her personal papers to find the name of someone to call. Turned out to be her father down in Georgia. You want to know what his surname is? Smith."

"You never told me that," said Dixie. "Smith?"

"Can you believe it? Creedence Smith. He told me he was in his thirties when Savannah was born, so he's mideighties. If he's still alive. I called down there at Christmas to ask how Savannah was and was told that the phone company no longer had a listing for any Creedence Smith."

He sighed and offered me more doughnuts. I shook my head. It's too easy to keep reaching into the box until suddenly you realize you've eaten three without even noticing.

"The fact that she's come back to High Point without telling me or anybody at Mulholland—the way you say she's dressing and acting so weird? It makes me wonder if he died or had a stroke or something. Without any next of kin to be responsible and keep her there, maybe she checked herself out of the hospital before she was stable."

"You say she's never been violent?" I asked skeptically. "What about smashing her car or flushing jewelry? That sounds pretty violent to me."

"Oh, she could get in a rage at inanimate objects," he agreed, "but she never directed it toward people."

"Evelyn was a little scared of her," Dixie reminded him.

His face softened. "Only because she was in such awe of Savannah's talents and so diffident about her own."

Sudden tears glistened in Dixie's eyes. "Oh, God, Pell!"

He reached across the table and patted her hand. "I know, love. I know."

"How did she die?" I asked quietly, knowing that sometimes it helped to talk.

"She fell off the Park Avenue stairs," she said. "Pell was there."

"It's what we call one of our staircases at Mulholland," Pell explained. "It's about fifteen feet high, very sleek and *moderne*, sort of a long graceful modified S-curve that's flat on one side so that we can push it up flush against a wall, make it look as if we're shooting in an elegant duplex apartment. Evelyn was dressing a set we were going to shoot that afternoon. A rush job. The product was a Fitch and Patterson piece, an armoire, if I remember correctly. A last-minute addition to the line."

"A last-minute Widdicomb knock-off," Dixie said bitterly.

"Anyhow, workmen had rolled the staircase into place but for some reason they forgot to lock the brakes, although one guy afterwards swore that he had. I was in prop storage looking for something clever to jazz up the set. Evelyn went up to hang some pictures on a wall near the top and when she started to hammer in the tacks, the stairs slid away from the wall. There was no handrailing on that side and she went right over. They hadn't laid the rugs yet, so there was nothing to break her fall."

"Fifteen feet onto a bare concrete floor," said Dixie. "She died three hours later."

Pell's eyes were wet now, too. "A blessing really. There would have been massive brain damage if she'd lived."

"Another two weeks and the doctors might have saved the baby," Dixie said brokenly. "A little boy. He was just too premature to live. We buried him in her arms."

"Oh, Dixie," I whispered. "I'm so sorry."

"Don't you see, Deborah? I *can't* let Millie take Lynnette. She's all I have now."

I nodded. "I do see. The thing is, does Underwood know you well enough to understand all this?"

"Maybe. Why?"

"Look at it from his viewpoint. You're so frantic to keep Lynnette here, you'd do anything to stop Chan from taking her off to Malaysia."

"Not kill!" Pell said sharply.

"So say you." I turned back to Dixie. "A prosecutor could argue that after Heather and I left, Savannah came to your office and brought my bag, just as I first asked her to. You open it, find my tablets and a baggie full of brownies that she's dropped inside, and realize you've been handed a gift. You page Chan on his beeper, meet him at the deserted Swingtyme display, offer him a brownie and *voila!* When he starts having trouble breathing, you tell him to lie down and you'll go get help. Instead you rush out to your friend's office and while he's dying, you're establishing an alibi."

There was a moment of stunned silence when I finished talking. Dixie was shaking her head in denial, but Pell said,

"She's right, Dix. They could build a case if they wanted to."

He turned to me. "So it's up to us to find out who really did it."

"*Us?* What's this us, white man? I'm a judge. I can't get involved."

"You're already involved," he reminded me. "Soon as you didn't tell David Underwood we were out in my van late Thursday night, you became our accomplice."

"*Oh, Lord help us!*" groaned the preacher.

"*Yeah, you'd better pray,*" said the pragmatist. "*And while you're at it, pray that Dwight doesn't hear about this either.*"

17

"The term 'furniture,' which means nearly every article and utensil of household use, is so comprehensive that it includes many things which have been described in detail elsewhere in this volume."

The Great Industries of the United States, 1872

Since Savannah's movements Thursday night held the key to Chan's death, finding her seemed to be our first logical step. For all my theorizing with Drew Patterson last night, misplaced maternalism hardly seemed a valid motive for murder, even assuming Savannah wasn't cooking on all four burners. We needed to know when she left my bag at the Swingtyme showroom and who else was there at the time.

"I know she worked at your design studio," I told Pell, "but where did she live?"

"Furnished apartments all over the area. I don't think she ever cared about stuff beyond her cars, a few clothes and maybe jewelry. She kept most of her books and personal papers down at the studio. Said she didn't trust nosy landladies with no lives of their own not to come snooping."

He looked up her last address and the three of us drove over to Jerilyn Street and talked to the owner of a furnished garage apartment, a woman in her twenties who couldn't have had a spare moment to snoop. Not with three children under the age of four and, from the looks of her swollen belly, another due any minute.

"The police were here yesterday asking about her," said young Mrs. Eakes, balancing a baby on one hip and using the other hip to keep a toddler corralled on the porch. "I'll tell you the same thing I told them. She wasn't well, poor thing, and her daddy sent somebody up here to bring her home. It was right before Stephanie Leigh was born—'bout a year and a half ago? Anyhow, I've not seen or heard a word from her since I shipped her things down to Athens, Georgia, like her daddy asked me to."

The efficiency apartment was now rented to a college student who was waxing his car in the driveway. "Now that you mention it, there *was* an old lady came by right after winter break. Said she used to live here, wanted to see if any of her stuff was still here. Seemed harmless enough, so I let her look."

"Was there anything?" I asked, resisting the urge to buff a spot he'd missed.

"Just a little cushion." He measured a twelve-inch square with his hands. "Black velvet with gold tassels in each corner. Wasn't anything I used and Frances—Mrs. Eakes—wasn't here to ask, so I let her take it."

Underwood had told me that Savannah still had work space at Mulholland and that he was going to put the building under surveillance. I was on the middle seat behind Pell and Dixie as he finished circling the block and again turned his blue van off Main Street onto Mulholland. I didn't see a soul that looked like a police officer.

Traffic was thick and parking spaces around the design studio were at a premium. While Pell maneuvered into the employees' lot, Dixie and I craned our necks trying to spot a car with someone sitting motionless. On television, the surveillance people are always digging up the streets, stringing telephone wires or staked out in a van with dark windows.

Not here.

No workmen, no smoked windows, and all the cars looked empty.

"Maybe they're watching from inside one of the surrounding buildings."

"Look around you, Deborah," Dixie said dryly. "Do you see any windows overlooking this entrance?"

She had a point. I could see a corner of GHFM, but no windows broke its exterior walls. The same was true of smaller showroom buildings that backed onto this block. Glitter and shine might fill those endless interiors, yet none of it came from natural sunlight.

Pell parked in his assigned slot in front of an inconspicuous rear door and I realized that I must have passed the Mulholland Design Studio a half-dozen times this weekend without noticing it.

Not that they were trying to keep their location secret. The name was carved on a low stone slab next to Mulholland Street, and the stone slab sat amid a narrow strip of evergreens with a thick border of bright yellow pansies running around the whole thing. But the block-square building itself could have been a tobacco warehouse for all the care that had been taken with its design: four windowless cement walls painted mud brown and a pitched roof sheeted in what looked like ordinary barn tin.

Hard to believe that ads for some of the glossiest magazines in the world were shot right here in this building.

Or to realize that a home furnishings revolution had started here when a brilliant young designer made eclecticism a household word.

"Thirty years ago, furniture was still being sold in rigidly matched suites," Pell told me. "Your mother wore matched cardigan sets, right?"

I nodded as he expected me to.

"So did mine. So did Dix's. Handbags coordinated with her shoes, right?"

Again I nodded dutifully.

"Same with furniture. Chairs matched tables that matched sideboards which matched china closets. Beds, dressers, and bedside tables—all part of a perfect matched set. If there was a candlestick lamp on one end table, it was balanced by an identical candlestick lamp on the opposite end table. If your couch was upholstered in striped satin, so were the side chairs, and chances are that your satin drapes would be a solid version of the dominant color as well."

"Savannah changed all that?"

Pell slid back my door and gave me his hand as I stepped down from the van. "Savannah changed all that. Put the word 'eclectic' on everyone's lips. It was before my time, of course, when Mulholland Studio was only a quarter of the size it is now. I got here ten years later but everyone was still talking about the way she turned things upside down. She was a Sixties Happening right here in High Point. She bought her clothes at a thrift shop, did what she wanted, said what she wanted and made everyone want that look, that style. She used it to talk her way into old Mack Keehbler's office."

"Keehbler Couches?" I asked, remembering that his was one of the power names Dixie had linked with Savannah's.

"And case goods," said Dixie, who must have known the story by heart.

Pell unlocked the studio door and we walked into another of those drab concrete corridors so at odds with the glitz and glamour of the industry when on display.

"So Keehbler sent over two suites," said Pell. "A bedroom and a living room, and she mixed them like two decks of playing cards. A bedside table became an end table for the couch. She hung the dresser mirror over the sideboard, put the coffee table at the foot of the bed for a dressing bench, and instead of matching lamps, silver cigarette boxes and neat little bouquets of flowers, she rummaged in the junk shops for off-the-wall accessories: funky lamps, painted boxes, antique toys, a wall display of old hand mirrors."

"And Keehbler loved the ad she created for him?" I asked.

"Hated it!" Pell said cheerfully. "But Victoria Cumbee of Ashenhurst saw a copy in his wastebasket and hired her on the spot to style their new fall catalog. The rest is history."

He opened a door at the end of the corridor and I caught my breath in astonishment.

Outside, the place had looked like a warehouse; inside, the resemblance was even stronger. Row after long row of eight-foot-tall gray steel shelves met our eyes and each orderly shelf was full of *stuff*.

At the door where we'd entered, the subject was candlesticks. I hadn't considered there could be that many different kinds of candlesticks in the world: eight-branched silver candelabras, tall silver, short silver, simple and severe, heavy and ornate, delicate for slender tapers, chunky for thicker candles. And after all the changes had been rung in silver, you had the same thing again in brass, pewter, wood, cast iron, tin, glass of all colors, porcelain, ceramics and crystal. Shelf after shelf after shelf.

There were shelves of cats and dogs of all sizes and all materials; twenty feet of antique painted iron, mechanical banks and toys; a section devoted to teddy bears of graduated sizes and all periods; another to boxes made of wood, paper, leather, metal, glass, marble or plastic, from matchboxes to painted breadboxes; yet another held bowls, from simple Revere silver to reproductions of Chinese porcelain. I saw old-fashioned wind-up clocks, Seth Thomas grandmother clocks, plastic dogs with clock faces for bellies, and even a few hourglasses. Taller shelves held the studio's extensive collection of table lamps (floor lamps stood in serried ranks along a far wall). Baskets, picture frames, vases, fire screens, books bound in colorful leathers, switchplates, bottles, silk flowers—I was already dizzy from looking at it all when Dixie touched my arm and said, "Look up."

Hanging from the rafters fifteen feet above our heads was a forest of light fixtures and paddle fans, swinging lamps and chandeliers of faceted crystal, massive wrought iron, polished brass, cartwheels, even a chandelier fashioned from deer horns, which in turn brought us to a macabre section of stuffed animals, fish and mounted trophies.

The aisles were barely wide enough for two persons to pass and as I followed Pell and Dixie through the maze, a woman turned into our aisle pushing a wire shopping cart piled high with miscellaneous articles which she was returning to their proper spaces after a camera shoot. We had to flatten along the side to let her pass.

"Hi, Pell," she said, holding up a small iron pot. "Where do you think it ought to go? Vases or iron cookwares? Jordan used it for dried hydrangeas but I don't know where she got it and she won't be back till after Market."

He upended the pot. "What does the tag say?"

"No tag," she said. "It must have fallen off."

"Then I'd stick it in cookwares," he advised.

"Yeah, that's the logical place, isn't it?"

As the woman trundled away with her cart, Pell said, "Before Savannah, design studios wouldn't have a tenth of these props. She put Mulholland on the map and they should have given her a share of the business."

We were interrupted by a very tall, very thin young man, who had spotted us from the end of a distant hall.

"Sst! Pell!" he hissed. "Hurry up, they're waiting for you."

"Oh, God," Pell groaned, brushing his hair out of his eyes. "I forgot all about the reception this afternoon."

"Start SMart's new art director's been asking for you for the last twenty minutes. She's furious," the young man said in a strident whisper.

"Give her another glass of Rioja and tell her I'll be right there." He handed Dixie his key ring, then smoothed his hair again and straightened his vest and shirtsleeves. "You remember where Savannah's office was? Around the corner from mine, up on the second floor? This key ought to fit."

"Go!" said Dixie. "We'll find it."

Once he'd left us though, Dixie looked around hesitantly. "I haven't been down here since Evelyn died," she said, "and they were always moving the interior walls, but I think . . ."

We turned a corner past a huge stack of colorful carpets in a range of patterns from Persian to English cottage, and I had to watch my step. The space was cavernous, the fixed cement walls were painted light-absorbing black and the floor was crisscrossed with electrical cords that snaked around flimsy temporary walls to portable floodlights, power tools and various appliances.

I heard someone using an electric saw and the smell of wet latex paint hung in the air.

We passed sets in various stages of completion. On one, an elderly black man was carefully assembling a red vacuum cleaner that would be photographed against this scrap of deep blue carpet like a ruby in a blue velvet box.

Another set held a bedroom that looked ready to shoot. Even the camera was in place. Everything that the camera might see was brilliantly lit and as pristine as the set's new coat of paint. Two feet out of camera range though and it was back to darkness, shabby and ordinary. The bed was dressed in gorgeous linens, but when we walked around to view it from the other side, I saw that the comforter that looked so lavish from the front barely covered the back edge and that where a leg was missing, someone had substituted a gallon paint bucket.

It was like being backstage at a Broadway show, viewing the scenery from behind. The degree of clutter around the edges was astonishing and the corners were stacked deep in what seemed to be bolts of cloth, old pipes, broken light stands, scrap lumber and odd sizes of sheetrock.

"Umm. Nice kitchen," I said, pausing at yet another tableau that looked camera ready to my untrained eye. The modern cabinets glistened as did the place settings of potteryware in an eclectic mix of primary colors. A sleek stainless steel chandelier hung over the breakfast table. At least it was sleek as far as the camera would notice. A few feet up, just out of the camera's field of vision, the shiny steel rod became a utilitarian cable.

"What do you suppose the product is?" Dixie asked me. "Appliances, breakfast set, or lighting fixtures?"

"The ceramic dishes," I answered promptly.

"Wrong," said a half-familiar voice behind us. "It's the vinyl floor tiles."

I turned and there from my courtroom yesterday was young Randy Verlin all togged out in jeans, scuffed work shoes and a very professional-looking tool belt.

"Oh," he said. "Judge Knott. Sorry. I didn't recognize you, ma'am, without your robe. You know, I didn't get a chance to tell you, but I sure do appreciate what you did. Giving me Travis and all."

He twisted a screwdriver in his hands. "And I'm gonna try real hard to do like you said, all that about not bad-mouthing April Ann to him."

"That's good," I said warmly.

"I gotta tell you though. When I seen that you were a woman, I thought for sure you'd give him to her, but you made a believer out of me."

"Thank you," I said, choosing to take this as the compliment he obviously intended. "So this is where you work?"

"Yes, ma'am."

"Great, maybe you can help us." I turned to Dixie. "Where exactly do we want to go?"

"I'm completely turned around," she told him, smiling. "Where do y'all keep your stairs these days?"

"Oh, you must have passed them on your way in here."

He led us back the way we'd come to the stack of carpets. "Just on the other side of that wall there."

We circled around and Dixie stopped short. Blood drained from her face. "Oh, God!" she whispered.

It stood alone in the center of an empty space—a graceful, sinuous flight of steps that snaked up to nowhere.

"I'll be happy to move it for you," said Randy Verlin.

He kicked off a brake and tugged at the lower rail. The fifteen-foot-tall staircase moved smoothly on ball-bearing casters.

"Where do you want it?" he asked Dixie, and I realized that he must have assumed she was on Mulholland's staff.

"No," I said sharply. "She meant the stairs to the second floor."

By now, Verlin had caught on that something was very wrong, though he wasn't quite sure what.

"Sorry," he said. "I thought— But you want to *go* upstairs, right?"

"Right."

He pointed. "Down to the next opening and bear left."

Dixie strode off as I thanked a puzzled Randy Verlin and hurried after her.

The stairs to the second floor were of ordinary industrial steel, painted bright red. Dixie was almost at the top before I caught up.

"You okay?"

"I'm fine," she said, but as soon as I touched her arm, she turned to me in tears.

I held her till she stopped shaking, then offered tissues from my purse.

"Sorry. Each time, I keep thinking this will be the last time I cry for Evelyn. And then something like this will hit me in the face and I fall apart all over again."

She needed to put cold water on her eyes. There was a women's room halfway down the hall, but it was locked and the second floor seemed deserted.

"Never mind," said Dixie. "I think Savannah's studio had a lavatory attached to it. If hers doesn't, Pell's does and one of these keys is bound to unlock his door."

Pell had said that Savannah's studio space was around the corner from his but the hall seemed to dead-end in a tangle of cast-off furniture. Yet, when we looked closer, we saw that it was possible to snake through the clutter and turn the corner.

As expected, the door was locked, but the second key that Dixie tried unlocked it. It took her a moment to find the light switch.

When the lights flooded on, we saw a large room, about twenty feet square, complete with drawing table, file cabinets, chairs, a cabinet full of colored inks and drawing pens. The Persian rug on the floor looked authentic and the prints that hung beside the door had been professionally framed by someone who valued them. Bookshelves ranged along one wall and were jammed tight with both books and loose-leaf notebooks. The ceiling followed the slant of the roof and the short wall held a full-length mirror framed in heavy ornate gilt.

A corkboard covered one whole wall from floor to ceiling and was thick with sketches, ads, old photographs, and scraps of papers with phone numbers, names, addresses and memos that had been hastily jotted down. All were dusty and curling at the edges.

Dixie peered inside the adjoining lavatory and ran her fingers lightly over the sink. "Dry," she said, "but it doesn't feel dusty."

Yet the office itself had a neglected, abandoned air and had clearly not been cleaned in months.

The industrial-size wire wastebasket held candy wrappers, crumpled potato chip bags and wadded-up sketches of chests and chairs, but they could have been there for ages.

As Dixie splashed cold water on her face and freshened her lipstick, I smoothed out some of the sketches. Knowing nothing about furniture styles, I couldn't tell if these were new or from a past season. But then I smoothed another sheet and saw two unmistakable faces. Drew might not have changed much in eighteen months, but Lynnette's snaggle-toothed smile was quite recent.

"Look," I said as Dixie emerged from the lavatory.

"This was hanging behind the door," she said at the same moment.

It was a new green nylon tote bag with the logo of a waterbed company, identical to the one those Southern belles at Market Square had given Lynnette yesterday.

18

"The necessity for a place to sleep, by its daily recurrence,
has made the bed we use one of the most important subjects
for consideration."
                    The Great Industries of the United States, 1872

"Did the police search this office?" I asked Pell when he
rejoined us almost an hour later.

"Underwood knew it was here," he reminded me. "They
must have."

"Savannah may be using the place occasionally," Dixie
said, "but where does she sleep?"

I threw up my hands in frustration. "If you ask me, she's
starting to sound like the Phantom of the Market. Drew says

she pops up when least expected. Heather McKenzie says she went scurrying through the bowels of your building like Alice's White Rabbit. And—"

"Of course!" Pell exclaimed. "Through the looking glass."

"Excuse me?"

"I almost forgot about this." He walked over to the large, gilt-framed mirror. "Years ago, she was grumbling about the lack of storage. The owners wouldn't give her a bigger space, so she bribed one of the carpenters—"

He tugged at the mirror and it swung toward him on concealed hinges to reveal an open space between the wall of the office and the slanting roof. It was six feet tall at the doorway and several feet deep before rafters, studs and joists took over.

The storage space had been floored with rough plywood and Dixie and I immediately stepped inside, but it was much too dark to see anything beyond some sealed cardboard cartons. Heat had built up under the tin roof and the air was uncomfortably warm and stuffy.

"Look," Dixie said and pointed to an electrical box down near the floor.

"That carpenter must have known a little something about splicing wires," I said.

My brother Herman is an electrician and he would not have approved those exposed sockets, but the plug end of an orange drop cord lay on the floor beneath them and I could never resist an invitation. As soon as I plugged it in, a dim glow appeared about ten feet away.

Cautiously, Dixie skirted more cartons and walked through the hot still air toward the light. I was right behind her when she pushed aside some sheets that had been rigged to curtain off a small area. We found tote bags, a box of sketchpads and pencils, a bundle of winter clothes, and a deep mound of designer bed linens: sheets, comforters, blankets, and pillows (including a gold-tasseled black cushion) tossed together to form a human nest.

An empty human nest.

From behind us, Pell said, "Oh, my. You should have heard Jordan cuss when that whole Ralph Lauren setup went missing this winter. She thought one of the workmen stole those linens."

As I turned to let him in, I saw numerous scraps of paper pinned to the curtain. Some had been clipped from *Furniture/Today*, a few were from the High Point paper, but most of them were pencil sketches done by Savannah. All but three were of Drew Patterson—Drew on Chan's arm at a party, Drew and her father in a group at some Fitch and Patterson event, Drew's lovely face smiling, laughing, full of mischief, serene and thoughtful.

The odd three were of Lynnette.

"I don't think I like this," said Dixie.

"I think we'd better call your friend David," I said.

Detective David Underwood wasn't in his office, but when I called his pager he returned my call within minutes, so I guess the three-five worked.

Pell told him about the rear entrance and went down to meet him. Fifteen minutes later, after I'd signed the search warrant he'd brought along, Underwood stood before the gilt-framed mirror and shook his head.

"Now how the expletive deleted did we miss those hinges?" he asked, shaking his head at his own inefficiency.

This time, he made a thorough examination of Savannah's hidey-hole, sliding his hand down into each shopping bag (a handful of empty prescription bottles in one) and leafing through her notebooks (more sketches of furniture, Drew and Lynnette). The sealed cartons nearest the mirror looked as if they hadn't been opened since Savannah originally put them there, so he didn't bother with them.

But he did explore the surrounding attic space.

Only the part around her office had been floored, but by carefully stepping from one joist to the next, it was possible to walk the whole side of the building between the roof and office walls. The second floor covered slightly less than half the building. The other half, where sets were built, photographed and then torn down, was open from floor to roof except where high catwalks provided support to suspend chandeliers and other lighting fixtures.

At that end of the attic wall, several scrap pieces of boards had been laid across the joists to make a solid floor, and Underwood found a small hole in the sheetrock where someone could stand and look down into the studio.

Correction: where someone *short* could stand and look down into the studio.

All four of us had to stoop down in order to see through the hole.

It was like looking into a maze of ceilingless rooms and cubicles. No wonder Savannah could pop onto the floor whenever she spotted Drew.

I saw Randy Verlin screwing switchplates onto that "kitchen" wall. I saw the elderly black man position the newly assembled vacuum in the center of the blue carpet and polish away all his fingerprints from the gleaming red plastic body. I saw the movable stairs surrounded by a small semicircle of people who watched as the tall young man we'd seen earlier demonstrated how easily it could slide around. I gathered that the in-house reception included guided tours of the studio.

If Underwood thought it strange that I was here with Dixie and Pell, he didn't say so. In fact, he seemed to accept Pell's story about suddenly deciding to check out his colleague's work space. When we regrouped in Pell's work-room, he asked me to repeat what Drew Patterson had told me earlier.

"It's not that much," I said. "You really ought to ask her."

"I will," he promised, "but for right now . . ."

I shrugged. "We were discussing who could hand Chan brownies and get him to eat them without arousing his suspicions. Drew said any woman probably could, including Savannah because he knew her from when his wife—"

"My daughter Evelyn," Dixie interposed grimly.

"—from when Evelyn was working here. For some reason, Savannah's started believing that Drew is her daughter and by extension—because she's seen Drew with Lynnette occasionally these last few months—she thinks Lynnette is her granddaughter."

"*What?*" exclaimed Dixie and Pell together.

I was equally surprised. "Didn't y'all know?"

Pell shook his head and Dixie said, "Of course we didn't know. Why didn't you tell me?"

"I didn't realize there was anything to tell. Drew said that Chan often brought Lynnette over with him when he came and they would go out for ice cream or something while Chan was in conference."

Dixie nodded. "That I knew."

"Well, they kept running into Savannah and Savannah got it in her head that Chan and Drew were married and that Lynnette belonged to both of them."

"That's crazy!" Pell snapped.

"Delusional maybe," I said and Underwood's mustache twitched at that more politically correct term.

"Whatever she is," Dixie said, looking at Underwood like a protective tigress, "you've got to find her, keep her away from my Lynnette."

"For what it's worth, Drew doesn't think she'd hurt Lynnette and neither do I," I said and described how the little girl had slipped away from me to go to Savannah and how Savannah had amused her by sketching pictures until we found them.

But then I remembered something else. "You know how Lynnette likes to rhyme words and names? How Pell's Uncle Pelly-Jelly and I'm Judge Fudge?"

"So?"

"So she calls Savannah Savannah-Nana."

Underwood saw my point. "Savannah's probably heard other children call their grandmothers 'Nana.'"

"Oh, dear God," said Dixie.

Underwood gave her shoulder an awkward pat. "Now don't you worry, Miss Dixie. We're going to find her." He hesitated. "Still and all, if that little girl was *my* granddaughter, I'd keep her on a short leash till this is cleared up."

He asked us to stay out of Savannah's office and took Pell's key, then left to go find the security guards.

"Whups. I almost forgot." He turned back to me, slapping at his pockets and finally pulling a ragged scrap from the breast pocket of his neat shirt. "Judge Simmard asked me to give you a message if I ran into you. Wanted you to call him." He looked at the scrap of paper dubiously. "I *think* this is his number."

It was.

Pell offered the use of his phone and a gracious Southern male voice answered on the second ring, "Judge Simmard here. How can I help you?"

I identified myself and he said, "Ah, Judge Knott. Allow me to welcome you to the Triad. I've invited a few friends for dinner and would be so pleased if you could join us at Noble's at eight-thirty tonight if you will excuse the short notice."

"Why, that's awfully nice of you," I said, lapsing into my own gracious Southern female voice. "Just let me check with my hostess."

"We'd be happy to have her join us, too, of course."

I covered the mouthpiece and said to Dixie, "One of the judges here wants us to join his dinner party at someplace called Noble's. What do you think?"

Despite her concern for Lynnette, a shadow of regret passed across Dixie's face. "I can't. Not with Lynnette here. But you go."

"You sure?"

"Of course I'm sure. People *kill* for reservations at Noble's during Market Week. It's the only five-star restaurant in town, and the food is wonderful."

So I told Judge Simmard that I'd be charmed.

19

> *"We must distinguish between a general principle and individual acts, the character of which must, in many cases, be determined by circumstances."*
>
> *The Great Industries of the United States, 1872*

Dixie felt she ought to check by her office, so we dropped her there and Pell left his van in her assigned parking space while we cruised the Market, hoping to get lucky and run into Savannah again.

Our first stop was the Fitch and Patterson showroom on the off-chance that Savannah would be drawn like a magnet to any place that Drew might be.

Except that Drew wasn't there.

Jay Patterson gave me a distracted nod, but he was in deep conversation with what looked like corporate buyers. Indeed, Fitch and Patterson seemed to be doing a killer business. Most of the sales reps were huddled over order books with customers and calculators. As we passed, an attractive woman with short brown curls finished bowing two Japanese buyers out the door and turned to us with the happy smile of someone who's just sealed a profitable deal.

"May I show you anything?" she asked. Her smile widened as she read Pell's badge. "Mulholland Studios. I thought you looked familiar. Hi, I'm Tracy Collier."

So this was the woman who had tried to dislodge Chan from Evelyn. She was probably thirty, slender, but not skinny, with wide hazel eyes. Quite pretty actually, in a clipped, efficient way. And she had a certain intensity of manner that was irresistible. People like Tracy Collier can make you feel that all their attention is focused on you because you are so utterly fascinating that they have no other choice. No wonder she was a good sales rep.

And no wonder that Chan had bought what she was selling until she went too far and involved Evelyn.

"Drew Patterson around?" I asked.

"Why, no, I believe she had to run over to Market Square for a little while."

Her smile didn't lose a scintilla of its warmth, but something cold flickered in those wide hazel eyes. It was gone again almost before I had time to register it, but I wondered if Drew knew she had an enemy. And was it because Drew was one of the owner's daughters or because Drew had been her rival with Chan?

"Can I give her a message for you?"

"That's okay," we said.

As we walked away, I was glad Tracy Collier wasn't anybody I needed to watch my back for.

Going through the showrooms with Pell was twice as much fun as doing it alone. He knew all the names, most of the facts and much of the gossip; and as we browsed, he kept up a running commentary.

"D34's an Ashley knockoff. They never designed anything that clever on their own." His soft voice was amused.

"Lovely fabric display. Guess this pattern will be showing up everywhere before the year's out. See how many snips have been taken out of the bolt? Must be a dozen scissors walking around in pockets and purses in this room. Ah! See there?"

He nodded toward the mirror and I saw a man reflected as he surreptitiously snipped his own personal palm-sized sample from a length of expensive jacquard weave.

At one exhibit, Pell gave my arm a nearly imperceptible nudge that made me tune in on the confidential conversation going on beside us. Two men in suits, with briefcases.

"—may be sharp, but he's crooked as a dirt road," said one in a Virginia accent.

"I'm telling you. He's gotta be laundering mob money," said the other, whose accent placed him in New Jersey or Long Island, "'cause I don't care how sharp you are, you just don't make that kind of money selling RTA."

"What's RTA?" I asked Pell when we'd moved on.

"Ready to assemble," he said. "As opposed to RTO."

"That I remember from Thursday night: rent to own."

"Very good. What's MSRP?"

"Manufacturer's suggested retail price."

"And No, No, No?"

"No down payment, no interest, no payments for a year," I said smugly.

He brushed back the hank of long hair from his eyes and that elusively familiar smile gave approval. "You *have* been paying attention."

The aroma of hot buttered popcorn wafted from a nearby booth to tempt buyers into a display of Southwestern pottery. I'd eaten nothing that day except a banana and a doughnut, and those bowls of candy at each booth were starting to call to me as well.

"Hungry?" asked Pell. "Then we should hit some of the bigger showrooms for real food. Come on."

He led the way up the escalator and down a wide hall where one large exhibitor after the other had hospitality areas. Employees had to eat lunch, so did clients. Why not conduct a little business on the side at the same time? Instead of the usual candy and nuts, I learned that most of the big companies had food catered in. One showroom offered pizza squares, others had chicken drummettes or sausage biscuits, and still others provided a modest array of breads and salads. There was usually a bar, too, stocked with soft drinks and an occasional bottle of wine. Most were hosted by very attractive young women in very short skirts and very high heels.

At Redd-Peabody, all the hostesses wore red dresses.

"Because of the name?" I asked.

"So they would have you believe," said Pell.

The showroom down the hall and around the corner from Redd-Peabody belonged to Tart, one of the oldest furniture houses in the state. The whole length of the hall had been paneled in Tart's favorite walnut and the name of the firm was superimposed on the paneling in foot-high walnut letters.

Unfortunately, the Redd-Peabody hostesses in their tight red dresses chose to lounge against the wall and to take their cigarette breaks by the ashstand which stood directly beneath the wooden letters.

"I should have brought my camera," Pell murmured as we passed.

"Well, sex sells liquor, cars, and clothes. No surprise that it sells furniture, too."

"James was born in High Point," said Pell, unconsciously assuming I knew who James was. "When he and his friends were boys, their fathers used to take them out to the airport to watch the hookers fly in for Market. Some of the bigger companies had party buses stocked with bars and wide seats. They used to pick up their best clients, drive them around for a few hours and then deliver them back to their hotels, sated and satisfied and ready to sign on the dotted line of a quarter-million order."

"Used to?" I asked.

"Hookers still come in for Market, but they're not as flagrantly subsidized now. Probably the AIDS scare."

So far, neither of us had seen anyone remotely resembling Savannah, but I was convinced that she was probably somewhere loose in the Market, munching her way through the exhibits, too, and no doubt filling some of her plastic bags for a late supper or tomorrow's breakfast. As long as Market lasted, she wouldn't have to trek over to Yolanda Jackson's soup kitchen.

Ever since we left Tracy Collier, Pell had been greeted by friends and clients, but I saw no one I knew until I caught a glimpse of a tall, slender woman with blonde hair and a familiar walk. I thought at first that it was Drew Patterson, but she proved to be Drew's mother, Elizabeth, who accepted a kiss on the cheek from Pell and gave me a mischievous smile as she touched my badge and said, "I understand we'll see you at dinner tonight, Judge Sotelli. Chick Simmard's asked us, too."

"Sounds like fun," I said, thinking what a nice woman Elizabeth Patterson seemed to be. Too bad Drew hadn't inherited Elizabeth's aquiline nose instead of a thinner version of Jay's. On the other hand, getting that fashion-model body was nothing to gripe about. Better to inherit her father's nose than her father's chunky build.

The thought of one chunky build seemed to conjure up another. As Pell and I helped ourselves to fresh fruit cups from the Mindanao Wood Products Collective's hospitality counter, I found myself face-to-face with Heather McKenzie.

Or rather, chin-to-hairline with her, since she was so much shorter.

I smiled. "You have an interest in Mindanaon wood products?"

She held up her own fruit cup. "Nope. Just an appetite for pineapples and fresh mangoes."

I introduced her to Pell and we took our fruit out to a central hub of the building where benches were scattered around the balcony area.

She was dressed more seasonally today in a simple cotton tunic over blue straight-legged slacks. The tunic was severely tailored, with a stand-up collar, and the ivory color flattered her dark eyes. Her only jewelry was a single string of lapis lazuli and her lustrous black hair was braided into a single plait that hung down her back and reminded me of Lynnette's.

"Would Savannah talk to you yesterday?" I asked, spearing a chunk of banana with my plastic fork.

"Not a word. I met them as they were leaving Century's showroom. Drew Patterson had another appointment and I couldn't get Savannah to stay."

She sighed. "Maybe I should just forget about her and get on with my life."

"Your life?" Pell was amused by the all-or-nothing gloominess of youth. "Surely a single profile's not all that crucial?"

"It is when you've invested as much time and energy in it as I have. This wasn't a one-shot deal. I was going to get a whole magazine series out it. I know she hasn't been well, that she's gone off her medications, and—"

I glanced at Pell, who lifted his eyebrow.

"Look, I *did* my homework," Heather said. "I know all about the Hollytree Nursing Home in Athens, Georgia."

She stared moodily into her fruit cup. "It's so bloody unfair. I finally learn where she is and I'm too late. Her father died in December, did you know that? Her only living relative and he dies a week before I get there. I did meet a woman who knew her as a child and that was interesting. Her mother was extremely proper—white gloves and ladies calling on each other every afternoon for formal tea. That frilly dress she's wearing now could've been one of her mother's tea gowns."

I frowned. "I thought you said this was your first real trip south."

"I meant this whole assignment," she said hastily. "Besides, I was only down there two days. Just long enough to visit her in the nursing home and start to talk to her and Bam! Next day, she's gone. Just walks away without checking out. Her doctor said I'd stirred up too many memories. How was I to know she'd take off like that? When she's off her medications, she thinks Drew Patterson's her daughter. Did you know that?"

"Yes," Pell said quietly. "We know."

Heather suddenly looked at him with interest. "Pell Austin. Hey, you're a designer, too, aren't you? At Mulholland?"

Pell nodded.

"I bet you've known Savannah forever, haven't you?"

"Over twenty years," he admitted.

"What was she like back then?"

Pell started to tell her the same things he'd told me, but Heather brushed that aside.

"Other people have told me about her innovations," she said. "But what was she like as a person? As a woman in a man's world?"

"There have always been women in this industry."

"A few tokens," she said impatiently. "We all know the real powers in this business still wear three-piece suits and piss standing up. You think I haven't sat in restaurants here waving my empty cup for more coffee while any man gets his topped off automatically? Dish me some dirt. Who did she have to sleep with to get her first big break?"

"Sorry," he said lightly. "I wasn't here then. She was twelve years older than I and already an established name when they gave me the studio next to hers, so if there's any dirt, it was shoveled under long before I got here."

Heather smiled suddenly and her dark eyes glowed as she patted his arm as if she were the forty-two-year-old professional and he the tyro of twenty-four. "She must have been pretty special to keep a friend like you all these years."

Her tone was wistful.

Pell laughed and stood up. "Come on," he said. "Why don't you let me introduce you to Pasquale Natuzzi? Now there's someone colorful enough for a whole series of magazine articles. The man's revolutionized upholstered goods. Put affordable leather within everyone's reach."

"I've met Signor Natuzzi and I agree that he's interesting, but I really want to do Savannah first."

Pell threw up his hands. "Good luck to you then. Ready to go, Deborah? I told Dix we'd pick her up by five."

It was only a little after four, but I didn't argue. "Do *I* get to meet Signor Natuzzi?" I asked.

I didn't.

Instead, we wound up stopping past the Stanberry showroom where I was the one making introductions. I showed Pell the headboard I'd put a down payment on. He was quite interested, got caught up in the Stanberrys' enthusiasm and even suggested a couple of useful design modifications that had Mai and Jeff Stanberry nodding thoughtfully.

"You know, I can think of at least two chains who could fit these headboards into their stores very nicely," Pell said and rattled off the names of some head buyers. "Give me your card and I'll send them around."

The Stanberrys were so excited by the prospect that they almost didn't want to take my check for the balance I owed them.

Almost, but not quite.

Dixie was waiting for us in high good humor.

"One of my retailers finally got some of his own back," she said as we miraculously found a half-empty elevator after waiting only eight minutes.

"How?" we obligingly asked her.

"You know those flipping eight-hundred numbers?"

She'd lost me.

"Only because you haven't bought much furniture in your lifetime. Open any home furnishings magazine or tune into any home-shopping program and you'll see ads exhorting you to call a one-eight-hundred number—'Buy direct from the manufacturer at wholesale prices,' they say."

"That's bad?"

"Disaster for my people. In the first place, buying direct means a lost sale for my little retailer. In the second place, Ms. Bargain Hunter never buys sight unseen. She wants to see the piece, sit on it, feel the fabric samples, maybe even use the computerized video display to see exactly what that fabric will look like on the couch she intends to buy. So she goes to my retailer, ties him up for an hour or two, writes down the style numbers, thanks him sweetly, then goes home and dials one-eight-hundred."

"One of my retailers down in Columbus finally got fed up with a customer like that. She's been doing this to him for years and he's had to smile and pretend he doesn't know what she's up to, hoping that eventually she'd realize how much service she's been getting from him even though she's never bought much beyond a couple of lamps and some throw rugs.

"But this time, when the expensive couch arrives from the wholesaler, Ms. Bargain Hunter is horrified. She calls one-eight-hundred, finally gets transferred to a human voice and shrieks, 'I wanted pink rosebuds on my couch, not orange and purple plaid.'

"'I'm sorry, madam,' says the wholesaler, 'but you ordered fabric number 4879-J and that's what we sent you.'

"So she calls to scream at my retailer, who says, 'Did you think I said 4879-J? Oh, no, no, no, ma'am, I said 4879-A. 4879-A's the rosebuds. Orange and purple plaid doesn't suit your decor? Sorry, ma'am. If you'd bought it from us, we could make it right, but since you didn't, I'm afraid we can't help you.'

"'Sorry, madam,' says the wholesaler's customer service manager. 'But we sent what you ordered, so it's your fifteen-hundred-dollar problem.'"

"The customer is not always right," Pell told me as he unlocked the van.

"Damn straight," said Dixie. "'Specially if she's not a paying customer."

"Why does Savannah think that Drew's her daughter?" I asked as the porch swing moved gently back and forth like a small boat caught in the shallows.

Dixie shook her head. "I don't know. You, Pell?"

The sun was sliding down the western sky and I was again on Pell's screened side porch, a glass of wine in my hand. Dixie was in one of the wicker chairs, her long legs tucked under her as she waited for the Ragsdales to bring Lynnette back. Pell was in the kitchen putting together a coq au vin for their supper later, but he had opened the sliding glass window over the sink so that he could hear and be heard.

"It's only when she's off her medications," he said. His voice was muffled as he turned away to slide the casserole into his oven.

"Heather McKenzie said that, too," I said, "but why?"

We had told Dixie about Heather's trip to Georgia back in the winter, so she was up to speed.

"Crazy people have crazy ideas. That's how you know they're crazy," she said.

"No, I mean why Drew? Why not Evelyn or some other child?"

"I don't know," Dixie repeated. "We weren't here when it started and Evelyn was older by the time we moved."

But I was remembering something. "You said she had affairs with some of the biggest names in High Point. And Jay Patterson was one of them, right?"

"That's only gossip. I wasn't here then."

Pell had finished in the kitchen and as he joined us, I said, "You were here in High Point then, weren't you?"

"High Point, low point, what's the point?" Pell asked lightly as he poured himself a glass of wine. "There is no point."

"Yes, there is!" I said sharply. "The point is that Chan's dead and she may have killed him with my penicillin. Even if it makes no sense to us, there has to be a reason that makes sense to Savannah."

"Maybe." He turned his wine glass in his hands and stared into the golden liquid, then sighed. "Okay. Yes, she did have an affair with Jay Patterson. Two affairs, actually. The first one ended when Elizabeth announced that she was pregnant—with Drew, as it turned out—and that was the first time Savannah took off. I guess it hurt too much to stay around and watch him make like a doting king awaiting the birth of the heir apparent. They said she was gone four months. She'd been back about six months when I started working at Mulholland and it was still fresh enough for me to hear all the gossip. For a while, it was all very civilized. She and Patterson acted more like old drinking buddies than past lovers.

"And she certainly wasn't celibate. Back then she could drink like a sailor and swear like a lumberjack—or is it the other way round? What Heather told us about Savannah's mother? I didn't know it, but I'm not surprised. Savannah was always there with gracious thank-you notes, bread-and-butter letters, flowers at the appropriate moment. Underneath all the brittle cynicism, she was Old South proper. But she was always taking on various freelance projects for Fitch and Patterson and I remember her bugging him once because the pictures of Drew that he carried in his wallet weren't up to date."

He took a small sip of wine. "The first time I noticed anything odd though was when Patterson brought Drew out to the studio one day when she was about three. Savannah had someone bring up an armload of dolls from the prop shelves for Drew to play with, and after she and Patterson finished discussing business, she got down on the floor and played tea party. This was not a woman who normally went gooey-eyed over children, but she even got Patterson to sit down on the floor and sip imaginary tea, too. You know the way some men are about their daughters? Especially Southern men?"

I nodded. My own daddy has a little of it in him although he never played tea party with me. (And not just because I was too busy running after my older brothers to sit still with a tea set.)

"I think Savannah fell in love with Drew that day."

"And Jay Patterson fell for her again?"

Pell shrugged. "That I can't say, but they did become lovers again for a while. That picture you said Heather McKenzie had? It was taken around that time."

"What happened?"

"I don't know that anything dramatic actually happened. I've often thought they just realized that their moment had passed. Things were intense for a few weeks, then it was as if the sexual part simply burned itself out. They stayed friends and she always had a soft spot for Drew."

"Which probably ensured that he'd always have a soft spot in his heart for her," I said, remembering how he'd helped Savannah fill her baggies with fried chicken and cornbread on Thursday night.

It was almost dark when I left for the restaurant and the Ragsdales had not returned with Lynnette. The coq au vin had cooked and cooled and still they didn't come. Dixie was striding back and forth in her living room and beginning to think such anxious thoughts that it was taking all of Pell's gentle reasoning to keep her from calling the police.

"But what if they've decided to go ahead and just take her back to Maryland with them?" she said fearfully.

"Never," Pell scoffed. "The girls are probably having so much fun that they've lost track of time."

"It's none of my business," I said, "but did Evelyn leave a will?"

Dixie nodded. "Soon as Lynnette was born, I nagged them both till they went to an attorney."

"Who did she name as guardian in the event they both died at the same time?"

She didn't want to say it.

"She named his sister, too, didn't she?"

Dixie's head came up defiantly. "And what if she did? I don't care, Deborah! She never expected it to happen this young. She was thinking *years* from now, when I might be too old to cope with a teenager."

"You're going to be the same age when that time comes," I said mildly.

"I'll be here," Pell said with his crooked smile. "I'm two years younger. I'll help her cope."

I could make the usual arguments, but how valid would they be?

Besides, from my time in domestic court, I know that families come in all flavors these days.

Truth to tell, they probably always did.

20

"The democratic industrial movement of the present era of civilization tends towards increasing the circle of the consumers of luxuries."
                    The Great Industries of the United States, 1872

J. Basul Noble's is located across from the Radisson in what could have been a clothing store, judging from the full-length front windows. The interior walls were painted to suggest a stone farmhouse somewhere in Tuscany, the farmhouse perhaps of a prosperous peasant. Trompe l'oeil windows overlooked pleasant gardens and primitive "paintings" of naively drawn farm animals decorated the walls. The heavy walnut side chairs had rush seats and a rooster carved in the middle of each back. The dishes were colorful pottery pieces handpainted in rustic Italian patterns.

The snowy tablecloths, the soft lights, the flash of jewelry, the hum of conversation, the entrancing smell of herbs in unfamiliar combinations—it was a heady mix of money and power at play.

I later learned that there was a more casual jazz bar downstairs, but upstairs was clearly the place for fine dining during Market, the place to see and be seen.

By the time I'd driven downtown and found a place to park my car, it was a few minutes past eight when I approached the maitre d'.

"Judge Simmard's table?" I asked.

"Oh, good," said Elizabeth Patterson from behind me. "We aren't the last after all."

"Good evening, Mrs. Patterson, Mr. Patterson," said the maitre d', beaming at the three of us indiscriminately. "You aren't late at all. Judge Simmard has only been here a few minutes himself. If you'll follow me, please."

Easier said than done in that crush. The tables and chairs were so closely placed that we almost had to turn sideways to pass between. Happily, Judge Simmard's table for eight was near the front of the room—probably so that his wheelchair would disrupt the fewest possible diners as he came and went. We were tightly jammed against the wall, but surrounded by fewer tables.

The men were in dinner jackets and black tie. Elizabeth Patterson wore a beautiful champagne silk organza shirtdress with long full sleeves and gold embroidery on the cuffs and collar. Her diamond earrings were even more stunning than her rings. The other woman—in the confusion of round-robin introductions, I wasn't sure if she was Mrs. Simmard or Mrs. Craft or, indeed, neither—wore an understated rose brocade evening suit.

I was in my all-purpose black raw silk that could be dressed up or down. Local judges often invite me to dinner as a courtesy when I'm in their towns, and I never know if I'm going to find myself at a country club or sitting on a stool in a strip mall's bar-and-grill, but this dress can handle either. The skirt is short and the front has a simple square neckline that looks great with my chunky silver necklace. With the jacket, the dress is proper enough for a church funeral; without the jacket, narrow straps crisscross a back cut so low that I have to wear a special bra. Silver earrings, black stockings and high heels complete the look—and the look I got from my dinner partner, Mr. Han ("Call me Albert") Shu-Kai assured me that my dress could certainly hold its own with those of the other two women, with or without diamonds.

Superior Court Judge Cicero "Chick" Simmard frankly looked like Mr. Toad of Toad Hall, but he was an affable and considerate host. On my right, next to him, was Mr. Han, CEO of a Singapore company that exported huge amounts of rattan and wicker furniture to the U.S. On my left was Lester Craft, a thin, friendly-faced man with dark curly hair and glasses. Beyond him were Elizabeth Patterson; a robust Californian named Bob Something, who headed an international robotics company; Jay Patterson; and the soft-spoken woman they called Nancy, whose last name and connection I never did quite understand.

That's the trouble with tables for eight (tables for ten are even worse). Eight for dinner may be fine in a quiet private home, but dropped down in a crowded restaurant? There's no way, short of yelling, to be heard across the table, so you settle for conversation with the two on either side of you at best.

The cuisine tended toward northern Italian and ordering took time as Judge Simmard conferred with the waiter about appropriate wines.

A Beaujolais and a Macon Blanc arrived at our table and were poured and then lifted in toast. "Welcome to High Point, my friends," said Judge Simmard, "and here's to a killer market for everyone—figuratively speaking, of course!"

There was a moment of shocked silence, then Chick Simmard flushed like an embarrassed schoolboy. "Oh, my goodness! Jay, Elizabeth, I'm *so* sorry. How stupid of me to forget. I do apologize."

The Pattersons made appropriate murmurs.

"That's right," said Han in flawless, colloquial English. "Nolan was your VP of Sales, wasn't he, Patterson?"

Albert Han was solidly built, fortyish, and urbane. His gold watch and signet ring were clearly expensive, yet unostentatious. His dinner jacket was impeccably tailored and his nails were more beautifully manicured than mine.

"Do the police have a suspect yet?" he asked Simmard.

"I'm afraid I know nothing more than you," he said, smiling at Han blandly as he turned to Jay Patterson and the quiet woman between them on his other side.

Since he knew enough to send me his phone number through Detective Underwood, I appreciated Simmard's discretion.

As our appetizers appeared, so did three attractive young women. Drew Patterson and a couple of her friends stopped to say hello on their way to the jazz bar downstairs. There were shadows under Drew's eyes that hinted at the sadness of the past two days, but she was still lovely in a midnight blue dress that clung to her upper body, then flared at her knees for dancing.

"Ah, the Princess Patterson!" said Simmard as the other men rose. "Forgive me if I don't stand, my dear."

"Oh, don't get up for me," she said, her hand on the back of his wheelchair.

It was evidently an old joke between them and she dropped a kiss on his jowly cheek as she greeted her parents' friends and smiled at me across the table.

She really *was* a princess, I thought. Poised and well-schooled in graciousness, yet nevertheless basking in her position and their approval. And if there was a trace of "I'm entitled" in her smile, well, who could blame her for growing up a little spoiled when one saw such overwhelming pride on Jay Patterson's face and such uncritical love in Elizabeth's eyes?

They left, and the noise level in the room continued to climb until conversation was possible only with the persons nearest, so I turned to Albert Han and asked the usual questions. He volunteered interesting facts about rattan and wicker and some amusing anecdotes regarding the perils of international trade. And he was courteous enough to ask me about life as a district court judge. I responded in kind with the tale of two drunk hunters who shot up a strip of retread from a tractor-trailer tire thinking it was an alligator.

Chick Simmard was back for the punch line and chuckled

appreciatively. "I heard about that the last time I was down in Beaufort. Darlene Leonard was telling it. She speaks mighty highly of you, Judge Knott."

"Please, it's Deborah," I said. "And I think highly of Mrs. Leonard, too."

As he and Han began to exchange deep-sea fishing experiences, I glanced at Lester Craft on my left. He was at the fringe of a four-way conversation between the Pattersons, the Chicago robotics executive and the quiet woman who, I'd decided, was not Mrs. Simmard, and he seemed more than willing to turn to a one-on-one.

"Are you with the furniture industry, too?" I asked.

He smiled. "You could say so. I'm the editor of *Furniture/Today*."

Normally a slick, full-color weekly, the tabloid-size trade paper comes out every day during Market with fresh updates on what's hot, who's buying, national and international trends, and provocative columnists, along with who's hosting the best parties, and discreet gossip. Today's front page carried as much news as was known about Chan's death: *Chandler Nolan Dies at Market / Foul Play Suspected in Sales Veep's Death.*

"I understand you're a friend of Nolan's mother-in-law," he said. "And that you were with her when she found him."

"Is that what Heather told you?" I parried.

"Who?"

"Heather McKenzie."

He shook his head. "I don't think I know anyone by that name."

I smiled. "I wouldn't have thought your editorial staff was so large that you wouldn't know all your reporters."

He continued to look at me blankly, still shaking his head. "We don't have a Heather McKenzie on our staff."

"But she has a *Furniture/Today* press badge. She's a reporter—"

"Not for me, she's not," he said emphatically.

Could he be right? I remembered thinking her word choice was odd at the Century showroom when she said "I may actually get a *real* article after all." And what else had she told me? "I think she's on assignment from your Massachusetts office? Writing profiles of important Market figures?"

Massachusetts was the magic word. His face cleared as he finally recognized Heather's name.

"Oh, yes," he said. "The freelancer. Right."

I decided that it might be fun to get Lester Craft into a poker game.

Except that it would be taking candy from a baby. His face was much too expressive to run a bluff.

Two things were now quite obvious: 1) he did remember Ms. Heather McKenzie; 2) she was not a reporter.

Not by Mr. Craft's definition anyhow.

21

The dinner party broke up a little after ten.

Outside the restaurant, we thanked Judge Simmard for a delightful and delicious dinner and waited while he hydraulically hoisted himself and his chair into his van.

The April evening had turned too chilly to linger on the sidewalk after he'd driven away. Lester Craft said goodnight and headed for his own car in the Radisson parking garage and, to my surprise, boisterous Bob and quiet Nancy went off together.

The Pattersons were going on to a private party at the Emerywood Country Club and insisted that the hosts "would be delighted if you and Mr. Han came with us."

But Albert Han had a car and driver idling at the curb and he wanted to go dancing at a lounge over in Greensboro.

The Pattersons accepted my regrets with polite regrets of their own and departed. Han was a little harder to dissuade. For all his western dress and speech, he seemed to have rather eastern ideas about women and I finally had to speak quite sharply before I finally convinced him that I was not a party favor thoughtfully provided by Judge Simmard.

I didn't want to party or dance. I wanted to go sit quietly and consider all the things I'd seen and heard these last two days.

Driving back to Dixie's house, I gave serious thought to Drew Patterson. Certainly she could have given Chan those penicillin-dusted brownies even though she claimed she hadn't known how serious his allergies were. She said Chan was merely an old friend who had treated her like a kid sister, but had been fun to play with. Dixie said she'd wanted to marry him, but Dixie seemed to see would-be stepmothers to Lynnette at every turn.

Yet, say it was true. Nevertheless, even if Drew had been head over heels for Chan, was his leaving High Point without her motive enough for murder? In this day and age, are there really women who tell themselves, "If I can't have him, no one will?"

Then there was all that love and pride the Pattersons had invested in their only child.

Dixie thought Jay Patterson was angry at Chan because

Chan was leaving Fitch and Patterson, going to Malaysia, and perhaps taking with him valuable proprietary information about Fitch and Patterson business deals. But what if he'd also come to believe that Chan had trifled with his daughter's affections? An aggressive, pugnacious man like Patterson—

"An aggressive, pugnacious man would have punched him in the nose and been done with it," said the pragmatist in my mental ear.

On the other hand, as Chan's employer, he might have known how serious Chan's allergies were.

And Savannah seemed to trust Patterson. He had helped her take food at the ALWA party Thursday night and he might have seen me pick up that baggie from the floor, the one with my fingerprints all over it. I tried to remember if that baggie was still on the table when first Savannah, then Patterson and finally Drew walked away from the table, but it was just an insignificant little plastic bag and I had absolutely no memory one way or the other.

Dixie said Lavelle Trocchi had been there. She was accused of being Chan's dupe, of letting him steal a preview catalog of her company's new designs. She could be fired, her reputation within the industry destroyed. I suppose she could have heard the byplay on the brownies and seen me pick up the baggie.

No one mentioned seeing the Colliers, though. And while those two retailers—Kay Adams and Poppy Jackson—might cheerfully poison Chan, would they have known penicillin would do the trick and would Chan have taken brownies from them?

More to the point, would Savannah have given any of those people my tote bag?

Heather McKenzie said Savannah had immediately disappeared into the bowels of the building.

If Ms. McKenzie could be believed.

But she *had* followed right on Savannah's heels. And for a reporter, she showed a singular disinterest in Chan's death. Was that her way of averting suspicion? Or was it merely further proof that she wasn't really a reporter?

"Are you finished?" asked the preacher. "Or are you finally going to admit that Dixie Babcock has the strongest reasons to want Chan Nolan dead? She was there at the table with both the baggie and brownies, she knew that penicillin would kill him, AND she had the opportunity when he came to her floor."

But I was with her that night at the hospital. Her grief. Her bewilderment. Surely her reactions were real.

"A woman you haven't seen in ten years? How do you know she's not capable of faking grief and bewilderment?"

He was right. I didn't.

All the same—

Dixie was in nightgown and robe when I got back to the house. I found her in the living room amid a stack of those family albums.

"My dad's aunt was devoted to genealogy," she said as she reshelved the bulging scrapbooks. "Spent the last twenty years of her life trying to account for every leaf and twig on the family tree. When she died, she left all her research to me. For some reason, Lynnette's fascinated by the family stories. She'd rather hear about a great-grandfather milking cows or how *his* mother shot a copperhead than any regular bedtime storybook."

"So she wasn't stolen by the Ragsdales and forced across state lines to Maryland?"

Dixie gave a sheepish smile. "Okay, so maybe I overreacted."

Her chestnut hair gleamed in the lamplight. "How was Noble's? What did you have to eat?"

"Grilled chicken with lemon and watercress. It was wonderful. Interesting conversation, too," I said and described the table. "It was too crowded to say much to the robotics man, but it's such a bizarre concept when you think about it."

"Think about what?"

"Well, take stressing, for instance. They used to have a guy at the factory who would bang up new furniture to make it look old, right?"

She nodded. "Only it's called *dis*tressing."

"So he'd spend day after day *distressing* this new wood: gouging it, banging it with pipes and hammers, nicking the edges, the whole nine yards. Now he's been replaced by a robot that'll do the exact same thing. You could say that a man's been put out of work by an artificial intelligence, except that the work he was doing was artificial to begin with. His fake marks were random though, and customers, according to Bob, want the exact same thing they see in the store. If there's a wormhole three inches in on the floor model, they want theirs to have the wormhole three inches in. I mean, robots are faking something fake to begin with and then *standardizing* it?"

Dixie grinned. "What's your point here, Knott?"

"The point is, you could probably buy original antiques for about the same as you'd pay for high-end reproductions."

"*Real* antiques? Someone else's castoffs? My dear, you don't know *where* they've been. Reproductions are new. Sanitary!"

Albert Han and his after-dinner persistence made her laugh. "I don't know if special pains are being taken for the Chinese, but when the Japanese first started coming to Market, some of the exhibitors wondered if they ought to supply geishas. Actually, I think a couple of them did. An American version anyhow."

"I wonder if some of those hostesses working the hospitality rooms will show up in my courtroom this week."

"Not this week. The police usually do a sweep the week before Market and they'll do another the week after Market, but during Market? Huh-uh."

I stepped out of my high heels and perched on the arm of the couch. "Changing the subject, what's your take on Heather McKenzie?"

"That reporter? Seems like a nice kid, why? Was she there tonight?"

"No, but the editor of *Furniture/Today* was and guess what? He kept saying he didn't have a reporter by that name."

"So?" She shoved the last of the albums back into its slot. "I bet the guy from Home-Lite in New Jersey doesn't know he's got a sales rep named Jacki Sotelli. People shuffle badges like cards."

"Maybe. But when I mentioned that she was down from

Massachusetts, he suddenly remembered who she really is. He tried to cover, but it was clear she's not on his payroll."

Dixie sat on the couch with her knees drawn up to her chin and her feline eyes were thoughtful. "So who's payroll is she on and why are they so interested in Savannah?"

We mulled it over a while, then Dixie said goodnight—"Lynnette will be up at first light"—and I toddled off to the guest room where I lay awake another hour trying to make some sense of things.

It kept circling back to Savannah, her delusions about Drew, her instability that began—

Sudden illumination pierced the darkness. Not for nothing had I sat in all those sessions of traffic court since coming to the bench.

Pell and Dixie and Jay Patterson, too—all agreed that the first major manifestation of Savannah's bipolar disorder was when she destroyed her Porsche with a sledgehammer and then disappeared for nearly two years.

What if that sudden, violent destruction had been to hide evidence of a hit-and-run? When seventeen-year-old Drew was at the wheel?

The trouble, of course, was that I didn't have enough facts. I really needed to ask David Underwood some questions, even though I didn't have much hope that he'd answer.

22

*"The Egyptians had metal mirrors, and a great profusion of
kitchen utensils, and dishes of all sorts for the table."*
The Great Industries of the United States, 1872

Next morning, I discovered that Detective Underwood
had a few questions of his own.

He called first thing and invited me to come out for coffee, pancakes and some informal discussion at the local
IHOP.

"Don't you ever take a day off?" I asked, sliding into the
other side of his booth.

"Not during Market Week," he said.

"Have you found Savannah yet?"

"Nope. You?"

I checked. The smile was there, hidden beneath that bushy brown mustache.

"You told me not to meddle, remember?"

"And I appreciate your restraint."

Coffee and juice arrived and when the waitress had gone away with our order, Detective Underwood said, "I was hoping you might've remembered if that baggie was still on the table when you walked away Thursday night."

"Sorry. I've been over it and over it and I just can't see it again after I laid it on the table."

As we talked, Underwood proceeded to lay waste to the table. When he tore open the sugar packets, the first one ripped badly and showered sugar grains everywhere except in his cup.

I couldn't understand how the man and his clothes stayed so neat and pristine, how his shirt and tie remained spotless.

Not the table though. By the time he had sugared and creamed to his satisfaction, it was littered with sugar papers and little empty cups of non-dairy creamer and their lids. (Every time I eat in a fast-food place, I'm always glad I take my coffee black.)

The coffee wasn't anything to rave about, but at least it was strong and scalding hot. I sipped cautiously before asking, "Haven't you made any progress at all?"

"Now, I didn't say that. As a courtesy, since you're involved, and sort of officer of the law to an officer of the court, you might say—I'm going to trust you not to let this go any further."

"Of course," I murmured.

He drained his orange juice and blotted his mustache on the napkin, then tossed the crumpled napkin toward the heap that was building at the end of the table and cleared a space for a tattered legal pad. I had seen this very same legal pad, crisp and unsullied, less than forty-eight hours ago. Now, its dog-eared pages hung precariously from the top and curled up at the bottom. Loose sheets covered with scribbles slid out of either side like straws sliding from a pitchfork of hay.

"We've checked out all the major players that were there Thursday night," he said, paging through his messy notes.

"And?"

"Starting with Chan Nolan. He left the ALWA party about 8:50 and went next door to the Fitch and Patterson reception where he exchanged strong words with Jacob Collier, who was drunk and belligerent. Then I gather that more words passed between Nolan and Patterson. Mrs. Patterson and Drew broke that up before it turned into anything serious. Mrs. Patterson, who's a real lady, asked Nolan to dance and Drew took her daddy out to the lobby to cool off. When the dance ended, Nolan cut out. The best we can narrow it down is that he left between 9:30 and 9:40. The 911 call was logged at 10:07, but the ME says that with that much penicillin, he'd have started reacting almost immediately and would have lapsed into a coma within minutes of ingesting it."

"Have you learned why he came down to Dixie Babcock's hall?"

He shook his head. "His car was parked at her house and he caught a ride to Market with her on Thursday morning. She says he was supposed to let her know if he wanted a ride back. Otherwise, he'd make his own arrangements. She says he didn't mention it at the ALWA party, so he could've been planning to go home with one of those women he'd ticked off."

"So instead of coming to borrow Dixie's antihistamine tablets, he might only have wanted a ride back to her house?"

"Probably. I'll get to her in a minute. First though, Kay Adams and Poppy Jackson. They left the ALWA ballroom with two other small retailers around nine and caught a shuttle bus over to one of the satellite parking lots. They drove in three cars back to the Howard Johnson on I-40 where they're all staying, went directly to the bar and talked and drank till nearly eleven."

Two down, but I never seriously considered those two anyhow. Our food arrived, waffles and sausage for me, French toast and bacon for Underwood. (He immediately turned a page right into his bacon.)

"Lavelle Trocchi left the room about the same time Savannah did, with six people who know her by name. She partied at the Radisson till midnight with those same six people and she did not leave the bar alone."

Okay, so if Lavelle Trocchi was carrying a grudge, she had immediately found someone to soothe her ruffled feelings. Nice for her, but the circle was shrinking.

"Jacob Collier had words with Nolan at the Fitch and Patterson party but we can't find anyone who saw him or his granddaughter at the ALWA party. Tracy Collier walked her grandfather back to the Radisson, then she joined the Trocchi party for an hour."

"What about the Pattersons?" I asked.

More turning of pages, some of which were now stuck together with smears of maple syrup. The pile of dirty paper napkins continued to grow. Every time anything got on his hands, Underwood fastidiously wiped it off at once and pulled a fresh napkin from the dispenser.

"Patterson left the ALWA party a few minutes after Savannah, and Drew joined him back at their reception between 8:40 and 8:45. The band was hired till ten, and that's when Mr. and Mrs. Patterson left, even though there were still people in the ballroom. Drew left with them and before you ask, she was returning to the ballroom when Chan was leaving. They spoke just outside the doorway, he gave her the same kiss on the cheek he'd given her mother a minute before and left. She came back in and remained there till her parents were ready to go over to her house in Emerywood where they're staying rather than drive back and forth to Lexington."

I didn't like the way this was shaping.

"So that brings us down to your friend Dixie."

"She's your friend, too, isn't she?" I asked.

"Well, sure. I mean, we don't go fishing together, but my boy dated her girl a few times when they were in high school and we ran the PTA's haunted house a couple of Halloweens." He speared a piece of his French toast. "But that doesn't mean I won't haul her into court if I find she's the one put your penicillin in his brownies."

"She didn't do it," I said earnestly.

"Maybe not, but you have to admit she could've if she was so inclined."

He knew he didn't have to lay it out again for me and when I nodded, he said, "So what it comes down to is Savannah, Dixie, or you, Judge."

"*Me?* I thought we agreed—"

"Well, ma'am, what I agree is that it doesn't seem likely, but you did have means and opportunity, even if there's no apparent motive." He took a swallow of his orange juice. "Yet."

"If you don't mind my saying so, Detective Underwood, it seems to me you're not taking Savannah very seriously. She's the one with the baggies, brownies and my penicillin. She obviously changed her mind about bringing my tote to the soup kitchen. Instead, it winds up next to Nolan's body. She's the only one who could have put it there."

He put the last morsel of bacon in his mouth and chewed a moment. "Maybe. Good thing for that Heather McKenzie that you thought to dial your cell phone, else I could argue that she took the bag from Savannah and—"

"No, you couldn't," I said. "She was with me from the moment we ran into each other till she dropped me off in front of the GHFM building."

"Oh, yeah. That's right."

"Just the same, there *is* something odd about her," I said and told him how the editor of *Furniture/Today* couldn't place her at first. "I wish you'd check her background."

"Anything else?" he asked dryly.

"Actually, there is. If I had time, I'd go sit in the public library and read all the microfiche editions of your daily newspapers from six years ago."

He frowned. "Why?"

I'd spoken with Pell that morning and he'd narrowed down the specific time for me. "For the week after the spring Market, six years ago, to see if there was any mention of a hit-and-run that week involving a black sports car. That was the first time Savannah flipped out really badly. Did you know that she took a sledgehammer to her black Porsche after Drew put a little dent in it?"

Underwood nodded as he discarded yet another napkin. "Yeah, I did hear something about that."

"What if there was more than a little dent? What if there were blood and threads picked up when Drew hit a pedestrian, or paint smears from another car?"

"She really smashed a gorgeous car like that with a sledgehammer?"

"Savannah's been obsessed with Drew almost since the day she was born," I said. "From all I've been told, she might well have trashed her car to protect Drew. And now, when she believes that Chan is married to Drew and Lynnette is Drew's daughter? If you think his taking Lynnette off to Malaysia is a motive for Dixie, you have to think that same motive's just as strong for Savannah."

"Something to consider," he agreed, but he didn't sound convinced.

Why?

23

"The education of our children has a mental and moral value, but its importance as a matter of every-day business, in dollars and cents, is not so often mentioned."
        The Great Industries of the United States, 1872

Back at the house, Dixie and Pell had both gone to Market, leaving Lynnette with a baby-sitter who was in deep panic over tomorrow's French test. I couldn't help her with irregular verbs, but I could keep an eye on Lynnette.

"Lynnette's barrette/ has come unset," I teased, and refastened it so that the side wisps of her sandy blonde hair were held away from her face.

"Let's go walk/ and talk/ and gawk," she giggled, which sounded like something Pell would say.

So we took a walk around the block, stopping along the way to pet the neighbor's friendly golden retriever and to speak to a haughty Persian cat, who condescended to let Lynnette stroke under her chin. We talked about the latest Disney movie, her first-grade teacher, and why boys always thought it was so funny to burp and break wind.

We came back through the kitchen for something to drink and commiserated with the baby-sitter, who was sure she was going to flunk and never get accepted to the college of her choice. In the living room, Lynnette briefly longed for her electronic games, "but Grandmama's got some great games, too."

I was amused to realize that Parcheesi, played with real dice on a three-dimensional board, was now a novelty. I beat her there, but she wiped me out in Mancala, easily capturing most of her stones even though she's just turned seven and the instructions say that it's for ages eight to adult.

When games palled, she offered to "read" to me from their family albums.

What Dixie's aunt might have lacked in formal training, she more than compensated for with vivid thumbnail sketches. Dry genealogical charts suddenly popped to life when, in tiny meticulous letters, there appeared beside a name and date: "Always sang around the house." "Gentled his first horse when 10-yr-old." "Her quilts had 20 stitches to the inch."

Now I've never broken a horse, but I have quilted on occasion and merely thinking of the patience it takes to make tiny, even stitches through lid, batting and lining was enough to make my fingers sore. I'm proud anytime I can consistently do six to the inch. Twenty? She would have been welcome round any quilting frame.

Lynnette's favorites though were the bulky scrapbooks that held letters and physical mementos. "Here's the last boll of cotton my great-grandfather picked before he went to work at the mill," she said.

Stapled to the page was a lump of dirty gray cotton that still had its seeds caught in the lint. Next to it was a blue satin ribbon that Dixie had won in a spelling bee when she was eleven.

"And here's David Henry," said Lynnette, opening the flap of a yellowed envelope that was pasted to the page.

Inside was a tress of fair hair tied with a pale blue ribbon.

"David Henry went to look for gold out West and nobody ever heard from him again. He fell right off our family tree. See?"

She pointed to the words on the envelope and seemed to read them aloud although I couldn't be sure if she was actually reading or parroting words that could have been read to her so often that she'd memorized them: "Gone from this family in 1853. His mother mourned for him until the day she died."

There were marriage certificates, birth certificates, tintypes of stiff-faced Edwardians, a copy of what must have been Chan and Evelyn's wedding picture.

Lynnette stared at it for such a long time that I said, "Do you remember her, honey?"

"She used to rock me on her lap," Lynnette said, "and she always smelled good, but sometimes I can't remember." Her lips trembled and fat tears formed in her eyes. "I remember Daddy, though. I wish he didn't die. I wish he didn't!"

Sobs racked her thin body as she buried her head in my lap. I could only hug her and make wordless comforting noises until she fell asleep with her head still in my lap.

While she slept, I turned the pages in one of the photo albums. There were pictures of Dixie with Evelyn as a baby, as a toddler, first day of school, a first-grade picture and her own crooked, snaggletoothed smile. There were even a couple of pictures of Evelyn standing by the Old Well on the Chapel Hill campus, then Evelyn in a body cast after that car hit her. The background shifted to High Point and this house. Evelyn seemed to go from preadolescence to womanhood in the turn of a page. There was an eight-by-ten of her wedding picture, then another baby girl. The proud grandmother. The first birthday. The third birthday with Evelyn and Pell poised to help Lynnette blow out her candles.

I sat lost in thought for several long minutes, then glanced down at the sleeping child and smoothed her long thick braid.

Since you were in your bassinet,
Your family's loved you, sweet Lynnette.

24

"Long before the days of the first Pharaoh the Egyptians had
carved couches, bedsteads of iron, and, it is believed, of
bronze. Carpets were on the floors of the wealthy."
The Great Industries of the United States, 1872

As a district court judge, I don't get a lot of jury trials, nor
do I often get to pass judgments on civil matters where damages are more than ten thousand dollars. But this Monday was
different.

Sylvia Cone Westermann versus Kurkland's Quality Carpet Cleaners in a civil action for negligence.

Mrs. Westermann's attorney had filed to have the matter
heard in district court because it was quicker than waiting
for a date in superior court, and neither attorney moved to

postpone when they learned I'd be hearing the case rather than Judge Dunlap, who was still out of town.

Mrs. Westermann was claiming that Kurkland's had improperly cleaned her Turkoman rug and had, in the process, irreparably damaged it so as to render it unsalable. Previous to Kurkland's cleaning said rug, its market value was placed at sixty thousand dollars. Current value? Two thousand.

Plaintiff was asking sixty thousand in damages and ten thousand in punitive damages for her pain and suffering. (Kurkland's had impugned her two Lhasa Apsos.)

Jury selection can take weeks in a capital case and even selecting a civil jury can eat up more than a day if either of the parties is well known in the community. But none of the prospective jurors called knew either party and only one had ever experienced dissatisfaction with a carpet cleaner. I allowed that one to be dismissed for cause. No peremptory challenges were issued.

The jury was seated in less than an hour, which has to be some kind of record.

Mrs. Westermann was one of those permanently indignant women, compact and pugnacious. Her steel gray hair was fashionably clipped, and the pearl buttons on her navy silk suit matched her pearl choker and pearl drop earrings. She immediately took the stand and told her story. She had called Kurkland's Quality Carpet Cleaners and asked for an estimate to clean her authentic, hand-loomed, seven-by-ten Turkoman rug that lay under her dining-room table on top of a rose Berber wall-to-wall.

She had been put through to Mr. Kurkland himself and, after some negotiation, they agreed upon a price for his services. Upon arrival at her home, Mr. Kurkland had noticed her two Lhasa Apsos and asked if there were any possibility that they could have soiled the rug.

"I told him absolutely not!" Mrs. Westermann testified. "My dogs are quite well trained and they are *never* allowed in the dining room. He wishes to blame them for his own incompetence."

According to her testimony, Mr. Kurkland proceeded to lay a plastic sheet between the rug and the Berber carpet. The description of his cleaning process sounded careful enough to me. He had first tested for colorfastness, then handwashed the rug on his hands and knees, rinsing and toweling as he went. According to Mrs. Westermann, though, "he left it so wet, it took two days to dry and when it did dry, it was faded and splotched."

"Describe your rug before Mr. Kurkland cleaned it," said her attorney.

"It was beautiful," she mourned. "Vibrant and glowing with jewel-like colors."

The rug had been entered as Exhibit A and her attorney now asked for permission to show it. I agreed and it was unrolled on the floor in front of my bench. I must say that while I know almost nothing about Oriental rugs, they do appeal to me and I'd been into several of the showrooms devoted to them here at Market, wondering if I could afford a decent reproduction of my own. This one had a dark red background woven in an all-over geometric design. Mrs. Westermann's authentic article might have been vibrant and jewel-toned at one time. Now it seemed to have faded unevenly in places, so that four or five areas were almost gray, as if someone had sprinkled a light dusting of ashes over those places.

Mr. Kurkland's attorney seemed curiously non-combative.

"Mrs. Westermann, did you comparison shop for a carpet-cleaner?"

"Yes, I did."

"Was Mr. Kurkland's the lowest price you got?"

"Well, yes. I saw no point in spending extra—"

"Thank you. Did Mr. Kurkland advise you that it was best to have the rug cleaned at his establishment where he had a proper drying table?"

"Well, yes, but I was planning a dinner party and I was afraid it might not be returned in time."

"And you are convinced it was his ineptitude that caused these spots instead of your Lhasa Apsos?"

"Absolutely. They know they aren't allowed in there. Mr. Kurkland got my rug too wet. That's all there is to it."

"I see. No further questions."

Her attorney now called a carpet expert, a small tidy man who described how a fine Oriental should be cleaned: by hand, on a drying table, one tiny section at a time.

"If a rug has been frequently vacuumed and properly cared for, what soil there is should lie mostly on top of the pile. You only want to dampen the upper surface, using the mildest soap possible. Then you immediately sponge it with clear water and blot up all the excess dampness with clean white rags or white paper towels. No patterns or colors," he warned the jury earnestly. "Only white."

"So there should have been no need for that sheet of plastic between the rug and Mrs. Westermann's wall-to-wall carpeting?"

"Technically, no. But if he was in the habit of using too much water, then it was certainly a necessity to prevent soaking the undercarpet. On the other hand, plastic would hold the excess water next to the rug and prevent the rug from drying more rapidly."

In his expert opinion, Mrs. Westermann's fine Turkoman had indeed been damaged by improper cleaning.

Since Mr. Kurkland's attorney had not challenged the man's credentials, I wondered what sort of defense he planned. On cross-examination, his only questions pertained to how one cleans away dog urine.

"Unfortunately, there *is* no way," said the expert. "The ammonia and uric acids soak right into the wool and attach themselves so that they're impossible to get out in any way that wouldn't do more harm to the rug itself."

He was asked if the faded splotches on the rug might not be due to dog urine. He hedged. When finally pinned down, he grudgingly agreed that they were not entirely inconsistent, but it remained his firm conviction that the rug had been damaged by too much water.

His was the longest testimony and when Mr. Kurkland's attorney finished with him, Mrs. Westermann's attorney announced that the plaintiff rested.

Mr. Kurkland's attorney rose and made a pro forma request for dismissal, citing a lack of conclusive evidence to prove his client's negligence.

I refused and broke for lunch at that point, after warning the jurors not to discuss the case among themselves.

Detective Underwood was waiting out in the hallway when I exited the courtroom. He said he was there to testify in a case being held in the next courtroom and thought that as long as he was so close, he'd put my mind at rest about Savannah's black sports car.

"I ran a check on all vehicular incidents in a fifty-mile radius for that week. Not one single hit-and-run reported."

I was deflated. I'd almost talked myself into a scenario of teenage carelessness and delusional mother-love and sacrifice.

Beyond a casual "poor dears" shrug when they were mentioned, Drew had seemed indifferent both to the Colliers' cut in income and to the loss of business Kay Adams and Poppy Jackson would experience if Fitch and Patterson withdrew from their stores. I was almost convinced that such indifference signified a deeper callousness that would allow her to shrug off a hit-and-run, especially if Savannah had urged her to; and now Underwood was telling me that the hit-and-run never happened?

What did that do to my theory that Savannah had killed Chan in a misguided attempt to protect Drew from the heartache of his many affairs?

"Shoots it all to hell, don't it?" the pragmatist said sourly.

"What about Heather McKenzie?" I asked.

"Well, yesterday being Sunday, she was a little harder. But not much. Turns out her father was a personal friend of someone at the parent company of *Furniture/Today*."

"Was?"

"He was CEO of a large freight-forwarding company in Boston. Had a massive stroke and died last summer. Nice guy, according to our source. Devoted to his wife and daughter. She's their only child. Still lives at home, but that may be because the mother's not well. Has her own desktop publishing business there in Boston where she puts out newsletters for various organizations all over New England. Occasionally sells small feature articles to the *Boston Globe*, but not really considered a reporter."

"So why is she researching Savannah?"

He shrugged. "Who knows?"

For lunch, I drove away from the center of town and found a relatively uncrowded neighborhood lunch counter. It was no J. Basul Noble's, but I had a slice of meatloaf with a dab of mashed potatoes and string beans and still got back in time for court to reconvene at one o'clock.

Mr. Kurkland took the stand first and his testimony echoed Mrs. Westermann's except that he was sure her Lhasa Apsos were not nearly so well trained as she insisted.

"And how can you speak with such certainty, Mr. Kurkland?"

"Number one, on account of I could smell it. Number two, on account of when I lifted up the rug to put my plastic tarp under it, I could see the stains where they wet through to the carpet."

Mr. Kurkland was tubby and clearly perspiring. He also spoke with a distinct Bronx accent and I had a feeling he wasn't winning many friends in the jury box. Especially during cross-examination when Mrs. Westermann's attorney, sensing victory, made him admit that plastic tarps did imply the possibility of too much wetting of the rug. Nor did it help when he was forced to admit that those stains on the Berber carpet could have been caused by wine or juice spills that had soaked through.

It seemed to me that the acids in wine or juice would be pretty damaging, too, but no one asked my opinion.

Like the plaintiff, defense called but one witness, another expert on rug cleaning, and I sat back expecting to hear claims that Mr. Kurkland's methods were entirely acceptable. It would probably come down to which expert the jury chose to believe.

He began with a mini-lecture on the nature of fine wool rugs, how the yarn is colored with natural vegetable dyes, and how damaging the acids in dog urine could be. Thus far, he sounded like the Westermann expert.

"Now, sir," said Mr. Kurkland's attorney. "There has been much talk back and forth about dog urine. Is there any way to say decisively whether or not the dogs did indeed use this sixty-thousand-dollar rug as a fire hydrant?"

"There is. While I did inherit the rug-cleaning business established by my father, my degree is actually in textile chemistry. Over the years I have discovered that certain stains manifest themselves in different colors when exposed to black light."

Like me, the jury sat up in renewed interest.

"And how does dog urine manifest itself?"

"If it is present, it will show up as a green tint."

"Your Honor, if it please the court, my witness has brought a black light with him today. If we could lower the lighting here in the courtroom, he could demonstrate his testimony."

"Any objection?" I asked counsel for the plaintiff.

He was clearly taken by surprise, but he could read the eagerness on the jurors' faces and knew what would happen if he prevented them from seeing the expert's show-and-tell.

"No objection, Your Honor."

I turned to the bailiff. "Mr. Dow, will you please find a plug for his extension cord and then cut the lights?"

"Yes, ma'am!" he said and turned off all the lights in the courtroom. There were windows in the rear doors and enough light came from the hallway to make out the expert as he approached the rug and switched on his black light.

The jury sighed and Mrs. Westermann sank back in her chair as big lime green splotches suddenly glowed all over the rug.

The jury was out less than thirty minutes. Their verdict? "The defendant is not liable for negligence."

I thanked them for performing their civic duty, explained how the clerk would sign statements to take back to employers for those that needed them, then released them from further jury duty for two years.

Since this case had been expected to last two days, there was nothing else on my docket, and I adjourned for the day at a little past three.

25

"In the progress of civilization, the tendency of which is to secure for mankind better conditions of comfort and health,
there is no special department the advance in which presents
a more satisfactory record than medicine and the modern in-
ventions which are allied to it."

The Great Industries of the United States, 1872

The first intensity of Market must have been wearing off.
How else explain that I found a legal parking spot within
two blocks of the GHFM building on my first pass?

I managed to evade the shoe shine offers from kids lining
both sides of the street, but I wasn't quite as skillful at avoid-
ing all the leaflets thrust upon me by college students
dressed as everything from space aliens to purple dogs. (It

reminded me of trying to get past the skin shows in Times Square without accepting a flyer.)

Chan's death had moved to the inside pages of *Market Press* and *Furniture/Today* both, but when I got off the elevator at Dixie's floor and passed the swing where I'd found him, I saw two exhibitors staring at the cushion.

"Wonder if it's the same cushion?" asked one man.

"If it is, whatever they're using for fabric protection is really effective," the other replied in utter seriousness. "Want me to ask? It could solve some of the problems we've been having with our current system. *If* it's not too expensive per unit, of course."

Dixie was too busy to take a break, but she recommended a coffee bar a couple of floors up, across from the Fitch and Patterson showroom. "Pell and Lynnette were there with Drew a little while ago, but they were going on to Mulholland. He had to pick up a fax and Lynnette loves to play with the toys."

I found the coffee bar with no trouble. It was the most popular spot around at the moment and I didn't see an empty chair at first, nor Pell and Lynnette; but Heather McKenzie was there alone, looking like a small dark cloud. She brightened marginally when she saw me and gestured for me to bring my espresso over and join her.

The little round metal tables and airy wire chairs were finished in a shiny white enamel. They mimicked those of an old-fashioned ice cream parlor and, according to a bold sign, were sold by the same company that sponsored this coffee bar. Some people got up from one of the tables and I confiscated a chair, which I carried over to Heather's table where she was finishing off a latte.

"Having any luck?" I asked.

"Do I look like it? I'm thinking of staking the Princess Patterson out in a field somewhere like a goat and see if that'll bring Savannah out into the open."

I was startled by the bitterness in her clipped New England accent.

"What've you got against Drew Patterson?"

"Not a goddamn thing."

"No?"

"No! And could we change the fricking subject?"

"Okay. We could discuss your real reason for stalking Savannah. And please don't hand me that 'profile' tale. You're not a real reporter. You run a newsletter-publishing firm in Boston."

She stared at me blankly. "How the hell do you know that?"

"I'm a judge," I said. "Judges hear things. And I'm still waiting to hear your answer."

"She's my mother."

"Your *mother*? I was told that your mother's in Boston."

"My adoptive mother," she said glumly. "Savannah's my birth mother."

Now it was my turn to stare. The heavy black hair, the dark eyes, the short stature? Yes, this could be Savannah's daughter. And I suddenly knew where that broad nose came from, too. Pell said Savannah had disappeared for four months when Jay Patterson dumped her after Elizabeth announced her pregnancy with Drew. She hadn't just gone off to lick her wounds, she'd gone to Georgia to have a baby and then immediately give it up for adoption. No wonder she'd fixated on Drew when her mental illness grew worse. Drew was Jay's legitimate daughter, unlike her own child, the child she could never acknowledge.

"Can you say ironic, boys and girls?" Her Mr. Rogers imitation was dispirited. "I'm trying to get her to sit still long enough for the big discovery and reconciliation scene and all she wants is ten minutes of Drew fricking Patterson's time."

Ironic was the word for it. Clearly Heather had no idea that Drew was her half sister.

"What's so goddamn bloody awful is that she's probably got her medications totally screwed—if she's even taking them. If she's not taking anything, her doctor said she should be okay physically, but if she's taking them without getting her blood levels monitored, she could wind up killing her fricking self. And why the hell should I care?"

She put her head down and the long thick hair swung down on either side of her face to hide the sudden tears.

"And here I thought Bostonians were always so proper in their speech," I said, trying to lighten the moment.

It didn't work. And to make things worse, wouldn't you know that Drew Patterson would pick that moment to stick her pretty head out of the Fitch and Patterson showroom, spot me and come strolling over through the crowds to say hello?

She immediately noticed how upset Heather was. "Is something wrong?"

"Not a damn thing." Heather fumbled in her purse for a tissue.

I handed her a paper napkin for her nose and started to introduce them, but Drew said, "It's Heather McKenzie, isn't it? You interviewed my dad about Savannah."

Tactfully, she pretended not to see Heather's tears.

Unfortunately, Heather was past pretending. "I should have interviewed *you!*" she snarled. "That's as close as I'm ever likely to get to her as long as you're around."

Drew recoiled as if she'd been slapped and looked at me in bewilderment. "Did I do something wrong?"

"Oh, hell," Heather said wearily. "Sorry. It's not your fault."

"You know," Drew said brightly, "there are lots of celebrities here at Market. I could introduce you to a dozen even more interesting than Savannah. And they're not crazy either."

"She's not crazy," Heather told her. "If she'd take her medications properly, she'd be as sane as you or me."

Drew's blue eyes went from Heather's face to mine. "Am I missing something here?"

It wasn't for me to say. Instead I glanced at Heather, who said abruptly, "She's *my* mother, okay? Not yours. Deborah can explain. I'm going to go wash my face and when I come back, maybe you'll tell me how I can find her."

She got up and headed for a restroom down the hall.

By the time I finished explaining that Savannah was Heather's birth mother, Drew looked even more stunned than I had felt a few minutes earlier. But then I knew her father'd had an affair with Savannah years ago and I rather doubted that it was something anyone had ever told her. Although how she could spend five minutes looking at a woman whose nose was slightly broader but otherwise identical to her own and not notice was beyond me.

"Savannah once had a real daughter?" she whispered.

"Evidently."

"I thought it was part of her craziness. She talks so much rubbish. No one listens to the rantings of a mad person, do they?"

"She talked about having a baby?"

"Indirectly." Drew twisted the end of one blonde tress and her blue eyes were worried. "She seems to think the reason I won't admit that Lynnette's my child is because I'm afraid of scandal. She keeps saying that it was shameful back in her day, not in mine. That she couldn't keep me back then, but things are different now."

"She thinks you're that baby."

"But she *knows* that Dad's my—" Her eyes widened in sudden dismay. "Oh, my God! Is *he*—? He is, isn't he? Oh, sweet Jesus! Does Heather know?"

I shook my head. "I don't think she knows anything. And neither do you, if it comes right down to it. Look, forget about who her father might be. All Heather wants to do is find Savannah and talk to her. Savannah trusts you. Will you help? It'll help Savannah, too. Heather seems to feel responsible. If she can establish a relationship, she can probably help Savannah get the mental treatment she so desperately needs."

But I had overlooked how young Drew still was. As bright and poised as she may have been under normal circumstances, she was not handling this very well. "I can't," she whispered. "I can't."

We both saw Elizabeth Patterson come to the front of their showroom and scan the passing crowds. She held two purses, one of them probably Drew's.

Drew stood up abruptly. "I'm sorry. I wish I could, but don't you see? How could I—? I have to—I promised Mother—"

She seemed to hear herself gibbering and somehow managed to get her tongue under control. "Give me some time to think about all this. I really do have to go. I'll call you tonight at Dixie's, okay?"

As Heather returned, I saw Elizabeth hand Drew her purse, then mother and daughter disappeared in the direction of the elevators. From behind they were almost indistinguishable, both tall and blonde, both in white silk slacks and navy blazers.

Golden.

"Did I shock the crap out of her?" asked Heather, who now had her Yankee tough-girl defenses back in place.

"You could say that."

Her sturdy shoulders drooped for a moment. "Well, then, the hell with her. I'll find Savannah myself and put her in a hammerlock."

I had a feeling she probably could.

"Let me buy you another latte," I said.

As I stood in line to give my order, I tried to decide whether or not it was all right to tell Heather about Savannah's hiding place. Underwood had asked Dixie and Pell to keep it quiet, but he hadn't exactly sworn me to secrecy.

A technicality and you know it, scolded my internal preacher.

"On the other hand," argued the pragmatist, *"think about it: Underwood's gone out of his way to tell you things even Dwight might not have. What's his game?"*

And why didn't he have an APB out on Savannah? Market was crowded, yes, but surely he could have reached out and touched her if he'd really wanted to. Especially if he thought she was a killer.

Ergo, he didn't fully suspect her.

Why?

She was there with my tote bag, my penicillin tablets, my—

Well, damn!

After all the time I've listened to DEA agents testify as to distinguishing a yellow Dilaudid tablet from a yellow Elavil, the differences between a green-and-white Donnatal capsule from Robins and a green-and-white Librium capsule from Roche? Every capsule or tablet has a stamp or imprint, a color combination, shape or size that's unique to the company that makes it.

That's why they weren't after Savannah: the fragments of the tablets they found in the baggie with my fingerprints weren't the same kind listed on my prescription bottle.

Underwood must have been snickering up his sleeve when I blustered that every medicine cabinet in America probably had leftover penicillin tablets.

And what were the odds that, in that stash of pills he'd found by Savannah's bed, four of them would be mine?

Neither preacher nor pragmatist wanted to bet against me.

In my mind's eye, I could almost see it happen: Chan takes the elevator down to Dixie's floor. He's going to bum a ride home with her. She's not there, but a note on her door says she'll be back for me at ten. He sits down on the swing to wait, remembers he has chocolate brownies in his pocket and swallows one down in two bites.

Immediately, his throat starts to close up as his breathing passages react to the penicillin. He gags, vomits, tries to get up, but already his brain is screaming for oxygen. It screams once more and then cuts out and all further struggle for air is lost in merciful unconsciousness.

Along comes Savannah, intending to return my tote— minus its loose change and pills—and finds Chan already unconscious. She drops the tote behind one of the chairs and flees.

And who had been with him only minutes earlier and had the opportunity to slip some brownies into his jacket pocket? Who was known to have had penicillin tablets at hand just last summer?

And who had a good reason to want Chan dead?

Right.

I stepped away from the coffee line, took out my flip phone and dialed Underwood's pager. At the beep, I said, "I don't know what you're up to, but I think I know whose tablets they were. I'm going to take Heather over to Mulholland to see if we can find Savannah and then I'll swing by your office. We really need to talk."

26

"*The improvement in the making of fire-arms is one of the most noticeable features of the modern era of industry.*"
The Great Industries of the United States, 1872

In stark contrast to the organized clutter that lay behind those double doors off to the left, the reception area of Mulholland Design Studio was clean-lined minimal, a high-tech setting for the large black-and-white photographs, each framed in chrome strips, that lined the walls. Each featured a single piece of furniture, photographed alone like a piece of jewelry or a work of art, and each carried a company logo. Widdicomb, Baker, Henredon, Fitch and Patterson, and Ethan Allen were there among other blue-chip names, but pieces of Benchcraft, This End Up and Hickory Hill showed the range of Mulholland's clientele and of the free-lance designers who used these facilities.

"I'm sorry," said the receptionist, "but we're closed now. All of our designers are gone for the day and I was just getting ready to lock up."

Indeed, she had already switched off the main lights in the reception area.

"We're here to see Pell Austin," I said. "He's still around, isn't he? I'm a friend—Judge Deborah Knott."

"Let me check." She pushed a button on her console phone. "Pell? There's a Judge Knott here to see you. Shall I send her up? . . . Okay, I'll tell her. You've got a key, right? Because I'm going to lock up down here."

She put down the receiver, smiled, and gestured to the chrome and glass staircase. "You can use those stairs or there's an elevator around the corner."

I must not have been the first to give her such a blank look because she immediately pulled out a floor plan from beneath the counter.

"Here's where we are. You go up these stairs, through the double doors, left, straight down the hall till it deadends in a cross corridor, take another left and keep going almost to the end. Pell's door will be open and he says to holler if you don't find him."

Beyond the sleek chrome-plated doors on the next level lay the shabby workaday reality I remembered from my tour on Saturday morning. The concrete landing was painted black, as were the industrial-steel steps that led down into the studio area.

"Wow!" said Heather as we stood looking out over the various sets in different stages of being built or torn down.

The whole lower floor was almost in darkness now. The main overhead fluorescents had been turned off and only a few security lights lit the main path through the labyrinth. Yet I could see a bright glow from somewhere over on the far side, as if a single floor lamp had been left burning.

Outside, I knew that the sun was still fairly high in the western sky. In here though, it might as well have been midnight for all the shadowy gloom.

At least the second-floor halls were brightly lit and we kept taking left turns till we fetched up at Pell's door.

"Ah, you found me." His long pleasant face warmed with a smile of welcome that included Heather.

"I thought Lynnette was with you," I said.

"She is. I told her she could go play in the toy section."

I frowned. "You're not worried about her wandering around down there in the dark?"

"Is she wandering? I told her not to go past the toys." He walked past us and out into the hall a few steps to where the landing was.

We followed him. Immediately next to the steps below, a dining room vignette was half built. Or half dismantled. It was hard for a layman to tell. Beyond that, Lynnette sat on the floor under a torchère lamp, about a quarter of the way down one of the long rows. She was surrounded by teddy bears and other stuffed animals.

"Hey, Miss Deborah," she called. Her braid had loosened and tendrils of fair hair tumbled about her face. "Look at all these bears!"

"You could be Goldilocks," I called back. To Pell, I said, "I'm all turned around. Point me toward the reception area."

"Over there." He pointed across the wide dim expanse to the red exit light. "You came the whole width of the building."

Like me, Heather was overwhelmed by all the *stuff* she could see from this landing: not just the movable walls or the two- and three-sided rooms filled with furniture or appliances, the cameras, table saws, workbenches, and so many aisles of accessories down on the floor, but also the chandeliers, paddle fans and hanging lights that were suspended from the catwalks and steel rafters that interconnected and crisscrossed the space overhead.

"And the door you brought Dixie and me through on Saturday?"

"Two aisles over and straight down to the back."

In the far distance, I could see another red exit light, but between the black-painted floor and walls and the dim lights, it was difficult to make out enough detail for me to orient myself completely.

"Rats in a maze," Pell said in his usual soft, self-deprecating tone. "Did you want to show Miss McKenzie around?"

"Heather," she corrected him.

"Heather." He smiled. "I can put more lights on for you."

"I do want to show her something," I said, "but not in the sense you mean. She wants to see Savannah's hiding place."

He stiffened. "I don't think that's a good idea at all."

Heather and I had discussed this and I said, "It's not for a news story, Pell. Remember how you told Dixie and me

about that time she went away for four months right before
you came here twenty-odd years ago?"

I could tell he thought I was betraying his trust and—by
extension—Savannah's.

"She didn't go away to get over a love affair," I said. "She
went away to have a baby."

"Ah." Pell looked at Heather a long considering moment,
then nodded. "Yes, I see."

"I brought pictures," Heather said, hefting a manila envelope in her hand. "Documents. I thought if I could just find
her, sit quietly for a few minutes and show her some of my
baby pictures, maybe she'd—"

"Clasp you to her bosom and tell you to call her
Mommy?"

"Pell!" I was surprised that he could be so harsh.

"Sorry, Deborah. Heather. But even when Savannah was
well, sentimentality was never her thing. And now we're
dealing with a very sick woman. She's not going to respond
in any predictable way. So I really am sorry, ladies, but I
can't let you in." He turned to me. "Besides, David Underwood took my key, remember?"

"I expect you found another," I said dryly. "And of
course, Savannah has her own. She's in there right now, isn't
she?"

"I mean it, Deborah, you can't go in." His long homely
face was distressed.

I held up my hands to calm him. "We won't. But, Pell, if
she's so sick, she needs help. You know she does."

"I'm trying to convince her—"

"You can't convince a delusional person. Believe me, I
know. I sit on mental health hearings all the time. There are

times when you just have to do what's best for the person until they're well enough to make their own decisions again."

"She didn't kill anybody," he said. "Not Chan, not—"

He broke off abruptly.

"Not who, Pell?" I asked softly. "Evelyn? Is that why Savannah flipped out eighteen months ago? You said she was here when Evelyn fell, and you meant that literally, didn't you?"

Heather was bewildered. "Who's Evelyn?"

"It was an accident." Pell's eyes were anguished. "It really was an accident. I was in the stacks rounding up a handful of things to dress the set when Evelyn went up the steps. Savannah was at the end of the aisle. I heard her gasp 'Oh, no!' just as Evelyn screamed. Then Savannah started screaming and everyone came running . . ."

His voice trailed off in memory. "She used to have cycles, Savannah did, and the highs kept getting higher and the lows were dragging bottom. She was near the end of a pretty bad low when it happened and she just couldn't handle the pain. Seeing Evelyn fall knocked her for such a loop that we had to commit her to the local hospital till her father could send someone to take her back to Georgia."

Pell turned to Heather. "You saw her in the hospital down there, so you know."

"Yes." She looked very young standing there, gazing up into his worried face. "But I also know I can't go back to Boston without seeing her and having at least one serious talk together."

Pell sighed. "Okay. I'll try. Why don't you sit down on the

steps here? If I can get her to come out, she might feel less menaced if she's taller."

"Should I leave?" I asked.

"No," said Heather. "She knows you."

I sat down and leaned back on my elbows. "Okay. Tell her Ms. Sotelli's here, too."

As we waited, we watched Lynnette play. She had found an antique wicker doll carriage and tucked a few teddy bears in, then set up a tea party on the floor for the others. We could hear her murmuring to herself, carrying on a lively conversation for five or six different characters. It was all very peaceful and quiet.

"She probably won't come," Heather said pessimistically for the third time.

That's when we heard footsteps in the hallway.

We had moved down a couple of steps to leave room for her to sit above us if she chose, but Pell followed behind her with a chair, which he placed on the landing.

Savannah stood looking down at us for a moment, then a formal smile crossed her lips and she took the chair as if it were a Hepplewhite in a formal drawing room. Her colorful chiffon scarves no longer looked jaunty, merely sad. Her pink ballerina slippers were filthy. Her hair could have used a good brushing, but her face and hands were clean.

"Ms. Sotelli, Miss McKenzie." Her voice was as husky as ever. "How kind of you to visit. I confess I had not—"

From out of the darkness came two gunshots in rapid succession.

The shots were so unexpected that even though I've been raised around guns and actually had a .38 locked in the trunk of my car, it took a split second to register what was happening.

A third shot hit the steel railing above, spraying me with enamel paint chips before ricocheting off somewhere.

"Uncle Pell!" Lynnette screamed in terror and got up and started toward us.

"No!" I yelled, ducking and running down the steps to her. "Stay there! Lie down!"

But Pell was even faster. He pushed me aside and raced to snatch her up in his arms.

Another shot shattered the concrete wall beside Savannah's head. Heather scrambled up the steps, grabbed Savannah's hand and pulled her back into the hallway, out of the line of fire. As they ran for cover, yet another shot zinged past.

Even while listening for more shots, my mind was racing furiously. The shooter must be after Savannah since Heather and I had been there several minutes and no shots were fired till Savannah appeared on the stairs. But why shoot a delusional old woman?

Mentally I tried to add up the shots. Five or six? And did the shooter have extra bullets?

In the sudden silence, we heard a crash, then staccato footsteps running at least three aisles over.

"He's getting away," I told Pell. "Quick! Call Underwood."

"Wait!" Pell cried, but I was already flying over the teddy bears, rushing toward the same door our assailant must be making for.

And would reach before me, unless I could somehow fool him into thinking someone was between him and the exit?

I grabbed a glass vase from the shelf I was passing and lobbed it as hard as I could over the shelves toward the exit. It landed with a satisfactory loudness and sounded as if it had taken a couple of other pieces of glass along, too.

And it worked!

The sound of running footsteps immediately swerved aside and headed out into the studio area. As he ran, crashes marked his direction. Glassware and metal fell to the floor as he brushed past them.

In the dim light, I saw a narrow cross aisle up ahead and put on more speed as I turned left and followed the sounds ahead of me. I stubbed my toe sharply on some metal object that he'd dislodged in the aisle. Broken glass crunched under my shoes and I almost tripped over a stack of baskets.

Then I heard another set of footsteps.

"This way!" called Heather. "He's heading for the front office."

I heard her roar, "Where the hell's the fucking lights?" Then a crash from her direction. She must have tripped over a cable.

The first footsteps vanished. Had he stopped short or was he hurrying across a carpeted set?

I came around a wall in time to see Heather silhouetted against the security lights near the front.

"Deborah? Where are you? Where'd he go?" she called, running blindly toward me.

"Sh-hh!" I hissed as I strained to see and hear.

Then I caught a flash of white legs mounting upwards in the darkness. Someone was on those movable stairs. Theoretically, the steps went nowhere. In actuality, someone agile could probably pull up and onto one of the overhead cat-walks and then run along a clear path to an unobserved exit.

Someone in white silk slacks.

Of course.

Although I was pretty sure that she killed Chan, I still didn't know why: but I could make a pretty good guess as to why she thought she had to kill Savannah.

"You can't get away," I called. "I know who you are!"

I saw a flash and heard the explosion in the same instant as the bullet destroyed a portable light stand off to the side. God, she was a lousy shot.

"Help me," I told Heather, who was puffing like a little steam engine as we both reached the sinuous set of steps at the same time.

I fumbled for the brake release, then we gave the thing a mighty tug and swirled it out into open space just as Pell finally found the lights.

Dazzled by the sudden brightness, I looked up into Drew Patterson's startled face the exact instant she lost her balance and tumbled down the steps. The gun went flying and she bounced a couple of times, then landed at the bottom, whimpering with pain.

"You bitch!" said Heather.

"Why?" I asked.

"It was an accident," Drew moaned. "An accident."

"Accident?" Heather was speechless with rage. "You damn near kill us and all you can say is it's a fucking *accident?*"

"Shut up, Heather," I said pleasantly. "Which was the accident, Drew? Chan's death or Evelyn's?"

"My shoulder," she moaned. "I think it's broken."

"Then tell me what I want to know and I'll see about an ambulance."

Her face was gray and twisted with pain, but I was having a hard time mustering up any sympathy.

"Both of them were accidents," she wailed. "Honest. I was mad at Chan."

"He was going off to Malaysia without you," I said, "so you killed him."

"I didn't know he was that allergic. I just wanted to make him a little sick. First I wasn't going to, but he was flirting with you, he was rude to Dad, rude to me—"

She tried to sit up, then gasped in agony.

"So while he was dancing with your mother, you went back to the ALWA party, put a couple of those brownies in a plastic bag that was lying on the table and smashed up some of your mother's penicillin tablets. Then, when he was leaving and stopped to say goodnight, you slipped them into his pocket."

"I told him to think about me when he was eating them. But I only meant to make him sick, not kill him. I swear it!"

"But you did mean to kill Evelyn so that you could have him," I said inexorably.

"No! It really was an accident. I tripped and bumped the stairs. You see how easy they are to move. I barely touched them, but they went flying and poor Evelyn— Oh, my shoulder! Please. *Please*."

I turned away, sickened, and saw Pell a few feet away. His hands were clenching and unclenching and his face was ghastly.

"You came rushing up to Savannah that day. I thought you were upset because of Evelyn, but you knew she'd seen you and you were afraid she'd tell. That's why you kept saying what a horrible accident it was, over and over, until Savannah reached out her hand and smoothed your hair and started crying. And cried for two days until they came for her. You did that. To both of them."

Then that gentle man spat on the floor beside her and turned to go let the police in at the rear door.

27

*"The enjoyment of light in darkness could not be realized
practically to any great extent without the means of vessels,
or other mechanical devices of some sort, to contain in place,
or convey to the action of heat, the fuels, oils, gases, etc.,
from which light is drawn."*

        The Great Industries of the United States, 1872

I met Savannah again at the end of the summer.

That's how long it was before I could borrow one of my
brothers' pickup truck and go pick up my headboard at Mulholland where Pell had stored it for me.

When I called Dixie to see which weekend would work
for her, she mentioned that Savannah was going to be in
town. "She's going to stay with Pell while she clears her
stuff out of Mulholland."

How could I resist?

Dixie invited me to spend the night, so I took the three of them out to dinner at Noble's—a much less crowded Noble's. The food was even more delicious when you didn't feel as if you were in the middle of the conversation at the next table.

The changes in Savannah were astonishing. Her hair was still gray, but shingled to take advantage of its coarse texture. Gone were the layers of pastel chiffon, but she was not totally dressed in black either. Instead, she wore chic black pants with thin white pinstripes, a black short-sleeved silk sweater over a white cotton shirt, and shiny black patent high-heeled sandals.

"Maybe I'll graduate to purple by next year," she said sardonically when she caught me staring.

They brought me up to date on things that happened after my week of court was up last April. Some of it I already knew, of course. When I made my original deposition, Underwood admitted that he'd given me all that information for a reason. "From the things Major Bryant said, I figured you must be a pretty good catalyst."

I also knew that Drew was out on a very high bond while her attorneys kept stalling the actual trial, that Dixie and Pell had "found" Chan's signed and witnessed will, and that Lynnette was now living with the Ragsdales in Maryland— "But she and Shirley Jane are coming to spend a week here before school starts."

"And you're in Boston now?" I asked Savannah.

"Heather and her mother talked me into giving it a try," she said.

"You should see the McKenzie homestead," said Pell, who had visited when up on business a couple of weeks earlier. "You could fit my house and Dix's, too, on the first floor alone, never mind the other two floors. It's in a historical section that's just ten minutes from the statehouse."

I was surprised. "You're living in the same house with Heather and her mother?"

"Old Home Week," Savannah said dryly. "Caroline and I were roommates at a prep school in Atlanta when we were girls. That's how the adoption was arranged in the first place. She has a tricky heart, which is why she sent Heather to find me—so the kid would have some family when she dies. Some family, huh? A mother dying of congestive heart failure, a mother living with a bipolar disorder, a father who wants nothing to do with her, and a half sister who's 'accidentally' killed two people."

"You can't choose your relatives," Pell said softly and I, who sometimes feel as if I'm drowning in family, wondered what it would feel like to have only one or two relatives.

Liberated or isolated?

Dixie's eyes were shadowed with pain. "At least you got your real daughter back."

Savannah shook her head. "No, I didn't. Caroline is Heather's mother, not me. And Heather herself is still the daughter of a childhood friend. We *want* to love each other and maybe we will . . . eventually. But feel for her what I felt for Drew all those years? I don't count on it."

"Give it some time," said Pell. He brushed back that long strand of hair from his blue eyes. "At least you're working again. What did you say your new project is? Redesigning a gourmet cookshop in Cambridge?"

It was as if Savannah didn't hear him. "She's a nice kid though, even if someone does need to wash her mouth out with soap. There's a live-in nurse to take care of Caroline and she and Heather make sure I keep my medications balanced."

She took a couple of pills from a little gold box in her purse and weighed them thoughtfully in her small hand.

I remembered the first time I met her and how she'd laid out a row of pills on the table beside her plate. "So you're well now?"

She shrugged. "I'll never be *well*. What I can be is sane."

"But?"

"But I miss my manic highs. I miss feeling the energy of line and color in my fingertips, the dance of fabrics and textures in my brain, the—" She broke off with an ironic smile. "I'm a seventy-eight rpm record that knows it's going to be played at thirty-three and a third the rest of its life and I'm not totally convinced that normal and sane is worth the trade-off."

"Yes it is," Pell said. He nudged her glass of water closer. "Take the damn pills."

"You sound like Heather," Savannah grumbled, but she swallowed them.

Later that night, Dixie changed into ice blue satin pajamas and I to a long white batiste nightgown. We curled toe-to-toe at opposite ends of her long comfy couch with a half-empty jug of white Zinfandel on the coffee table in front of us, talking girl talk.

I took a slow sip of wine and asked, "What made you decide to give up Lynnette?"

"No one thing," Dixie said, stretching out a long leg. "More a combination. Millie and Shirley Jane, and even Quentin, I think, do love her and she loves them back. Pell convinced me that it was probably better for her to be in a young household rather than watching us dodder through middle age. And then there's Tom. Did I tell you about Tom?"

"Tupelo Market? Thinks you're special? Makes you laugh?"

She grinned and kicked me. "Did I say all that?"

"Yeah. So does he still?"

"Yeah," she mimicked. "The thing is, it's hard to be spontaneous and go flying off to Mississippi when you have a young child in the house. Besides—"

"Ah, here it comes. The real reason!"

"Is it?" Dixie's slanted eyes grew thoughtful and her chestnut hair swung forward as she gazed down into her glass. Then she nodded. "You may be right. The truth is, even going to the gym three times a week, it's hard to work all day and then come home and try to keep up with a seven-year-old."

"You and Pell miss her though?"

"Oh, God, Deborah, you don't know!" With her free hand, she gracefully tucked her hair behind her ears, making her look nearer twenty-five than forty-five. "But most of all, we miss Evelyn being over there in Lexington and dropping in with her a couple of times a week."

I'd drunk just enough wine to loosen the restraints on my tongue. "Did Evelyn know?"

"Know what?"

"That Pell was her father?"

Dixie cut her brown eyes at me sharply. "Where on earth did you get that idea?"

"During Market. Lynnette was showing me the family albums and there was a picture of Pell with Evelyn and Lynnette and I realized that all three of them had the same lopsided smile and the same blue eyes even though both girls inherited the shape and tilt of your eyes. And once the idea was planted, everything fell into place. You two were so close all through childhood and high school—he said you were like his big sister—yet he didn't know Evelyn existed till he bumped into you in Chapel Hill. After that though, *he* became the protector. Found you this house, found you a job—"

"Co-signed the mortgage. Helped me move. Was always there across the alley in any emergency."

"But you never told Evelyn," I said, guessing.

"No." Her voice was sad. "Pell's choice, not mine. He was so sure that a teenage girl would rather have no father than one who was gay. Then when she married Chan . . . Well, you've seen Quentin Ragsdale, you know the homophobic culture Chan came from. Not that he was ever snide to Pell's face. Evelyn loved Pell too much to stand for anything like that, but he understood and again he didn't want her to know, to risk Chan's throwing it up to her."

She took a swallow of wine and I followed suit.

"Obviously he wasn't always so totally committed to same-sex sex," I observed.

"Too bad I wasn't Deborah Kerr," she said wryly.

"Deborah Kerr?"

"As in *Tea and Sympathy*. Or is that before your time?"

I made a mental note to rent the video sometime.

"Under other circumstances, it would have been so funny that night when you were practically shrieking at Millie that no nineteen-year-old woman would make love to a seventeen-year-old kid. Yet that's exactly what happened with us. He was late to mature and he wanted so desperately to be as straight as all his male friends. I was just as ignorant. I honestly thought that he could choose, that friendly sex with me would prove to him that he was as hetero as anybody else."

She lifted her glass to her lips and drained it. "We did it twice, but all we proved was that he really didn't have a choice. He was having such a hard time dealing with it that I couldn't lay a baby on him, too. He really was just a kid. I was going to do like Savannah did—have the baby and then give her up for adoption. But once I held her in my arms, I couldn't do it."

Tears were streaming down Dixie's cheeks. "I just couldn't do it," she whispered.

I started to crawl down to her end of the couch to put my arms around her, but she shook her head and got up to get a tissue. "I'm okay. Honest."

She topped our glasses and sat back down again. "I'm sorry Evelyn never knew, but I did tell Millie that Pell is Lynnette's grandfather and I'm going to tell Lynnette when she comes next month. I think she'll be glad."

Her smile was indulgent and downright grandmotherly. "Did I tell you what she did?"

"Millie?"

"No, doofus, Lynnette."

"What did she do?"

She gestured toward the bookshelves across the room. "You know those family albums?"

I nodded.

"When we finally decided that she was going to go live in Maryland, she got cold feet at the last minute. Started saying she didn't want to be David Henry."

"The relative that went West during the gold rush and no one ever heard of again?"

"God, you *do* have a memory, don't you?"

"I love family stories," I murmured defensively.

"Well, you're right. That was David Henry. Fell completely out of our family tree. And Lynnette was afraid the same thing would happen to her if she went North."

"What did you do?"

"Explained that David Henry didn't have telephones and E-mail and a grandmother who knew exactly where he was every step of the way and could hop in her car and be there in no time."

"And that reassured her?"

"Not completely." She walked over to the shelves and pulled out one particularly bulging scrapbook. "We were in such a tizzy that morning, getting all the bags and boxes packed up, so they could get on the road before lunch. I noticed something odd about her, but I thought it was because she'd pinned her braid up in a ball on top of her head. Later, after she'd driven off with Millie and Shirley Jane, I came in here to straighten up and I couldn't fit this scrapbook back into its usual slot. Here's why."

She opened the book and I saw a thick, four-inch length

of braided hair the color of beach sand held firmly to the page by many crisscrossings of Scotch tape.

Beside it, in her best promoted-to-second-grade printing: DONT FORGET LYNNETTE.

You bet.

More
Margaret Maron!

Please turn this page
for a
bonus excerpt from

Home Fires

available as a Mysterious Press hardcover
in December 1998

1

*Fire cleanses but the Blood of the Lamb
Washes whiter than snow*
— *Jones Chapel*

Flames are already jetting through one side of the roof. Daddy brakes sharply and pulls his old Chevy pickup right in behind Rudy Peacock. Before he can switch off the truck, I have the door open and am running towards the fire.

The West Colleton volunteer fire truck swings in next to that blazing corner and half a dozen men swarm to unreel the hose connected to its water tank. No water mains or fire hydrants this far out in the country. I doubt if there's even a garden hose. Most buildings this old and this poor, the best you can expect in the way of on-site water is probably a rusty old hand pump out back.

No electric pump and nothing much else electric, judging by the outdated transformer on the light pole and the single thin line that runs down to the small one-room structure where flames leap up against the darkening sky. Where it started, no doubt. Frayed wires. A power surge or maybe a short. The wiring here probably hasn't been inspected since it was installed fifty or sixty years ago.

Typical rural complicity. Long as you pay your bills and no one complains, Carolina Power and Light won't bother you. But get cut off for letting your payments lapse, and they'll make you bring your wiring up to code before turning the power back on.

All this and more rushes subliminally through my mind as I race for the open front door.

Daddy hollers for me to stop, to come back, and I hear one of the firemen call, "Reckon they's still any gas in them old tanks?" Then I'm through the door and into the smoke-filled room.

Someone in protective gear pushes past me with a rough-hewn cross. "Get out!" he yells, but a young, barrel-shaped man gestures urgently from across the smoky room. "The Bible! Grab the Bible!"

I snatch up the big open book and the white lace runner beneath it just as he hoists the wooden pulpit, slings it over his shoulder and heads for the door. Two more men try to move a monstrous upright piano but they can't get the casters to roll and the thing's too heavy for them to pick it up.

Flames lick the exposed rafters only nine or ten feet above our heads and sparks shower down on us, stinging my bare arms. One of the pews in the middle of the room is burning like a solitary bonfire, although the most intense heat radiates from the corner. Smoke chokes me, the skin on my face feels tight and hot, and my eyes are streaming as I look around for something else to save. Adrenaline pumping, I scoop up a stack of paperback hymn books. Some old-fashioned hand fans are heaped together at the end of one pew and I pile as many as I can on top of the hymnals and the pulpit Bible, then stumble towards the door and out into the humid night air as a burning rafter crashes somewhere behind me.

Daddy breaks free of restraining hands and grabs for some of the fans that are sliding out of my control.

"Don't you never do nothing like that again as long as you live," he says angrily as I cough and cough and try to clear my lungs. His hand is rough as he brushes at my hair where sparks have singed it. "You hear me, girl? I'm talking to you!"

"I'm okay," I gasp between coughs. "Honest."

But then I look back at the burning structure, and like Lot's wife, I am struck dumb and motionless.

More people have arrived and their headlights light up the front of this makeshift church. For the first time

I see the swastika and some large dark letters: *KKK* and *NIggERS*.

Small g's and the capital I is dotted.

The tin roof gives way with sharp cracks as metal sheets twist in the heat. Flames shoot heavenwards and my silent, involuntary prayer follows them. *"Oh God! Not A.K.?"*

It's the second time in four days that my nephew had me begging God's mercy.

2

When things go wrong,
Don't go with them.
—Faith Freewill Baptist Church

Four days ago, I was in New Bern. In Kidd Chapin's bed.

Kidd's a tall skinny game warden from down east. He's my reminder that there's more to life than courtrooms and campaigns. He's also the main reason I'm finally building my own house out in the country and why I came to wake up that hot Sunday morning to feel him nibbling at my ear.

"I thought you said you bought bagels for breakfast," I murmured sleepily.

"I did. But then I saw this tasty little ear just laying here . . ."

His unshaven cheek brushed mine as he kissed my neck, then moved on to my shoulder and from there to my breasts.

Air-conditioning had us snuggled under a heavy comforter but flames began to kindle along the length of my body and small brushfires erupted wherever his hands and mouth touched. I turned in his arms and stoked the flames that were building in his own body while the fire between us grew and raged and blazed white-hot until we were consumed by wave after fiery wave and came together in a blazing conflagration that left us lying naked on top of the comforter, breathing in cool drafts of frigid air.

His long thin fingers traced the features of my face. "I missed you."

"Me too, you," I said inanely as our lips met again.

It had been way too long. Things keep coming up: his job, my family, his teenage daughter, my political commitments—judges do a lot of after-dinner speeches. A dozen different obstacles had kept us apart since the middle of May, but this late June weekend was ours. I'd driven down to New Bern Friday night and got to his cabin perched above the Neuse River while it was still light enough to see small boats heading upriver after a day of fishing in the Pamlico Sound.

We'd spent most of yesterday in bed, making up for

lost time, and though today was Sunday, church was not on our docket.

He pulled the comforter back over us and we lay twined together in post-coital laziness. The whole day stretched before us. Later we would shower, make coffee, have honeydews and toasted bagels on the deck.

But not now.

Now was the afterglow of tenderness and sweet intimacy.

And then the damn phone rang.

Kidd sighed, took his hand from my breast and reached for the receiver.

I lay quietly against his chest, almost certain that it would be Amber, Kidd's fifteen-year-old daughter. She must be slipping, I told myself. Normally, her radar lets her catch us in the middle of making love, not at the end.

From Kidd's casual grumbling, I know that she usually goes five or six days in a row without calling.

Unless I'm in town.

He's always so happy to hear her voice that he doesn't seem to notice how her calls pick up when I'm down and I'm too smart to point out this recurring coincidence.

But this time he wasn't speaking in his indulgent-father tones.

"Just fine," I heard him say with country politeness. "And you? . . . That's good. . . . Yes, she's right here."

He handed me the phone. "Your brother Andrew. Sounds serious."

My heart turned stone cold and a silent prayer went up—*Dear God, no!*

Andrew's nine brothers up from me. He hates any show of emotion and while he did plenty of catting around in his own day, he's like the rest of the boys in wishing I'd quit mine and settle down. Even so, despite his relatively recent respectability, he'd never take it upon himself to confront me head-on about my love life. I could think of only one reason why he'd call me here.

(Please not Daddy. Not yet.)

"What's wrong, Andrew? Is it Daddy?"

"Daddy?" My brother's voice came gruffly over the line. "Naw, Daddy's fine. It's A.K. He's really stepped in it bad this time, Deb'rah."

A.K. is Andrew's oldest child by his third wife. He's seventeen now and will be a senior in high school this fall if Andrew and April can keep him from quitting. Unlike his sister Ruth, A.K.'s not much for the books. Too near like Andrew used to be, from all I've heard.

"What's he done now?" I asked apprehensively. I've been on the bench long enough to see some of the messes a seventeen-year-old can step in and A.K.'s already dirtied his feet a time or two.

"I swear I feel like taking my belt to his backside. He knows better'n this."

His paternal exasperation couldn't mask the worry coming to me through the line.

"What'd he do?" I asked again.

"You know old Ham Crocker?"

I said I did, even though Abraham Crocker must have died around the time I was born.

"Well, A.K. and a couple of his buddies sort of busted up his graveyard Friday night."

"*What?*"

"They got hold of some beer and I reckon they got drunk enough to think it was funny to knock over the angel—you know the one on Ham's mama's grave?—and then Charles or Raymond, one had a can of spray paint. A.K. swears he didn't do no writing, but he's charged same as the others."

"Charged?"

"Yeah. Bo Poole sent a deputy out to bring him in this morning and me and April don't know what to do. John Claude's gone off to Turkey."

He made it sound as if Turkey was the dark side of the moon and an outlandish place for a Colleton County attorney to visit under any circumstances.

"Did you call Reid?" I asked, since Reid Stephenson is John Claude Lee's younger partner.

"I thought maybe you could come and take care of this," he countered.

Though no kin to the sons of my father's first marriage, John Claude and Reid are both cousins on my mother's side and they're also my former law partners, but the boys have never quite trusted Reid the way they trust John Claude. Maybe it's because John Claude has silver hair while Reid's two years younger than me. Or maybe it's because Reid's personal life is such a shambles and John Claude's stayed respectably married to the same woman for thirty years.

"Call Reid," I said firmly. "He knows us and he'll do just fine."

"But can't you—?"

"No, I can't." I thought I'd made it clear to him when A.K. got caught with marijuana a second time after John Claude had made the first offense go away. "I told you that last year, remember? Judges aren't allowed to represent anyone or give legal advice."

"Not even to your own family? Now that just don't make no sense."

Incredulity was mixed with suspicion and right then's when I knew my weekend was over. If I waited till tomorrow morning to drive back as I'd originally planned, Andrew and the others would think I cared more about my own pleasure than a brother's need, even though there was absolutely nothing I could do except hold his hand and April's while Reid did all the work.

"His probation's not up yet on that marijuana possession, either, is it?" I asked.

"And he got hisself another speeding ticket last night," Andrew admitted glumly. "I swear I'm gonna lock that boy up myself."

I was ready to hand him a key. A.K.'s not really a bad kid but bad luck and bad judgment aren't helping him these days.

It was going to take all Reid's skills and a kind-hearted judge.

"Try not to worry," I told my brother. "I'll be there just as soon as the speed limit lets me."

"I ain't worried," he said doggedly. "It's his mama that's worried. But you'll get him off, right?"

"I'll do everything I can," I hedged, since I clearly wasn't getting through to him about the legal restraints on my help. "I'll call Reid myself and he'll have A.K. out of jail before I get to Kinston, okay?"

"Okay. And, Deb'rah?"

"Yes?"

"I'm really sorry 'bout messing up your weekend."

So was I, but there was no point grousing about it. If you have to do something you don't want to, you're not going to get any Brownie points unless you do it with a willing air. The Lord's not the only one who loveth a cheerful giver and holdeth it against you if you aren't.

My only sour compensation was rousting Reid from *his* bed and hearing a woman's sleepy complaints at being awakened so early. Eventually Reid agreed to go see what Bo Poole, our longtime sheriff, and District Attorney Douglas Woodall had in mind for A.K., but he wasn't happy about it.

"This is not how I was planning to spend my Sunday morning," he grumped.

"Tell me about it," I said heartlessly.

Kidd wasn't happy about it either, but he'd had to cancel out a couple of times himself because of Amber's last-minute demands, so he tried to be a good sport.

He poured me a mug of coffee for the road, stowed my overnight case in the back of my car, and even managed a crooked smile as he watched me fasten my seatbelt, but his voice was wistful.

"You ever wish you were an only child?"

"Frequently," I sighed.

MARGARET MARON grew up on a farm near Raleigh, North Carolina, but for many years lived in Brooklyn, New York, where she drew her inspiration for her Lieutenant Sigrid Harald mystery series. When she returned to her North Carolina roots with her artist husband, Joe, she began thinking about a series based on her own background and went on to create the award-winning Deborah Knott series. In 1993 Margaret Maron swept the top mystery awards for her bestseller *Bootlegger's Daughter*—the Edgar, Agatha, Anthony, and Macavity Awards. *Southern Discomfort* was nominated for the Agatha Award for Best Novel. *Shooting at Loons* was also nominated for an Agatha and an Anthony Award.